TROUBLE
Girls

ALSO BY JULIA LYNN RUBIN

Burro Hills

TROUBLE
Girls

A NOVEL

JULIA LYNN RUBIN

WEDNESDAY BOOKS
NEW YORK

First published in the United States by Wednesday Books, an imprint of St. Martin's Publishing Group

TROUBLE GIRLS. Copyright © 2021 by Julia Lynn Rubin. All rights reserved. Printed in the United States of America. For information, address St. Martin's Publishing Group, 120 Broadway, New York, NY 10271.

www.wednesdaybooks.com

Designed by Devan Norman

Library of Congress Cataloging-in-Publication Data

Names: Rubin, Julia Lynn, author.
Title: Trouble girls / Julia Lynn Rubin.
Description: First edition. | New York : Wednesday Books, 2021.
Identifiers: LCCN 2020056431 | ISBN 9781250757241
    (hardcover) | ISBN 9781250757234 (ebook)
Subjects: CYAC: Best friends—Fiction. | Friendship—Fiction. |
    Sexual abuse—Fiction. | Fugitives from justice—Fiction. |
    Lesbians—Fiction. | Love—Fiction.
Classification: LCC PZ7.1.R827573 Tro 2021 |
    DDC [Fic]—dc23
LC record available at https://lccn.loc.gov/2020056431

Our books may be purchased in bulk for promotional, educational, or business use. Please contact your local bookseller or the Macmillan Corporate and Premium Sales Department at 1-800-221-7945, extension 5442, or by email at MacmillanSpecialMarkets@macmillan.com.

First Edition: 2021

10 9 8 7 6 5 4 3 2 1

For all of those who've never reached the ocean . . . may blue waves appear on your horizon

This book contains discussions and off-page depictions of sexual assault, as well as on-page violence. If you think you might need extra support while reading this book, please reach out to your guardians and friends, and see the resources below.

The Trevor Project
1-866-488-7386
Available 24/7 Free
If you are a young person in crisis, feeling suicidal, or in need of a safe and judgment-free place to talk, call the TrevorLifeline now.
www.thetrevorproject.org

RAINN
1-800-656-HOPE (4673)
Available 24/7 Free
Call to be connected with a trained staff member from a sexual assault service provider in your area. www.rainn.org

National Suicide Prevention Lifeline
1-800-273-TALK (8255)
Available 24/7 Free
The Lifeline provides support for people in distress, prevention and crisis resources for you or your loved ones, and best practices for professionals.
www.suicidepreventionlifeline.org

Crisis Text Line
Available 24/7 Free
Text from anywhere in the United States, anytime. Crisis Text Line is here for any crisis.
Text HOME to 741741
www.crisistextline.org

I ALWAYS KNEW
THIS GIRL WOULD BE TROUBLE.

The diner's full of hogs today.

Hog men, that's what I call 'em. Men with their gazes creeping up my thighs and across my chest. Men with their smarmy grins, their slimy, leering eyes. Men in suits who're clearly passing through on the way to the city. They think they're better than the rest of these boys, but they're not. There're men in dusty overalls with lobster-red sunburns. Farmhands and field workers whose skin doesn't sizzle, just gets leathered by the sun. Men in biker gear with wild beards, smelling of diesel oil, trying hard to look mean. Some of the hogs are shaven and well groomed. Some have greasy ponytails that look days unwashed. Some are bald or just balding.

Don't matter one way or another. They're all hog men to me.

Hot dogs and hamburgers sizzle on the kitchen grill in the back, and the whole place reeks of grease and burning meat. It's way too hot in here with the AC broken. Boss Man said he'd fix it, but he's useless as anything, so I expect it won't get sorted out until the end of the month, at least.

I wipe my sweaty lip on my sleeve, my palms on my apron. I smile, write down another order, serve them cherry pie and root beer floats and cheeseburgers, ignoring the leers and stares and wolf whistles from the hog men as best I can, counting down the nanoseconds until my break.

Any minute now. Judy is the only other waitress on duty who's not hiding out back smoking. She can handle the hog men. She's in her late fifties, with charcoal gray hair she rinses with purple shampoo that gives it this nice lavender shade. She's never been married, as far as I know. No kids. Nothing to save for. No one to answer to, except her boyfriend.

Judy snaps her gum and rolls her eyes and tells the hogs to shut the hell up and order already, don't be wasting her whole damn day, and they laugh and holler and eat it up like the pie they love so fucking much. Then she goes in the back near the kitchen to pop the pills she likes. She thinks I don't see her taking them, but I do. I don't blame her for it, either. There are times when I want to go in the back and ask her to slip me one.

I love Judy. She's probably the only reason I haven't quit all year. That and my half-brained plans of saving up for a year abroad. She's the reason I have a car, too. She sold it to me for two hundred bucks, and while it's more or less an old clunker, and it can't go below a quarter tank of gas before it starts to wheeze like an old man with emphysema and shut itself down . . . hell, it's still mine.

Sometimes I wish I had the guts to steal the keys to one of the hogs' big monster trucks and ride off into the sunset, flipping off this dying town as I go. But for now—and maybe forever—Blue Bottle is where I'm stuck.

Anything else is only a pipe dream.

One of the hogs beckons me over. I consider pretending like I didn't see, but Boss Man is in a sour mood today, and he's been all eyes on deck. So, I take out a pen from my apron and approach.

The hog man is maybe forty, maybe my daddy's age if he

were still alive today. He looks me up and down, grunts. I imagine the wheels turning in his head, rusty squeaky wheels in desperate need of some WD-40. "Can I ask you something?" he asks gruffly.

You just did, asshole. That's what I really want to say. But instead I force my mouth to make the closest thing it can get to a smile and ask in my Real Nice Girl voice: "What can I get for you?"

Now who's asking questions?

His lips twitch into a grin, and for a second I feel like he's gonna give me the answer he secretly wants to give. He runs his fat pink tongue across his lip instead and goes: "What's your favorite thing on the menu, Trix?"

Trix. His eyes are on my nametag now. I brace myself. Most of the hogs make a joke of it, ask me if "Trix are really for kids" or if I have any "tricks" up my sleeve. Some shit like that. But this guy doesn't say any of that. He leans forward on his elbows and studies me closely.

What's your favorite thing on the menu?

I shrug and give him my best tight-lipped grin in return, like a nervous dog with its teeth pulled back. "I don't know. I don't really eat the food here."

If Boss Man heard me saying that, he'd have me drawn and quartered. But damn, the food here really is terrible.

The hog man quirks an eyebrow and licks at the side of his mouth, slowly, his eyes never leaving mine. I can read in his gray gaze what he wants to say: *I'd love to taste* you. The chatter of the diner lowers to a dull buzz. It's only us here now, in this space, alone, and he wants to suck the life out of me. I can taste it. I feel my heart quickening, little black dots blinking in front of my vision. It's getting harder to breathe. He stares at me, dumbfounded, as I choke back an oncoming sob and then gasp as a hand from behind suddenly slaps my shoulder.

It's just Judy, looking all concerned. "Hey, kiddo, why don't you take your break now, huh? You look a little bushed."

Judy always seems to be in the right place at the right time. She has a sense about things, just kind of knows when something's about to go down. It's probably why last night right before my shift ended, she gave me the knife. It's double-edged. Sharp as a hornet's sting. She put it in a little protector case for me and slipped it into my hands while I was out smoking, irritable and hot from a long night of hog men leering and Boss Man yelling.

"Keep this for me, will ya?" she asked, stepping away moments later. I could still smell her cedar perfume.

I'd held big knives before, sure, but never outside a kitchen. Never *hung on to* one before.

Now Judy is standing in front of me looking all Mama Bear concerned, the wrinkles around her thin gray eyebrows creasing as she frowns. The hog man is saying something, probably frustrated at being interrupted in the middle of his order, but I can't hear him. His voice is static now. Judy tucks a lock of hair behind my ear and pinches my cheek.

"Go," she whispers, giving me a wink. "I got this."

I nod and hurry outside into the late spring air, still dizzy from the attack. My mama always called them the "jitterbugs," but I suspect it's something more sinister. Men like him make them come on.

Men like him are men I need to steer clear of.

Every few weeks or so, Judy shows up at the diner with another eggplant bruise blooming across her skin. I've seen them on her arms, her legs, her collarbone. She once came in with a black eye badly hidden behind drugstore powder. There are bite marks sometimes, too.

I know her boyfriend beats her. She doesn't talk about it. She blames the bruises on anemia and low vitamin C if anyone dare make a comment. Most people don't seem to care or notice. But I know it's him. I also know she and Boss Man were having an affair. I caught them out behind the dumpster more than once, sucking face like horny teenagers. Her boyfriend knows it, too. I don't know how I know he knows, but I know he does. He swaggers into the diner sometimes, his big blue eyes never leaving Judy, a roguish smile on his face and venom in his voice. She always gives him leftovers. She speaks to him all sweet and syrupy, like he's a little baby in need of looking after. He looks at her like he wants to bite her. A rattlesnake. Hungry and waiting.

Why does a woman like Judy put up with a man like that? It makes me sick to have thoughts like this, but I can't help it. I wonder it all the time. What does Judy get out of it? Why doesn't she just up and leave?

These questions spin around and around in my mind until I feel nauseated.

Outside the back of the diner the air is so clear that I can breathe again.

Naturally, first thing I do is suck down a Marlboro Light. Blame my daddy for passing on those addiction-prone genes. My cell phone buzzes in my pocket, and pretty soon, Boss Man is barking at me to get that damn cancer stick out of my mouth and get back to the front line. Customers are waiting! The hogs are hungry!

I check my phone and my heart stammers again, but for a different reason this time. I swallow hard.

It's Lux.

Lux and I have plans to head down to Fever Lake for the long weekend. Despite its name, the water is actually clean and fairly cool, and it's not meant to get you sick or anything. The plan is, we'll rent a cheap motel room by the water, or maybe camp out in the glen if the weather stays nice enough. We'll grill burgers

and dogs and make tea over an open flame. She'll snap photos
of the trees and the woodpeckers and the bumblebees screwing
the flowers or whatever it is she likes to do with her beloved '89
Canon, while I lie out in the sun and work on my tan. We'll
skinny dip at night. Make s'mores. Scream our favorite songs at
the stars while the Blue Ridge Mountains watch over us. Maybe
we'll even try shrooms together for the first time. Lux said she
could snag some from an ex. And best of all, if it rains, we can
put down the seats of my hatchback at night and sleep in the
warmth of the car.

Lux. *The lake.* A whole weekend with me and her, together.
Alone. The hammering in my heart reaches my throat.

I answer.

Before I can even get a "hello" in, she's all: "You're coming
over right after your shift ends, right?"

It's pretty quiet on her end overall. No TV blaring in the
background, no stereo blasting '80s music. Her dad must not be
home yet. Thank the moon and the stars.

"Yeah, I'm coming over," I say, clearing the smoke out of my
voice. I stomp out my cigarette. No use smoking the whole damn
thing and making my breath smell bad. Not when I'm about to
spend the whole weekend alone with Lux.

———

I slather sunscreen on the new stick-and-poke tattoo on my
wrist—the one Judy did for me two weeks ago after I slipped
her a week's worth of tip money—and drive down in my copper
clunker of a hatchback to pick up Lux. Fuck the diner. Fuck this
town. It's hot as hell, but the lake will be cooler.

I can't remember the last time we had rain. All the rhododen-
dron that bloomed so full and bright earlier this spring are now

brown and shriveled. Thirsty for a droplet. Husks of what they used to be. The heat is unrelenting, like the earth is punishing us for using everything up. Now we get nothing back.

Fuck Blue Bottle.

And fuck that leering, menacing hog man. And Judy's boyfriend. And Boss Man and all his glares.

All of them can go right to hell.

We planned it all last minute. Just the two of us. We'll be back by Sunday evening at the latest.

Judy promised to look after Mama for me. I offered to pay her, but she refused. She knows how much it means to me.

Mama lives in a dream world now, a limbo her mind can't quite escape. She hears and feels but doesn't really understand. She can make her own peanut butter and jelly sandwiches, let's say, but gets confused and leaves the stove on and wanders around the house when she wants to cook anything more complicated. She almost started a fire once. She has night terrors, too, times when she crawls into my bed at four a.m. dazed and confused and asks me what house she's in. Where she is. Sometimes she knows me, other times Judy keeps trying to tell me she's declining fast, that she'd probably do better in a facility, but any facility would be too far and I'd never see her.

If the good old state of West Virginia ever finds out how far gone Mama really is, surely they'll take me away from her. Put her in a hospital or a home and me in the foster system until I turn eighteen. I asked Judy once if she could adopt me, on a cold December night when Mama was wailing and crying for hours and my head hurt and I had two essays due the next morning. I called her up in a panic and begged her to take me in if she could, but she just sighed sadly and said: "You know that's not how it works, kiddo."

Mama can be difficult, yes, but she's my mama. I've been handling her mood swings and false memories and occasional late-night runaways for years. I just need a break. A spring break. Only for a little while. One weekend. Judy will watch her while I'm gone.

At the next stoplight, a hulking minivan pulls right beside me, stuffed with rowdy kids. One little girl smushes her face against the window and sticks out her tongue. I stick mine right back and make the funniest face I can. She giggles and it makes me giggle, too. Then the little boy next to her whacks her over the head with his monster truck toy. The girl grabs it from him, rolls down the window, and tosses it right out into the street.

I let out a cackle I didn't know was inside of me. The boy's mouth falls open. The light turns green.

The boy points and cries out for his toy, but it's too late. His mama yells something at them before speeding away.

Hey, don't hit your sister, kid.

I stare at the toy a moment too long, this big red plastic truck left all alone in the sun, ready to be crushed by someone's tires. I consider grabbing it, following them or something crazy like that and giving it back. They're only kids, after all. Then the car behind me honks and I jump in my seat and hit the gas.

I never had siblings, and part of me is grateful for that. No brothers to pull my hair, no sisters to steal my clothes. No one to fight with over toys and attention. It was nice, having my parents all to myself. Daddy could be a real jerk, but on his best days, he was the most fun person in the whole world. He took me to water parks and the mulch store and we'd go home and plant flowers, me running my fingers through the soil bursting with fat pink worms. Mama was always so loving and patient. Always happy to see me when I came home from school. Always ready with a slice of her famous homemade pie and the radio playing classic rock. She used to dance around the kitchen in her apron, light on her toes. Effortless. Beautiful.

Mama.

A pang of guilt and sorrow sears through my gut so painful that I wince. *Fuck.* No siblings means that no one will be there for Mama if something ever happens to me. I'm all she has left.

Checking on her one last time before I leave for this trip is the least I can do. Make sure she hasn't set the toaster on fire or whatever before Judy comes over after her shift is done.

And while it's hard to see her like she is now, I still miss her. Or what's left of her.

I'll swing by the house and grab a few blankets in case Lux and I need to sleep in the car. The thought of her curled up on her side next to me . . . it gets a little hard to concentrate on the road.

I swallow down the mountains of guilt that rise up from my heart and fill my mouth, giving me that familiar sour, bitter taste. The mountains are always watching, waiting, threatening to consume every inch of me. They're as old as time, like the Blue Ridge. Been somewhere inside of me forever. They'll never leave me. I know that now. I'm old enough to understand it, no matter what happens with Mama and when. But underneath, there's a fast-flowing river of something else pooling into me, now that I know I'm driving away for a long weekend.

I know this feeling. I haven't felt it in so long. I hate to admit it.

It's relief.

As I make a U-turn, I pass the red monster truck on its side, right where it was dropped. I don't know why, but it's the loneliest-looking thing I've ever seen.

———

We left the trailer park I grew up in not long after Daddy died.

Our new house on the edge of town promised so much hope, with its fresh white paint and stabilized rent. Mama planted vibrant flowerbeds of gold and yellow and orange by the dogwood trees in the front yard. I helped her install a new mailbox we'd gotten that was hand-painted by a local artist. I used to love coming home after school, seeing the mailbox with the cheerful foxes painted on it, running up the dirt path, knowing inside it would smell like Mama's baking, her raspberry pies and chocolate soufflés. Not anymore. Now the sight of that house makes my stomach lurch. The foxes are slowly wearing away.

Our little one-story house is located at the end of a long, winding cul-de-sac in a neighborhood tucked into the center of town, about a ten-minute drive from the diner and a five-minute walk from the Sunset Shopping Center. It's small but sturdy, with pink wooden panels and shutters faded and peeling from the sun. There's a little porch alcove where I like to curl up on the rocking chair and blast music on my earphones, watching the neighborhood kids play in their yard and the elderly Miss Belker walk her grizzled Chihuahua up and down the street five times a day. Flower pots filled with wilting daisies and peonies sit perched in the kitchen windowsill, right beside the brand-new AC unit Judy installed last week.

First thing I notice when I unlock the door and step inside is that the shiny new AC is off: it's almost as hot in here as the diner was. Hot and stuffy, and something smells like it's burning.

Beads of sweat pool on my upper lip and down my lower back. The kitchen is dark, as is our cramped little living room. The TV is off.

"Mama?" I call. The house gives me its silent, sullen reply, save for the leaky sink that goes *drip-drip-drip.*

There's a light glowing from under the bathroom door. I knock.

"Who is it?" Mama asks. Her voice sounds tired and craggy, laced with suspicion. "Who's in my house?"

I press my face against the door and sigh. Who else would it be, besides me or Judy? "It's me, Mama," I say, making my voice as bright and cheery as I can. "Trixie. Your daughter. I came to check on you. See how you're doing. I'll be gone a few days but Judy will be here soon."

"Who?"

"Judy. You remember Judy." I pause and wait for a response, but there's nothing. Then the sound of glass shattering and Mama cursing, things being knocked onto the tile floor. "Mama? Are you okay in there? Can I come in?" I jiggle the doorknob. It's locked. "Mama, why did you lock the door if no one was home? Can you open it, please? Let me in."

She begins to sob, muffled and low at first, and then her voice cracks into a tight, high wail. "Mama, please open up!" I pound on the door again and again until finally it swings open.

Mama stands in her silk pajamas—the ones I got for her birthday two years ago special—her dirty blond hair a tangled mess, tears running down her face. That's when I spot the red all over the floor. For a minute I startle, thinking that it's blood, but when I step inside, I see that what broke was a giant glass jar of tomato sauce. The homemade kind Judy brings over. The bathtub is running, steam rising from the faucet. The tub is filled with water, uncooked spaghetti floating in it. I turn off the water and drain the tub, collecting as much spaghetti as I can, fighting back the pinpricks of tears behind my eyes.

"I . . . I thought . . . I was trying to make something. To cook. I . . ." Mama's face falls, deeply embarrassed, ashamed. She knows what she did was wrong somehow, but she can't quite formulate why or how. In a way, it was creative, inventive: trying to cook spaghetti in the boiling tub water. I can't help but crack a smile and laugh. It's not really funny, but it's all I can do.

I take her in my arms and hold her for a moment, letting her cry into my shoulder. I stroke her back. "It's okay, Mama. Why don't we come lie down for a bit? Maybe a rest will help."

Her bedroom is a dusty mess of clothes and half-eaten cartons of snacks, bags of chips and cookies, crumbs littering the carpet. The shades are drawn. I pull them open, letting in the afternoon light, and she squints and covers her eyes. "What time is it?" she asks, her voice groggy and so, so tired. I help her into bed and gently tuck the blankets around her like I'm the mother and she's the child. I'll have to text Judy and ask her to clean up the mess in the bathroom and Mama's bedroom a bit. I feel bad, but I want to get to Lux as soon as possible, and standing in this room for too long makes me dizzy and sick.

After Mama is all comfy in bed, I hold her hand in mine for a few minutes, watching her stomach move up and down as she breathes, her eyes slipping closed. This isn't fair. *This is isn't fucking fair.* She's only forty years old.

After a while she blinks and stares up at me, wide-eyed, as if she didn't realize I was still in the room. "Are you Angela?" she asks.

"No, Mama, it's me, Trixie," I say gently. "Angela is your sister."

"Mm," she says. "Tell Angela I miss her."

"I will." Angela died of a heart attack a year ago. We couldn't afford to fly out to her funeral in Louisiana, where Mama's from. "She misses you, too."

Mama seems satisfied with that answer, but then suddenly jerks her hand from mine. "Are you Willow?"

I don't know who Willow is. It's getting hard to breathe, my chest constricting. "No, Mama. It's me, Trixie. Your *daughter*."

She squints at me and studies my face, long and hard, then reaches out and gently strokes my cheek. Her skin smells like raspberry lotion, like it always has, ever since I was a little girl. The tears drip down my cheeks and I let them. I can't help it.

"I think I remember you," she says, voice thick with honey and love. I feel it deep in my bones. "I'm going to nap now, if that's okay. I'm a bit tired. Maybe if I get some sleep, I'll feel better."

"Yes, Mama." I lean down and gently kiss her eyelids shut, my tears dripping onto her skin, but she doesn't notice. I close her door as softly as I can and go into my room, grabbing some blankets from my closet.

I should go get Lux.

I should—

I collapse into my closet, curling up into the two blankets I'll be bringing, bury my face in the soft fabric, and scream.

———

A part of me is always waiting for Mama to die.

Another part wishes she would hurry up and do it.

Not because I want to lose her, but because in so many ways I already have. Mama is a ghost now, existing in fragments of the woman she used to be.

Mama, who loved raspberries and baking pies in the summer with the windows open, leaving them out to cool on the sill. Mama, who beat me at Scrabble every single time, except for the few times she let me win and pretended like I didn't know.

The Mama who laughed loudly and openly, unashamed of her crooked teeth. I always thought they were beautiful.

And once she's really, fully gone, buried in the family plot beside Daddy and Grandpa Joe, maybe I can finally let her go and fly free. I can run and run and leave all the pain behind in a big whirlwind blur, and slowly work on my own version of learning to forget.

⌒

There's Lux.

She races down her front porch two steps at a time, nearly tripping on a toy her baby brother, Milo, left out by the rocking chair. Her curly, faded bubblegum-pink hair is up in a bun, wrapped in the star-spangled bandanna I gave her last Fourth of July. She's in denim overalls, blue Keds, and a white crop top, her skin clean of makeup. She's glowing. Nothing like me in my simple denim shorts and big yellow T-shirt. Big boobs but I always try to keep them fairly hidden. My short hair the color of used coffee filters, cut asymmetrically at the sides. Mama used to say I looked like a middle school boy. She never understood that I wanted it that way.

My fingers itch. Lux's expression is hidden behind opaque cat-eye sunglasses.

I don't know how else to say this: Lux Leesburg is smoking hot.

I honk the horn for her three times hard, even though there's no need. The old guy across the street watering his marigolds turns to scowl in my direction.

"You ready, cowgirl?" I call, hanging out of the side of the window.

"*Moo!*" she yells, and I laugh.

Lux swings open the passenger door and bounces inside, bringing with her the smells of freshly mown grass and sunshine. She kisses my cheek, tosses her travel bag in the back, and pops open a can of fizzy Diet Coke, nearly spraying me in the face with it.

"Jesus! Careful!"

"Want one?" She gives me this sheepish grin that makes my heart flutter.

"Always."

Lux pulls another can out of her bag and we tap them together in a toast.

She leans her seat back and sighs like she's at the goddamn spa or something. "God. I've been waiting all damn day for this."

I love seeing her happy. The freckles on her nose and forehead seem to shimmer in the light of dusk.

"We should take a picture," I say, nudging her with my elbow. "With that stupid camera of yours."

She rolls her eyes and chugs some Diet Coke, then kicks her Keds up on my dashboard. I don't even care that she's getting dirt all over. "*Stupid*, yet you want to use it. Why don't we just use your phone?"

"Because this trip is special, you know? Don't you want a 'real photo,' Dorothea Lange?"

She laughs, and it's like clanging bells with a little bit of snorting thrown in. I love that laugh. "I'm a touch surprised you know who that is. Fine. You're the pilot. Let me get my Canon."

We get out of the car to take the photo, Lux holding the camera up and angling it for the perfect selfie shot, grinning while I keep my lips closed in my best sultry stare. What I love about these kinds of selfies is that she can't see what kind of face I'm making, and we won't know how it looks until the photo is ready. No time to waste angling the camera and making stupid kissy faces and all that, trying to get the perfect picture. Trying to look *pretty*.

It's all so exhausting. Sometimes I just want a right to exist, to look however the hell I look and not feel a damn bit of shame.

The wind flutters our hair and she presses the button, and then we're locked in time, me and Lux, Lux and me, and my stomach is doing somersaults and my face is burning red hot. We get back in the car and I sip my Diet Coke to hide my blush and she plugs in her iPhone and we're off, Lux screaming with joy as she flips her daddy's house the finger, "Supercut" by Lorde blasting from my shitty speakers.

That was the very last time I saw her so damn happy.

─────

We're on our third Lorde song and already making good time along the main highway, if you can even call it that. Blue Bottle isn't exactly a one stoplight kind of town, but stretches out for miles and miles, flanked by groves of maple and chestnut trees, valleys that stretch their fingers out to the Blue Ridge Mountains that are always there in the near-far distance.

We breeze past the old Coke factory—crumbling and weathered red brick—and the trailer park where I spent most of my childhood. Where He was. Lux gnaws at her pinky nail. There's still the emerald green polish I painted on it two weeks ago, but it's chipping now.

"I like your stick-and-poke," she chirps, gesturing to the new tattoo on my wrist. It's a tiny hummingbird, with gossamer wings spread wide. The line work is pretty decent, all things considered. "Did Judy do it?"

"She sure did."

"And she's looking after Mama, right?"

I swallow down the bubble of anxiety forming in my mouth and nod. To Lux, my Mama is basically her mama, since her mama left years ago. Which reminds me.

"Hey, Luxie?"

"Mmm." She turns down the music.

"Your dad? Lux, you told him we'll be gone, right? Like, even if you didn't tell him where exactly, you at least told him you're leaving?"

She hides her smirk behind her hand. Poorly. Flashes me mischievous eyes.

"Shit, Lux! You didn't tell him!" I admit I sound both bewildered and deeply impressed. Lux tends to have that effect on me.

She snorts and snickers. "I left a note."

"Oh my *God*."

"It's fine, Trixie!" She waves absently at the cluster of maple trees we pass. Her window is rolled down, hand snaking up and down in time to the music as she mouths every single word.

"He's gonna murder you."

She snorts. "Probably. But not until I get back. Anyway, he'll get over it. I deserve a break. I've babysat Milo *five weeks* in a row after school. It's like, hey, dude, how about you take care of your own damn kid for once? Just 'cause Mom left doesn't mean you aren't a parent. I might have maybe said a few of those things in my note. I sprayed it with some of his Axe. It's fine. It should calm him down. He loves that shit." She laughs, bright and open and full of bells.

I grip the steering wheel tightly.

I imagine what my daddy would've done if I'd skipped out on him like that. Face dark, eyes mean. The things he'd say . . . No, no, I can't go there. The little black dots dance in front of my eyes and Lux gasps and grabs the steering wheel to steady us.

"Jesus, Trixie, you're driving like a drunk!"

"Sorry," I mumble.

"Are you thinking about it again?"

It. Only Lux knows what It is.

I run my tongue over my crooked top teeth. The same kind Mama has. "Maybe," I admit.

"Possibly," she says.

"Absolutely," I finish, and then finally smile. She smiles back and reaches over to ruffle my hair. I practically melt as her fingers weave over my scalp. "Are you hungry?" I ask.

Lux sighs dramatically and throws her head back against the seat. "*Famished!* I didn't have anything to eat except the leftover Jell-O mold Aunt Sybil brought over. Like, lady, this isn't the sixties."

I wrinkle my nose. I hate Jell-O. Too wiggly. Tastes like nothingness with a little sugar forced into the mix. "Gross. What was in it?"

"Nothing but nightmares." The way she bites her bottom lip and grins at me makes me shiver. I cough into my hands to hide the champagne feelings bubbling to the surface, the ones that make me want to lean across the cupholders and kiss her on the lips.

"We could stop at the nearest Cracker Barrel or Dunkin' or whatever," I say, trying my best to sound casual. But there's a little hitch in my voice.

She sticks out her tongue at me. "Nah, it's *vacation,* Trixie. Have you ever been on one of those before? I don't want coffee or some shitty buffet food. Let's stop and get a *cocktail.*"

"Oh, sure," I say, rolling my eyes. "That'll definitely happen. There're *so* many good places around here that'll most definitely let in two underaged girls."

She shakes her head and clicks her tongue. "You underestimate me, Trixie Denton! I know a real good place, not far from Pinesborough State. It's practically on campus. They have a live country band some nights. Cheap drinks, open late, and they don't card. College bars never do."

I already know this. Pinesborough State students frequent the diner during the fall and winter months, all decked out in their university sweaters and scarves, typing furiously on their fancy laptops. They're always gossiping about the latest late-night shenanigans at frat parties and the famed Eagle Water Outpost, which is clearly the place Lux wants to go to.

When I don't respond, Lux swats my arm. "*Come on.* Just one drink. Maybe two. And a dance! God, I really need to dance off some of this pent-up energy." She kicks her dirty Keds against my dashboard, and this time, it kind of bugs me. I notice she's covered them in blue glitter. That or her brother did it. Her dad's always saying he's worried his boy's gonna end up "queer."

God, I really hate that motherfucker.

"*Hello?* Did you hear me, Trixie?" Lux waves her hand in front of my face, and I snort and swerve a little out of the lane to scare her. She giggles and whips a shiny blue piece of plastic from her purse. "Plus, I swiped one of Dad's credit cards! I found it in his jeans last month while doing the wash, and well, he hasn't asked about it. Earth to Trixie? I *said* we'll go and get one or two drinks, then we're back on the road again to Fever Lake. What do you say, cowgirl? Moo?"

Bars are full of hog men, especially bars like that. Drunk hog men who want to watch me. Leer at me. Hurt me. I'm sweating hot and cold just thinking about it.

But she looks so damn cute with those puppy dog eyes, lit up like a firecracker, clutching her dad's stolen card. How can I possibly say no?

Lux is so much like a can of soda pop. It's all still and placid inside until you shake it up enough, and then she's about ready to burst. Ready to spill everywhere and leave a big, sticky mess.

───────

As dusk settles in, the sky turns an indigo blue, that last grip on the light before it melts away into a blackness full of salt-and-pepper stars. They burn and glow and seem to stretch out forever, watching over whatever happens down here on Earth, be it good or bad.

I think it's the thing I like the most about dusk in Blue Bottle. That and the fireflies. The way they hum and buzz and glow like sparklers. I like the way the air smells like sage and ash right before the last rays of the sun inch off and let go of its grip.

It's always the same here. That sky, that blue dusk sky light.

The stars. Glowing and humming.

The fireflies, like sparklers.

Always the same. The record of our lives scratches as time keeps on going. A film on repeat. Stories played out over and over again, bliss and laughter and sorrow and death.

Remembering.

Forgetting.

But the sky remains. It watches over Blue Bottle, over everything that grows up from the soil and survives on the crust, and everything deep down rotting away beneath.

───────

We pull up and park in front of the bar, a total dive with a tin metal roof and a neon sign glowing out front, only some of the letters fully lit to read: EAGLE WAT R O POST. It's a fitting name, I guess—the bar is indeed nearly on Pinesborough State University's campus, and the university mascot is a proud and soaring American eagle—though it's far from clever, if you ask me.

Lux rests her head against my shoulder. I could melt right into the hot concrete below. "Thanks, Trix," she says. "I really appreciate you stopping here. Seriously. I know these places make you . . . well, you know." I relish the warmth of her against me and resist the urge to reach out and stroke her hair, caress her cheek.

Loud music pulsates from inside the dive, and traffic roars on the highway behind us, but for just a moment, the two of us are locked in a beautiful stillness. I wish it could go on like this forever, that we could freeze time and never leave this moment, like when we took the selfie outside her house.

"It's been such a stressful year, you know?" She sounds so worn out and sad. "My dad . . . Trix, you know he's the *worst*. He never lets me do anything, or go anywhere. And he always wants more from me. More babysitting. More cleaning and cooking and chores done while he's at work or off golfing and drinking with his friends. Like I'm his wife or something. Or his maid. It's so goddamned ridiculous." I nod. *Of course*, I know, but I also know she likes to vent. Lux doesn't ever really get to hang out with me unless we're at school, or she's sneaking out at night, climbing through her bedroom window or sleeping over at my place, where Mama doesn't even know we're there.

"Sometimes I feel like this completely imperfect daughter." Her face crumples and I touch her hand. She's on the verge of tears. I hate seeing her like this. "This imperfect *person*. Like I can never be enough." She traces lines in my upturned palm and I shiver.

I shake my head. "Fuck that, Lux. Your job isn't to be the perfect daughter, or the perfect person. There's no such thing as a 'perfect person,' anyway, and even if there was, why would anyone want to be perfect? That's so boring. Besides, soon you'll be out of there and doing your own thing and your dad won't be able to say *nothing* to you."

She shakes her head and sniffles. "But who will look after my brother?"

"Um, your *dad*. Milo is his son, not yours."

"I guess," she murmurs, pulling away from me and leaning her head against the window. I wince because I've said the wrong thing again. I have a habit of doing that with her.

I clear my throat. "Should we go in?"

She grabs my hand again and manages a half-smile. I wish I knew what was going on inside her head.

We should've stayed in that car. Turned around. Driven straight to Fever Lake. We should've never gone inside.

Shoulda woulda coulda.

As much as Lux wants to drink, I want to eat, so we compromise and make a dinner stop at the McDonald's across the parking lot. Lux wants to use her dad's credit card, but I insist we pay in cash. We should have more than enough for the weekend if we're smart about it.

After downing two greasy burgers, a vanilla milkshake apiece, and a giant box of fries drenched in ketchup, we finally step inside the dreaded college bar. Immediately, I'm assaulted by the stench of bad beer and sweat. They're playing some terrible bro-country song. It's hot as hell in here, hot as the diner with the AC on the fritz. It almost makes me miss the place.

Still, someone tried to make the interior look halfway decent. White tea lights are strung up around the concrete walls, and everywhere you look, neon bulbs and colorful inflatable animals hang from the ceiling, or are perched on cardboard boxes and metal shelves. Elephants, camels, donkeys, turtles. It's a goddamned zoo.

Lux loves it here, I can tell. She pulls me right toward the bar, which is thankfully not too crowded, and once again whips out the stolen piece of plastic.

"Seriously, Lux?" I groan. "We have cash."

She shrugs and bites down on it like it's a piece of candy.

"You're gross."

"Finders keepers! No sense wasting your cash on this, anyhow."

I shake my head in disbelief but can't help but grin as we take a seat at the bar. "Won't he see the charges? Won't he know?"

She sighs impatiently at me and taps the credit card on the counter, catching the attention of the bartender. I relax when I see it's a woman, maybe college-aged, with fiery red hair and cherry-red lips. She eyes us both for a second, then lays down two coasters and asks: "What can I get you girls?" When she spots Lux's credit card, she adds: "Cash only." Lux pockets her precious card and pouts at me until I get out my wallet.

Lux leans forward on her elbows and tells the bartender with pure, adult-woman confidence: "A dirty martini with extra olives. Two shots of Fireball. And whatever my friend here wants."

"A beer," I say. The bartender blinks at me and I clear my throat, cheeks burning. *This isn't a goddamned sitcom, Trixie, you have to actually* name *the brand.* "Pabst Blue Ribbon on ice," I stutter. "Please. Thank you." I've never had Pabst before, and I've got no idea of how it tastes "on ice," but hey, it's a lyric from a Lana Del Rey song. That's about as far as my booze knowledge extends.

The bartender looks like she's trying not to laugh at me, but nods and moves to fill our drink orders. I slide a twenty across the counter, hoping that'll be enough.

"How do you know how to do all this stuff, anyway?" I ask Lux.

She turns an inch, our noses brushing, her eyes glowing and boring right into mine. Her hair smells like fresh melons and mangoes. Suddenly the heat, the bro-country, the twinkling string lights . . . they all evaporate. My hands shake.

"There are things you don't know about me, Trixie Denton," she purrs. Our lips are so close. Fuck. If I tilt my head one way, lean in a little bit closer . . .

"*Here you go, girls!*" the redheaded bartender hollers, slamming our drinks down in front of us, and I jump, startled. "Four drinks for two young'uns." She winks at us and moves to help the next person, some ugly frat boy. I notice him eyeing Lux. The music and heat and sweat all come flooding back into focus.

"Well, that was shockingly easy," I say, grabbing one of the shot glasses to steady my hand. "Do you think she knows *how* young we are?"

She shrugs and tosses back her shot. Effortlessly. I do the same.

Only mine doesn't taste like the one shot I've had before in my life, like burning cinnamon candy, sizzling all the way down. It tastes like soda water with maybe a splash of juice or ginger ale. The redheaded bartender locks eyes with me and winks. In front of me is a cherry-red concoction full of ice that is most certainly not a Pabst Blue Ribbon. I take a sip: a Shirley Temple.

Fuck. She definitely knows we're underage. It sets off butterflies in my stomach and makes my palms slick up with sweat, but I choose to play it cool.

I watch Lux stir the toothpick festooned with olives around

and around her martini glass, or whatever's really inside of it. Maybe soda water, too. You know what, who cares. As long as Lux is happy, I'm happy. As long as she thinks she's getting drunk.

I don't know why I love Lux Leesburg so goddamned much. Sure, she's beautiful, but so are a lot of girls at our school. None of them can make me laugh like her, though, until my sides ache, until I giggle-snort. She's sharp and funny and she calls me on my shit in the most loving way when I need to be called out.

Why does anyone love anyone? There's an endless list of reasons to love her, the more I think about it. Her talent. Her passion for photography and dreams of becoming a world-famous artist. Her quick-witted jabs and her kindness and compassion for everyone, no matter who they are.

I don't know when it started, really. It crept up on me slowly, like a soothing lullaby that lulled me into dreams of always her.

She makes dry observations about this rinky-dink place, gives out witty one-liners about the college students and bad lighting that makes this look like, in her words, "a 7-Eleven with barstools." I laugh until my sides hurt and enjoy her warmth, soaking her in, her closeness to me. The way she rests her hand on my knee while she speaks and it makes every part of me tingle. For about twenty minutes it's like this, just me and her, me listening and nodding and her chatting on, the two of us suspended in time once more.

God, I wish I could kiss her right now.

Then I feel a hovering presence behind us. I shut my eyes tight and grimace, smell the cheap beer and body spray and know damn well who it is before I open them. "You ladies doing okay tonight?" he slurs. It's the frat boy, the one who was eyeing Lux a minute ago. He's so uncomfortably close to us that I shiver.

Lux takes it in stride, biting an olive off the toothpick and sizing him up. "We're good, thanks. We just got here."

"I can *see* that," he says, like it's this huge revelation he's had. His voice is slimy. His skin is slimy. Greasy and bearded all the way to his neck. He's wearing a backward baseball cap with the Pinesborough State University logo emblazoned across it, an ill-fitting polo shirt, and cut-off denim shorts. His fucking elbow is in my face.

"Um, can you—"

He ignores me, inching closer to Lux, literally shoving me to the side. My stool squeaks as it moves. I want to slap him. I want Lux to tell him to fuck off and leave us alone. Defend me, at least.

But instead she twirls her curls around her finger and smirks up at him, like he's something to be ogled back at. They're speaking now in low voices. The music is getting louder and I can barely hear them.

He asks her something about one quick dance. She nods and grins, but as our eyes meet her face drops and the grin fades. She mouths: *Is it okay?* She chews at her lower lip, staring at me with this strange intensity.

What, does she think it bothers me that she gets attention at the bar and I don't? Does she think I'm envious of her position? I sigh and shrug like I don't care, fiddling with my straw. Let her do what she wants with who she wants. The hog boy tugs at her arm. I can feel her gaze on me again, like she's waiting for my permission.

It nips at me like a gnat in the heat of July. Why does she think she needs my permission to dance with some boy? She danced with plenty of boys back in Blue Bottle. *It's fine*, I mouth back at her, and flash her a fake happy look. Something softens in her face, but she doesn't quite return my forced smile.

Lux lets the strange slimy hog boy sweep her away and onto the tiny little dance floor in the corner, full of college girls, a few hog men here and there, and many more hog boys just like him.

Then Lux's favorite country song comes on and she squeals, throwing her arms around the greasy bearded hog boy. He lifts her off the floor and twirls her around, and they start swaying and dancing together to the music, bodies pressed together as they move. Every now and then, she turns and gives me this pointed look that I can't quite decipher, and I've seen just about every Lux Leesburg look there is.

I watch her dance for a while, then stare into the martini glass she left behind, the one she barely drank from. I gulp it down and yup, there's not a drop of booze in it, either, as far as I can tell, and I'm not even a drinker. Has Lux ever had a drop of alcohol in her life, or was she just blowing smoke? Sometimes I really don't get her. I chew the ice in my empty Shirley Temple glass and order a refill. I'll take a sugar high and a headache over getting wasted in this slimy college bar any day. Anything to get rid of that hollow, shitty feeling in my chest.

The redheaded bartender smoothly slips me back my twenty bucks. God bless her. I only brought two hundred dollars' worth of tip money for this trip, and Lord knows we need it all.

A few more bad bro-country songs play, one after another. A group of drunk sorority girls in matching Hawaiian leis and T-shirts shriek shimmy to the music. A hog boy bumps into them and spills his beer all over their shiny cowboy boots. They holler in protest, ready to fall on him like a pack of lionesses. I flinch in anticipation as if expecting someone to start swinging.

The bartender slides a sweating glass of ice water over to me along with a coaster. "You okay, kid?" she asks.

I shrug and stare into my Shirley Temple, swirling the ice around with my paper straw. Everything is made of paper now. Save the turtles and all that, I guess. It's a nice sentiment, and I'm all for it, but it's kind of funny how we're trying to save the planet now that we're in what feels like the end times.

"You know, it's a little slow in here right now," the bartender goes on, snapping me out of my racing thoughts. Her face is covered in a smattering of freckles, birth marks dotting a constellation across her rosy cheekbones. She's movie-star beautiful, except her front teeth are a little bigger than the rest, and it suits her really well. Probably would be a model or an actress if she didn't live in this Podunk town.

The bartender leans her elbows up against the counter and shoots me that knowing look that Judy always gives me. The one with the little twinkle in her eyes, the little *"I see you, girl"* in it. "Can I get you anything else, love?" she asks.

I stall, not really wanting to go search for Lux in the sweaty crowd full of people yet. My eyes land on a pack of Tarot cards near the register, tucked right behind a stuffed platypus and a disco ball.

"You read fortunes?"

The side of her mouth turns up in a smirk. "I do."

"How much?"

She drums her fingernails on the countertop. "Usually five bucks on a slow night like tonight. Two if you're nice."

I swallow the last drop of my Shirley Temple, letting the ice clink against my teeth. "Do I qualify for that discount?"

She chuckles. "I'll do you one better. This one's on the house." She winks at me and grabs the deck.

I watch, hypnotized, as the beautiful bartender opens the pack of gorgeous, hand-illustrated cards and shuffles through them. They're all done in black and white, with symbols of spears and sharp sticks and horses with shining eyes. The bartender closes her eyes, appears to concentrate hard for a moment, then begins to place some cards facedown on the counter so I can't see what they reveal.

"Flip this row over one at a time," she says, in that voice teachers use when they want you to know this is serious business. "We'll talk about it."

I won't lie, it's pretty spooky.

I chew my lower lip. I want to know, but I also kind of don't. Do I really even believe in this stuff? Why am I getting goose pimples all up and down my arms?

One card she calls "the Hermit" is inverted. The next two are facing me. Next there are two in the top row, one in the middle, one on the bottom, all of them fairly benign-looking. She has me flip them over one at a time before giving me vague interpretations of the cups and swords and strange illustrated men: *Trust your gut. Don't fall for fool's gold. Be careful with money.* Some of the anxiety melts away. This isn't so bad. It's like reading your horoscope: it can mean anything you want it to mean. The advice can apply to anyone. We laugh and chat, and she tells me a little about bartending next to a college campus, how she deals with getting hit on night after night. How she handles the rowdy, drunk patrons. I can't imagine all the hogs she has to deal with, their eyes moving up and down her body, drinking her in along with their cheap college beer. But her voice is so soothing, so assured. I feel myself start to relax. This weekend will be fine. Lux and I will get to Fever Lake and everything will fall into place.

I don't know how long it's been, but the combination of hanging out with this pretty bartender and the sweet, fizzy Shirley Temples I've been downing has made me lose track of time.

"All right." She cracks her knuckles and winks at me. "We're at your future card. You ready?"

I reach out to flip it over, then hesitate, pulling my hand back like the card might bite me. Whatever terrible song is playing suddenly slips away, like we've both gone underwater.

"Don't worry," she says gently. "Whatever you pick, whichever side it turns up, you still have a choice. You always have a choice in your future."

I swallow hard and flip it over.

It's a knight riding a white horse, a banner clutched in his hands. Only the knight is a skeleton. A dead man riding. Bodies with missing limbs are strewn across the grass below his horse's feet. The image on the banner is of a white flower with five sharp points. It makes me think of this picture I once saw in one of Lux's photography books: a lake with thousands of white cranes floating down it, white lanterns hanging from the tops of long-fingered trees. It unnerved me.

On the card, flames burst from the windows of a high tower as terrified people leap to their deaths.

I don't know its name but I know its meaning instantly. The card spells disaster.

It's horrifying.

"It's bad," I hear myself say, voice trembling. "It's so bad, isn't it?"

The bartender opens and closes her mouth, like she wants to say something but really doesn't want to upset me. "It's not bad, per se," she says delicately, but I can hear the stutter on the last few words. She clears her throat, and even though she nods encouragingly at me, it's like the air's been ripped right out of my lungs.

"You always have a choice," she repeats. "And please don't think the Tower card represents any kind of physical death." She laughs, a little nervously, I notice. Or am I imagining that? "That's highly unlikely. But see, because it's facing you . . . well, that is key. It could mean failure. It could mean the end of something. It could mean letting go. But whatever it means, remember: *you* are ultimately the one in control. *You* decide your own fate."

Our eyes meet once more. She's looking at me so intensely. I'm sweating hot and cold.

Protection, I think. *I need protection.* I can smell the dirt from the pen, from where He kept the hogs . . .

The knife. I feel for it in my pocket. It's there. Judy's knife is still there.

She tilts her head at me and reshuffles the deck, erasing my fortune from view. "You should probably go find your friend. It's been a while since I've seen her."

That's right. Lux.

I feel a pang of guilt mixed with a stab of sheer annoyance. Lux *would* run off and leave me by myself at the bar forever. But maybe something is wrong. Maybe she needs me.

As I wade back into the crowd, someone accidentally bumps me. I slip on the wet floor and fall hard, a bright flash of pain shooting through my hip. Hog boys chortle and heckle: "Party foul!" and "Drunk bitch down!" Someone asks if I'm okay and helps me up. Someone with a kind, gentle hand. The room does a sickening turn even though I'm stone cold sober, and all I can think of is Lux. I need to find her and we need to get out of here. Now. She's not with the college girls, or with any of the frat hogs or men on the main dance floor. My teeth chatter. Why am I so damn nervous?

"You look like you're gonna be sick," a girl says in my ear. It's one of the sorority girls, in her Hawaiian lei and cowboy boots. Her voice is so kind and she smells like spearmint gum. "Do you need to use the bathroom, honey?"

I nod and she grabs my hand and takes charge, shouting *"Excuse me!"* and shoving us through the sea of bodies, a mix of women and girls and hog men and boys. Someone slaps my butt.

I whip around to see who it is but we're already going down a long, narrow hallway where the music is muffled and oh, there's the bathroom. Thank God. The sorority girl disappears back into the crowd.

I shove open the heavy door and call out for Lux. My voice echoes, bouncing off the dirty tiles.

I hear the sound of whimpering. A male voice, gruff. Dark.

There's a hog in here.

A bearded frat hog in a backward baseball cap, polo shirt, and denim shorts, lurking in the corner like a phantom. The same greasy hog who hovered over us. Who asked Lux to dance. One hand is wrapped around Lux's waist like a vise, another clamped over her mouth. *Fuck.* She cries out when she sees me, her voice muffled and terrified. There are hickeys covering her neck, red and raw. There are bruises blooming on her arms. She kicks at him but it's useless, a terrified tiny bird in a tiger's paw beating its wings. *Fuck fuck fuck.*

The hog sees me. I'm suddenly eerily calm, like this is all a lucid dream and nothing is real.

"The fuck you want?" he slurs, squinting at me with his creepy hog eyes. "Oh yeah, the lesbian. You want to join us or just watch like a weirdo?"

Lux shakes her head back and forth, back and forth. Tears flow down her cheeks and onto his ugly, hairy hog hand. I come closer and he smirks like I'm about to come and play.

I smell the dirt.

I hear the grunts.

It's thick and warm where Judy's knife goes in, like slicing down hard into raw meat. Which I guess is what this fucker is. Meat and flesh. Wasted oxygen. Lux gasps as his hands release her. Warm blood gushes onto my yellow shirt, like ketchup on mustard. Sticky. In a second, I'm back in seventh grade science class, where we sliced open cold dead frogs. It feels sorta like that.

The hog's mouth goes slack, eyes wide and terrified, a farm animal paralyzed at the slaughter. He stumbles forward.

I spy the open fly on his jeans, the dick he was about to get out. He reaches for me helplessly, clutching at his abdomen. He makes these gurgling sounds deep in his throat, blood spilling into his insides and out of his mouth.

I stab him there, too, where his fly is opened. He lets out an ugly, garbled scream. Maybe I scream, too.

Lux grabs my hand and we run like hell.

When I was little, I always wondered when rot settles in, exactly. How you know when something's really good and rotted after it's good and dead.

I guess I was always scared to ask those kinds of questions. I remember once accidentally smashing a fat pink worm in the rain with my bare toe as I played in a muddy puddle; it felt like a kind of savage violence. A horror I'd inflicted on something so innocent and small. I didn't really want to know what would happen to my own flesh and blood and bones, assuming that worm was the same as me.

I wish I had blacked out, that those Shirley Temples had been full of liquor instead of Sprite and cherry syrup. I wish I'd been as drunk as my daddy used to get so I would never, ever have to remember what I did.

But I remember every beat, every moment. The spins I started getting in the hatchback as Lux sped away, the ragged sound of her crying, snot running down her nose. The blood on my hands, all over my shirt, warm and sticky and wet. *Oh God, oh God.* Our headlights flashed blindingly across a long and lonely highway, the night sky burning with bitter stars. The blood was everywhere. His blood. Pig's blood. The smell of metal and rust and rot. My hands shook violently as I flipped the radio on, smearing it with blood, desperate for a shred of normalcy, for something to hear besides the screams of the hog boy that kept ricocheting through my brain on an endless loop.

John Denver's "Take Me Home, Country Roads" began to play, and I cranked up the volume. From the driver's seat, Lux gaped at me like I had gone and lost my damn mind as the bitter stars and warm night air whizzed past us. I guess in a way I had. But I needed it right then and there, this song about our home state. *My* home. Blue Bottle.

I'd stabbed someone. I'd watched him bleed and scream, the terror in his eyes. *His* terror washed over me, now my terror.

I'd stabbed another human being. I'd wanted to.

That was when reality smacked me cold across the face and I began to cry like I'd never cried before. I buried my head in my knees and sobbed as Lux pulled up to a nearby motel and the car came to a stop. Some ugly runt of a place off that long and lonely highway.

"Oh God," I moaned. "Lux, oh God, what did I *do*?"

She couldn't speak. Couldn't even reach out and touch me and tell me everything was going to be okay. She gripped the steering wheel and clenched her jaw, her gaze a thousand-yard stare out at the parking lot bathed in glowing street lights.

I remember everything. Lux whimpering and cleaning the blood from the seats and the radio as best she could with an old dishrag she found in my trunk. Me projectile puking on the sidewalk before I could go inside and lie down on the bathroom floor in the motel room she'd secured for us while I'd sat in the car and hyperventilated. The smell of mothballs and pipe smoke wafting through the thin motel walls. Pounding bass from a party next door. I didn't sleep a wink. I took a freezing shower and then stared up at the ceiling in the darkness, listening to Lux shudder and sob beside me, waiting for the spins to quit, for my sober mind to stop being so damn intoxicated. My heart hammered in my chest, the shock and terror giving way to a deep, dark feeling of stone-cold-sober dread. A horrifying dread-filled feeling. This was a waking nightmare. Oh God, oh God. What had I done?

I remember everything. What I did to that boy. How the knife felt going into his solar plexus, and then his groin. I wouldn't say I enjoyed it, not exactly, but the question of whether or not I regret it . . . well, that's something else entirely.

<hr />

Cold. It's so damn cold.

I blink and my eyes hurt and it's morning, sunlight streaming in through moth-eaten curtains. Lux is gone. I did doze off after all, if only for a little while. My teeth are chattering again, my stomach an empty pit of pain. I glance over at the AC unit in the window: it's set to 72 degrees. Why am I so damn cold? Maybe I'm in shock. It must be shock. Can you die from shock? Freeze to death?

I wrap the blankets around me tighter, cocooning myself in the sheets. Willing this bad dream to be over. My head hurts and the space behind my eyes aches from crying. I feel empty and hollowed out inside, the thought on a sickening loop in my head: *I stabbed someone. I stabbed someone.*

Lux comes back a few minutes later all downcast, the hickeys on her neck mostly covered up with concealer. I think of Judy and her eggplant bruises. Lux has brought me an Egg McMuffin and hash browns, my favorite breakfast. I devour it in bed like a slob. Lux sips a can of Diet Coke but doesn't eat a thing. Doesn't really speak. Just sort of stares at the old stain on the dirty carpet that's probably been here longer than we've been alive. Her mascara from last night is still smudged below her eyes. Her bubblegum-pink hair needs a wash, bad. The bruises on her arms from the hog man's fingers are deepening in color. She's changed out of the overalls and white crop top with the frat boy's blood splattered across the front. Sometime during the night, she changed me out of my blood-stained yellow T-shirt, too.

Ketchup on mustard.

I want to crawl across the bed and wrap my arms around her, whisper soothing words in her ear. But I chew and swallow the rest of my greasy breakfast as we listen to the buzz and hiss of the AC unit and the faint roar of morning traffic outside.

Lux mumbles something so softly I can't make it out.

"What's that?" I ask, mouth full of eggs and ham.

"We're fucked."

Oh.

The tension hangs between us, heavy and sharp. I glance around the motel room, see Lux's open duffel bag spilling over with bottles of sunscreen and bug spray meant for Fever Lake. I squeeze my eyes shut and try to breathe.

She touches my arm and I jump a little.

"He's fine," I hear myself say. It's like I'm hovering somewhere over my body, watching and listening from above. "I'm sure someone took him to the hospital."

Lux swallows. "We should call the police, Trix. We should tell them what happened."

"It was dark and no one saw us. I'm sure of it. He wasn't bleeding that bad. He could walk, probably."

"Trix—"

"Nothing happened."

The world tilts like I'm on a seesaw, and I can feel myself slipping off into the unknown. I'm on the edge of something big, something brewing and bubbling deep in my belly. If I don't hang on tight enough, I'll fall right off and never come back. Lux looks like she's about to cry again.

Somehow, Lux looks different this morning, like I'm seeing her without a sparkly filter. And I can't help but think: have I *always* seen her with this filter?

Whatever was there before is shattered now. It's like someone finally flipped off the lights, and my eyes are adjusting to the way things appear in the darkness.

"It's okay, Luxie." I inch closer to her and lean my head against her shoulder. Her skin is hot to the touch.

Then somewhere inside her the dam breaks and she's full on sobbing. I wish I looked that pretty when I cried, then instantly feel horrible for thinking that. There it is again, that filter. I blink and it's gone again and Lux is just Lux. And right now, she's not pretty and dreamy in her sadness. She's just distraught. My best friend is distraught because of me. "You did it to protect me," she moans into her hands. "I know you did. I know that's why you stabbed him."

"Where's the knife, Lux?"

She sniffles and heaves.

"Lux. *The knife.*"

She keeps her eyes on the checkered bedspread, fat tears dripping down onto it.

A ripple of fear slices through me, sharp as Judy's blade. When Lux speaks again, her voice is very small.

"I don't have it," she squeaks.

"*What?*"

"We must have left it behind. You were so angry and . . . not yourself." Her voice is so strained and faraway, it's like I dreamed it. "You really scared me. I got us into the car as fast as I could and I—"

Suddenly I'm tearing up the room, ripping apart her duffel bag and mine. Lux is screaming at me to stop, to calm down, be rational. I open empty drawers and slam them shut. There's a Bible in one of them, and it makes me laugh even though it's not really funny. I can feel the red-hot rage swimming through my veins. I want to break something. I could stab someone again.

The knife.

"Give me the keys."

Lux hiccups. "Trixie, it's not in the car! I checked. Please."

"Give me the goddamned keys, Lux!" I roar.

I'm being cruel, I know I am, but I need to find the murder weapon. No, the *attack* weapon. I didn't murder anyone. If I left it at the scene of the crime like a fucking idiot, I'm over. We're over. We're done.

"Please sit down," Lux begs, grabbing my hand. "Breathe. We can do this together. All we have to do is call the cops and everything will be fine."

"*IT WON'T BE FUCKING FINE!*" I scream. Her mouth flies open and she steps away from me. I've never yelled at her before. Not like this. When I speak again, my voice is shaky, but I try my best to keep it quiet, to keep the rage held down as tightly as I can. "They're going to find it. The cops. They'll do a DNA analysis or something and link it back to me. They'll come looking."

Lux's arms are wrapped tightly around herself. She can barely look at me.

"We should go to the police, Trix," she says again. "If we tell them what happened, that it was self-defense, they'll have to listen. They'll have to understand."

I think of cops, of their flashing cherry-red and Icee-blue lights, the screaming sirens and the cuffs and the rough voices and the hands all over me. I hear His voice and taste the dirt and shake my head no, no, *no*.

"No cops," I say sharply. "They wouldn't believe us."

She blinks at me. "You don't think so?" She takes a long breath and crosses the room, then approaches me as if I'm a wild animal that could launch at her at any minute. Maybe I am. I notice my fists are clenched at my sides. She lightly touches my wrist, the one with the hummingbird tattoo etched into my skin.

"Is it because of It? Him?" she asks gently. Lux knows a little bit about the Dark Place. She's the only one who does. It's the waking nightmare that haunts every dream, burning at the edge of every memory, good or bad or somewhere in between.

I nod slowly. Lux has brushed against my darkest haunts and traumas, and I just told her that she shouldn't get help for hers. That no one would believe her.

All the fury inside me evaporates, replaced by an aching, familiar mound of guilt.

The AC unit clicks and whirrs. A semitruck passes by, and somewhere, I can hear the distant shrill sound of sirens.

I sink down onto the bed. "Jesus, Lux. I'm an asshole. I'm so sorry I wasn't there when he . . . I'm a bad friend, I know I am. If you really want to go to the police we can totally—"

"No," she says firmly, sitting beside me. "No, no. You were right, they wouldn't believe us. Nobody would and nobody will. We're underage and were in a bar with drinks in our hands and tons of people saw me flirting and dancing with that guy. He didn't . . . he didn't even rape me." Her face darkens. "He hurt me, but he didn't rape me. I have no evidence, no proof that anything happened."

"But you have bruises and marks, and maybe we could—"

"No." She shakes her head. "No cops, like you said. They'll ask me if I was drinking, why I was in a bar underage. What I was wearing. If I let him touch me and kiss me. I *did,* Trix. I did all of those things. I didn't even want him. I was . . . you know what, never mind." She turns away from me. "I just want it to be over. And besides, if we turn ourselves in, they'll take us in for questioning and I guarantee you they'll turn us against each other faster than you can spit. I've seen the cop shows, I know how it works." She makes a helpless sound in the back of her throat and cradles herself protectively. I want to hug her so bad, wrap her up in my arms and never let go. "It'll be awful. My dad will *kill* me." I don't think she means literally, but the way her tongue wraps around that word, it's like it's a weapon.

"It'll blow over." She forces a plastic smile, and her dimples don't show so I know it's not a real one. "It just needs to blow over," she repeats with a huff, like she's trying to convince herself, to exhale away the pain and the horror. "Someone found him. You're probably right. He's probably fine. Though he doesn't deserve to be, you know?" She laughs a little. "Fuck him. But he's probably all right." It sounds so convincing, coming from her.

Or maybe I just need it to sound that way.

I shudder. "We need to get out of here. We need to move. Get away for a while. Put some road between us and them." I walk around, throwing things back into our bags, shutting drawers, tidying up.

Then Lux does something that surprises me. She stands up and grips my arm hard, steadying me. She turns me to face her. Her chestnut-colored eyes are solid, sure. "We'll destroy our phones, Trix. Then no one can track us either way. It'll be fine. We're fine."

I gnaw at my lower lip. I could run a whole triathlon right now. My skin is crawling and I want to sprint a thousand miles and keep on going until I get to the edge of the world. *We should get in the car and go*, I think. Go, go, go.

But Lux pulls me into a hug, strong and firm. I don't expect it, but I ease into the softness of her arms, letting go of some of the tension and fear roiling inside of me. I've been shaking, and not like when I was in the dive bar, when our knees touched and our lips were so close to touching, too. Not in the good way.

"Okay," I say, letting out a ragged breath. "Okay."

So, we do. We break our phones. Smash them right to pieces.

Lux and I stand on the shoulder of the main highway, me holding my outdated iPhone covered in scratches and water damage, her clutching the brand-new one her dad just bought her, the one with the shiny pink-and-purple case. She was so excited to get that case. I remember. Her dimples practically popped out of her cheeks when she first showed it to me. Now it's about to be roadkill.

Lux lays down the phones ceremoniously inside the white traffic lines, takes my hand in hers and grips it tight, then pulls us both back a step. I hear the roar of an engine, see the blur of an oncoming SUV, then count down from fifteen. Before I get to six, *whoosh*, the car's gone and both of our phones are shattered beneath its monster tires, glass and plastic case pieces flying every which way.

"Bull's-eye," Lux says with a grin. I laugh in spite of myself and she winks at me when I meet her gaze. It's not funny. Not really. But what else can we do? I stare at the glass and smashed plastic that's now baking on the glittering concrete. No more calls and texts from Judy with updates on Mama. No more gruff voice-mails from Boss Man pressuring me to take more early-morning weekend shifts. No way to dial 911. No more anything.

We might as well have gone back in time.

—

After the funeral of our phones, Lux and I go back into the depressing little motel room. She flips on the TV. This place doesn't have cable, only local access, the basics. The news. But it's fine. That's all we need.

Lux pounds the remote with her thumb, flipping around for ten minutes or so through commercials and infomercials and news segments until we see what we both need to see. It's on KGTV-9.

Onscreen sits a news anchor in a fitted blazer. "New reports of an assault late last night at the Eagle Water Outpost, a local Pinesborough State University bar," she tells the camera, her voice tight and urgent. A photo of the bar flashes onscreen and my stomach flip-flops. It doesn't seem real. "Police are investigating, but currently, they have no leads."

No leads.

No leads.

"Holy shit," Lux breathes. We wait to see if the story continues or develops, but it soon cuts to a segment about a local elderly woman who just celebrated her 105th birthday. Lux turns off the TV.

We stare at each other in disbelief.

"No leads," she repeats. A wicked smile blooms across her pretty face.

"We're okay."

"We're *definitely* okay."

"Maybe."

"Possibly."

"Absolutely!" we say in unison.

We stumble over each other's words, frantic, giddy with relief.

"They have no idea we were there—"

"—there's absolutely nothing to link us—"

"—we can go anywhere now. I mean, *fuck* Fever Lake! We can get out of here, go somewhere way better—"

"—we don't ever have to go back at all. We'll start over."

"A *new* life."

"We can do anything now."

"*Be* anything."

Lux is a can of soda pop, and I am her shaker. Shake. Shake. Shake.

———

We hit the road that evening, a dazzling new plan firmly set in our minds.

There's nothing for us here anyhow, nothing in this nowhere cow town county. Nothing for miles but wide-open fields and little rusty farmhouses that dot the flat, green-brown landscape. Tiny shopping plazas, a gas station, a drive-through carwash. Over and over, copied and pasted throughout the state. We can go bigger. We can do better. We'll head south, set up new lives somewhere like Austin, Texas, with its soaring skyscrapers and year-round gorgeous climate. Lux chatters on about becoming a wedding photographer, finally putting her Canon to good use. "Screw college!" she says, kicking her glittery blue Keds against my dash. She's on her fifth Diet Coke and is buzzing like a bee. We have to stop for her to pee every half hour, but it's fine, because *we're* fine. Everything is more than good. It's fucking grand. "Who needs an overpriced art school education and mountains of student loan debt to take *photos*? I mean, Jesus, what would I learn there that I can't learn on the job? All the best artists learn on the job and in their studios! School is a scam, if you think about it."

I don't know if any of this is true, but I nod and nod like it is, because I want and need it to be. "I can waitress for money under the table," I add, though I'm not sure how it'll work, but right now it all feels so feasible, so within reach that I could grab it and make it mine. We'll buy fake IDs, get a little apartment just the two of us, a tiny house, whatever we can find. We'll live in my car at first if we have to. But there's no rush now. We can take our time. Hurry up and go.

The thought of going home, back to Blue Bottle, the diner, normal life, Judy and Boss Man and Mama . . . it fills me with this deep, dark dread. It's like there couldn't be anything worse than going back, so why not keep pushing forward? Who cares where we end up, whether it's Austin or Mexico or Paraguay? The thought is so dangerous, but so tantalizing at the same time.

Lux and I stop at a local bank and max out the cash advance on the shiny blue credit card she swiped from her dad: $2,000 total. Her dad's PIN is 0924, her birthday. Easy money. We cut up the plastic and toss it without a second thought.

We have $2,000 in cash, plus the $115 we still have left for the trip. But this damn cash advance: I've never seen so much money at once in my entire life, not even when I counted the register after work. The hundreds are so crisp and beautiful I could kiss them, but I don't, because God knows where they've been. "*Bills have been up hookers' assholes,*" Judy used to tell me, always insisting that I wash my hands after dealing with the register. But thinking about it now, I'm damn sure there are far worse places those bills could've been.

Lux and I find a tiny post office. We get rubber bands and

string together our lumps of cash, stuff it inside a big manila envelope with the rest of what we have, then tuck that envelope safe inside my glove compartment. We buy paper maps at a gas station, load up on fruit, cheese, expensive bottled water, gourmet sandwiches, and plenty of Diet Coke. We'll follow the main highway, figure out the map as we go. How hard could it be?

With my windows rolled down, Lux's pink curls are free to bounce and glide in the warm breeze, held tight by her star-spangled bandanna. The one I got her. Her hair is freedom. We sing along loud and proud to my CD collection: more Lorde and Charli XCX, of course, and some good old-fashioned country and Johnny Cash. Lux made a CD mix special for the trip, just like the kind we used to make each other as kids. It's full of sparkling pop songs that shimmer and explode and rap songs with lyrics so sharp and brilliant they awaken new parts of my mind.

We can do anything now, absolutely anything. Buy $2,000 worth of goddamned chicken nuggets if we want to.

We crack jokes about nothing, the people we drive past, trucker hogs with beer guts and families with cars crammed with kids, people in stuffy suits on their way to the office, or overalls and denim on the long road to some factory job, a lifelong bone-churning grind that never stops or slows. That will never be us. We have no responsibility, no one to answer to, no one to care for.

This is freedom. This is it.

Lux and I see a sign for an outlet mall and she begs me to stop the car, so I do. We buy iced peppermint lattes from a fancy coffee shop, get a little too caffeinated and splurge on two hundred dollars each of clothes for our new life ahead: Lux buys pretty braided sandals, shorts, jewelry, and a full bag of makeup. I get two pairs of fresh new sneakers and a snapback.

"This is the best day of my life," Lux sighs dreamily as we fill my hatchback's trunk with our loot. She stands and admires the orange-pink ring I picked out for her at the jewelry kiosk. It glitters in the sunlight, makes me think of crushed ice and the orange Creamsicle bars we ate every summer in her backyard, as sweet and pretty as she is. "Seriously, can it be like this every day? Doing whatever we please whenever. Like a permanent vacation. No more ass-crack-of-dawn early mornings."

I laugh. "I guess if we get jobs we might have a few of those," I say, and her smile drops a little. I clear my throat and add: "But we'll set our own schedules now. No more school. It'll be fine."

No more school. We only have a few weeks left of the semester as it is, but it's hard to imagine the fall rolling around, leaves changing, air cooling. Sweater weather and new jeans and leggings, but no classmates to compare the first day's outfits to. No pep rallies, not that I ever liked those much. No classes or homework or impossible tests. No more sneaking onto the roof with Lux and tossing breakfast fast-food wrappers at the football team as they run their morning drills. No more Principal August on the loudspeaker, wishing us a "very, very nice day."

Autumn feels like a hundred years from now, but the idea of no graduation, no end cap to everything we've worked up to . . . impossible. I keep that all to myself as we climb back inside my hatchback and buckle up, waiting for the air-conditioning to kick in. We'll see way cooler things together than we ever could've if we'd stayed in Blue Bottle. *Just wait,* I tell myself. *You'll see.*

Lux clears her throat and pipes up, breaking through the storm cloud of my thoughts. "You know, when I was a kid, like really little, I thought I was destined to be famous. Don't laugh." I clamp my hand over my mouth and she grins and continues. "I mean, I don't know what I thought I'd be famous *for*, exactly, but I knew I'd do something special. I had, like, all these music videos in my head that I'd make myself star in when songs came on the radio. Visions of me on red carpets, trailed by paparazzi."

I cough to hide my snicker. "I didn't know that."

"*Of course* you didn't, dumdum. I never told anyone. Not even you. Because . . ." She takes a breath and there's this hitch in her voice. "This is gonna sound ridiculous."

"More ridiculous than what you just told me?" I'm kidding, but I can tell by the wounded look she gives me that I pushed it too far. "No, really, Lux. Go on. I'm sorry."

She shrugs. "Just that . . . one day, maybe if I became someone, did something really special, my mom would see me, wherever she was." Her eyes flutter closed for a long moment. "Like, on TV, or in the movies, in a magazine or on a billboard—it didn't really matter to me where or for what. But she'd see me, you know? And she'd think, wow, I really fucked up. I really missed out on my amazing goddess of a daughter. Look at her go. Look what she did without me."

I realize how tight I've been clutching the steering wheel, even though we're still in the parking lot and haven't moved an inch. I take a deep breath and push back my shoulders. "Oh," is all I can say.

Lux fumbles with the new ring I got her, twisting the orange-pink gem around and around her finger. No doubt it's a new nervous habit. I don't want her to ever develop a nervous habit ever again. "The night she left, your mama had driven me home. We'd been laughing so hard, yeah? Giggling about the stupidest shit. And your mama was laughing, too. And my dad was, like, standing on the porch, arms folded, face all stony, and my stomach dropped because I knew even before I went inside that something really, really bad had happened."

She's told me this story many times before, but not usually with this much detail. I perk up and listen closely.

"I came into the living room. He followed me and sat down in front of the TV, watching blankly, and said, 'Your mom's gone.

She left. All her stuff is gone.' I freaked. I panicked. I started hyperventilating, crying, looking everywhere for her. I begged for answers, for a phone number, a story, something. But he just kept watching TV, not answering me. And I fell to the floor sobbing and he told me to get up and go comfort Milo. He was upstairs crying himself to sleep in his little crib. He was barely a year old. He needed his mother."

I can see it all play out in my mind like a movie, and I feel a surge of white-hot rage, once again imagining Lux, *my* Lux, crying on the floor and her dad staring at nothing, doing nothing, and then going upstairs to comfort her infant brother while trying to hold herself together. My hands shake and I long once more for that fucking knife. I know it's sick, but part of me wants to stab her dad and let him bleed like I did the hog.

Lux takes a long, deep breath. "After she left, you were the only person I could really talk to about it. Not even Zarin or Crystal." They were both part of our original foursome before Zarin moved to Idaho and Crystal dropped out early to have a baby. I see her—*saw* her, I remind myself—every now and then at the grocery store, ringing up customers, her smile tired and wan where it used to be glowing. After the baby, she stopped inviting me over, stopped texting or calling. It hurt a lot at first, like maybe I wasn't good enough for her new mom life. Maybe we'd never been all that close after all.

"They didn't understand," Lux continues. "They were so full of themselves, so worried about who we'd all be when we started high school, how we'd get boys and 'be cool' and all that shit. I wished so hard I'd had my mom to help me through it, you know? Mean girls and petty drama and periods." I know. I do know, but right now it feels like my mouth is glued shut and I can't speak. Her voice cracks when she says, "I just wanted my mom."

For a while, I still can't find my voice, but finally I'm able to say, "I'm so, so sorry, Luxie." She reaches over and wipes a tear from my eye.

"Damn, I didn't even know I was crying. I shouldn't be crying." I sniffle and shudder back the sobbing ache in my throat, shaking my head. "You're the one who should be crying."

She laughs a little through her own tears. "That's what I always loved about you, Trix. You feel things so damn much."

It makes my heart flutter, the way she says it. "I love you, Lux."

She tilts her head and studies me for a moment, smiling shyly. "I love you, too, Trixie. You're my best friend."

It's so confusing, the way I feel right now. I take a deep breath. "Let me tell you something true.

"When my daddy died, I didn't feel a thing. My body kept on working, but everything inside of me was numb. Food tasted bland, like cardboard. Sleep was dreamless. Life was a haze of dark navy blue. Nothingness. People in town and in church kept telling me how sorry they were, but I didn't know how to respond. Mama was a mess. She broke things in the house. Screamed. Stayed up all night rewatching their wedding video, over and over again. At his burial, Mama's cries were piercing animal sounds, and she kept moaning over and over: 'Damn it, God, why did you have to take him from me?' I don't think I cried about it until one day, months later, 'Take Me Home, Country Roads' came on the radio. He'd always liked that song, but it was never his favorite, so I don't know why, but hearing it finally broke me. I felt every emotion there ever was, and after I stopped crying, I lay shaking in my bed, gutted clean like a fish."

Lux's lower lip trembles, her eyes glassy with tears. It shouldn't shock me but it does, the way she seems to feel for me so deeply. She places a hand on top of mine, and it feels so warm, so secure. I lean my forehead against hers without thinking. It feels right.

"Thank you for telling me, Trix," she says softly. I can feel her breath on my ear. "I never knew. I can't even imagine."

"I need a minute," I whisper, my voice shaky. She nods and we stay like that, foreheads pressed together, lips close enough to touch.

This shouldn't be the moment when I imagine kissing her, but it is. Her eyelashes flutter against my forehead, and she leans closer, and for a moment I think it just might happen, we just might finally . . . But no, she sighs and moves to rest her head in the crook of my neck, and I deflate a little, fall back down to earth and reality with dizzying speed.

I clear my throat, stretch my neck to back out slowly from the parking spot, navigating around a few sedans trying to give my hatchback a fender bender. I get us back on the highway, cheeks burning, heart pumping hard. I snap on the music, and Lux seems to understand. I want to change the subject, forget what we both said for a little while.

Forget what maybe might've almost happened.

We pick somber songs at first, but after a while Lux turns on the sugar rush pop goddess music of Charli XCX. We perk up and sing along at full volume, both of us feeling much better, like we've shed old, uncomfortable skin. By dusk, I'm road weary and badly need to stretch my legs. Luckily, after hours on the road, we've come across what to my small-town eyes looks like a blaze of Vegas emerging from the middle of nothing and nowhere: Middlesville, Kentucky.

It's cool, a little in-between place. A highway roadside tourist trap of a town, preluded by towering, colorful billboards advertising all the commercial junk your heart could ever desire: fireworks, baby-back ribs, fishing and camping equipment. There's a long strip of fast-food restaurants, gift shops, gas stations, liquor stores. There are motels and strip clubs tucked away from the main interstate, promising LIVE GIRLS and ADULT SHOWS, burning with their dazzling XXX marquees.

Lux and I splurge on a deluxe room at the Motel Grandeur even though we totally shouldn't. It's this dump of a building behind one of the strip clubs with a massive pool out back. The place is wicked ugly, with yellowing wallpaper, cigarette burns in the carpet, and TVs from the '90s. It's loud as hell here next to the highway. Sirens wail and horns blast, polluting an otherwise still and lovely late spring evening. The concrete outside is cracked and sprouting weeds. But here and now, Middleville, Kentucky, might be the most beautiful place I've ever seen.

The room's AC is on the fritz. It's hot and stuffy, so we yank open the rusty windows. I'm sweating and want a Slurpee bad, but Lux scoffs and goes: "What are we, eight?" She insists that if we get them, we spike them, so we decide to hedge our bets and wing it without fakes at one of the liquor stores nearby.

Perched on the waxy bedspread, Lux spends a good thirty minutes putting makeup on both of us. Some of it she brought for the trip—which I don't understand because we were going *camping*—but some of it she recently splurged on. She paints a thick pink gloss for her, crimson lipstick for me. We look years older, like those college girls back at Eagle Water Outpost. Lux swipes concealer over my eyelids and adds smoky shadows, browns and blacks, a touch of red and gold at the crease, then layers on the mascara that makes my eyes itch.

I scoff at her plastic bag full of colorful kits and brushes and odds and ends. "Jesus, Lux. Were you afraid the deer paparazzi would catch you at a bad angle?"

She snorts. "I like playing with makeup," she says, maybe a little sheepishly. "It helps me be someone else, change my face into something different. I figured I'd have plenty of time to experiment at Fever Lake, and hey, the deer wouldn't judge me if I looked like a clown."

I catch my reflection in the foggy wall mirror and nearly gasp. I'm a plastic girl, shiny and new. I'm not sure if I love it or hate it.

"I look like a goddamned Barbie doll."

"You look like you," Lux says tenderly, turning my chin with her finger and pressing blush to my cheeks with a fluffy brush. I relish the closeness of her face to mine, all of her attention glued on me. I'm free to gaze into her eyes, let myself float in the chestnut pools of them as she adds a layer of clear gloss to my lips. "You look like an enhanced version. You're beautiful. Go like this." She puckers her lips. I do the same and get that fluttery feeling again in my chest. "Perfect. Now when we get there, walk in like you've done this a million times before." She slides on her cat-eye sunglasses and straightens her posture, and we grab the room keys and race each other across the highway, nearly getting hit by a car on the way over, but we're laughing so hard we can't breathe so we sure as hell wouldn't care if we did.

The AC is turned up to arctic winter inside. Lux and I try to act cool at first, nodding sagely at the scruffy guy behind the counter while perusing the long aisles of liquor and wine as if we were connoisseurs. He barely pays us any mind, too busy with some game on his phone. We settle on two bottles of white rum and one handle of whiskey, more or less because the labels look cool.

The scruffy boy rings us up, eyes still on his phone. "$55.87," he mutters.

Shit. That's a whole day's worth of tip money, if I'm lucky. My mind runs through all the things that could pay for: groceries, gas, toiletries . . . but no, I tell myself, that's over now. A hundred-dollar bill is nestled deep in the pocket of my shorts. I fork it over like it's no big deal, like we do this every day.

His eyebrows rise slightly at the hundred-dollar bill. I do my best to keep my expression neutral and maybe a little bored. I imagine that I've spent the day at the office, that I'm bone tired and can't wait to get home and put my feet up and watch Netflix with an ice-cold rum and Coke in hand. I imagine who that girl would be, what she'd make for dinner, if she'd spritz on perfume before hitting the bar for a nightcap.

I'm so lost in my daydream that I barely notice he rings me up and doesn't even ask for ID. Thank goodness. I didn't know it would be, but it's still freeing, spending that much money at once. Just as exhilarating as the first time.

"Thank you kindly, good sir!" Lux trills in her highest voice, and it cracks me up. We grab our paper-bagged booze and race out of there, laughing until our sides ache. The 7-Eleven is shockingly out of Slurpees, so we take swigs of the rum and chase it with warm Diet Coke from my car. It tastes disgusting, and it burns like hell going down, but soon I feel super giddy, light like the little hummingbird etched on my wrist. I look up at the purple bruise of the sky and think, shit, I could spread my wings and fly up to those darkened clouds right now. I catch a glimpse of myself in my rearview mirror: Lux was right. I look *enhanced*. For the first time in my life, I feel something like beautiful.

We do end up getting chicken nuggets, and though it's not $2,000 worth, it's damn near enough to feed at least three families. Lux and I stuff our faces trying every sauce they have, then trip and stumble back to the motel where there's a party going on by the pool.

"That looks fun!" I shout, pointing.

Then I do something brave. I put my arm around Lux and squeeze her shoulder. She doesn't pull away.

Loud trance music thumps from someone's speakers, and with the hazy glow of the LED lights and the liquor swimming through me, everything feels easy-breezy. There are two girls in the pool, maybe our age, chattering and tossing a beach ball back and forth while sipping from red Solo cups. A beautiful boy with wavy black hair who looks just like them watches from one of the broken plastic pool chairs, a joint between his fingers. He wears winged gold eyeliner, a hot pink tank top, and a long, swooping sea-green skirt that shimmers in the outdoor lights. No one dresses like this back in Blue Bottle. Certainly, no boys do. Normally I would be too shy to approach him. But here, now, everyone looks so friendly and easy to talk to, like this is all a dream and no matter what I say or do, it won't matter in the morning.

"I love your skirt!" I blurt out.

"Thanks, babe," he says. "Love your eye makeup. It suits you."

"Oh, I keep forgetting," I laugh, touching my face, then realize my other hand is empty of Lux's. She's already scurried off to talk to the girls on the other side of the pool. They're waving and chatting with her excitedly, instructing her to pour herself something into one of the red Solo cups.

My heart sinks.

"You okay?" asks the boy. He takes a long drag off the joint and holds it out to me. "Want some?"

I've never tried weed before, but I smoke cigarettes all the time on break at work, so I figure, why the hell not? But inhaling this is nothing like a cig, and I cough and sputter as the harsh, funny-tasting smoke hits my lungs. Soon, though, a warm rush goes right to my head and I relax into the sensation. The boy pats the spot beside him, and I join him on the pool chair where we both watch Lux and the girls. They've both gotten out of the water now and seem to be her new best friends.

"Thanks," I say. "I'm Trixie."

"Arjun."

"Are they your sisters? You guys look so alike."

He nods and motions to the girls. "We're triplets, but I'm the oldest, technically. Anika's going to Brown for college—such a genius, it's disgusting—Zara's headed west to UCLA, and I'm going to state school here, because well, I'm decidedly *not* the family valedictorian." He laughs, but there's a sadness tucked there. "I'm the dancer. The family *artist*. My parents were never thrilled, but they accepted it around the same time they finally realized I'd never be bringing home a nice Indian girl." He smirks and rolls his eyes. "You know how *that* is."

My cheeks burn and my mouth flops open like a fish out of water, but I say nothing, even though inside everything is bursting with electricity. He hands me back the joint, and I take it with a shaky hand.

"We're having one last hurrah before we're split three ways," he says. I try to imagine being split up from Lux, embarking on a new adventure all alone. A future without her seems implausible, a big black void of uncertainty. "You know, party all night and dance till dawn. Senioritis gets to you."

Though her leaving me alone to deal with this . . . her going back to normal life. Maybe it is plausible. Maybe if she had the chance to be free of me—of this big old mess—she'd take it.

"Dance till dawn, huh?" This time when I take a hit, I expertly suppress my cough. "I look like one of those big plastic things they put in front of car washes when I try and dance." I wiggle my arms a little to demonstrate, and he laughs.

"Honestly, I doubt you look like *that*! When you love dancing, you don't really care what you look like, anyway. It's all about how it makes you feel. For me it's become an obsession. Our mom actually studied ballet for years before ending her career to give birth to us—but hey, now I'm just high and rambling."

"They say rambling is good for the soul."

Arjun cackles. "Where the hell do they say that?"

"West Virginia."

His eyes sparkle. "Go figure." He chuckles and shoots me these knowing eyes. His voice softens. "Bet it's hard there." We lock eyes again, but this time they're serious. Somber.

Now I know for sure that he sees me, *really* sees me. I've never been seen like this before. The electricity in my veins intensifies into shock waves of pure delight. For the first time, me and someone else are both in this one unspoken, special secret.

"I bet it's hard here," I say. "Bet it's hard everywhere." He nods sagely like he knows, and I realize that maybe neither of us really does know. Maybe in some places it isn't so hard to be fully yourself, doesn't feel like you're constantly walking a thin tightrope, keeping a smile on your face while holding your breath. Molding yourself with care to fit the scenery. Dull. Fully blending in.

But Arjun doesn't blend, and it's beautiful. He's not like me. He lets those sparks inside him fly free, even if he's still wobbling alongside the rest of us on that tenuous tightrope. I wonder how many places out there are filled with people just like him. Just like us. The thought is scary and brilliant and beautiful all at once.

I vow to someday find them.

I hand him back the joint and study Lux, the way she moves her hips so freely as she dances with Anika and Zara. The music is blasting now, a rhythmic hip-hop song undercut with a smooth synth beat. Zara or Anika—it's hard to tell, I'm tipsy as hell and the sisters are spitting images of each other—lifts Lux off the ground and twirls her around. Lux has always made friends so easily. Not like me.

Arjun points with the joint before handing it to me once more. "Trixie, right? How about we both get up, go join them, and set off some of the fireworks we've been saving for this very night? There's a field down the road, and if the cops come, we scatter. Deal?"

He holds out his hand, revealing shining gold nails that match his eyeliner and a stack of sapphire bracelets on his wrist.

We shake. He has a nice grip, strong and firm. He places the end of the joint in my mouth and waits for me to inhale.

It stirs something new in me. Something like hope. A roaring fire of emotion.

I take a long, deep breath, letting the weed buzz through me, then strut right across the pool to where Lux is standing with the girls, a red Solo cup in her hand. I grab her by the waist again and pull her close to me. Her mouth drops and her eyes light up like sparklers. Arjun and the sisters and the music and motel pool all fade away. I press my lips to her ear and whisper, "Let's go light some shit on fire."

The night blurs into a delightful symphony of sounds, smells, and candy-colored lights. I swear I never thought I could feel this happy.

Red, white, and blue fireworks shimmer in the heady night sky. Arjun lights them quick in the open field and then makes a run for it, Anika and Zara whooping and applauding in their bathing suits as the fireworks pop and crackle and simmer. They've brought their speakers over from the pool, which are now blasting a medley of energetic pop songs. To my surprise and delight, no hog cop comes by and tries to stop us. I guess no one's really making noise complaints in this part of Kentucky.

The triplets are cool as fuck, and the five of us share our liquor and light sparklers and get so drunk the grass beneath me starts to spin. Arjun and Lux talk makeup, squabble a bit over the best way to contour. Anika and Zara try to explain the easiest way to tell them apart: something about their birthmarks, and the bridge of Zara's nose is a little higher, but I'm so drunk I barely pay attention.

I stumble a little and Arjun steadies me. "You doing okay, kiddo?"

"I'm no kiddo. I'm, like, a year younger than you at most," I slur. This time when I stumble, I fall, hitting the ground hard. But I don't feel a thing, and I can't stop laughing. "Come with us. We're going to Texas. We're going on a grand adventure!" I uproot fistfuls of grass and toss them in the air like confetti.

"Here, Trix, let's take a break," Lux says gently, appearing out of nowhere like a goddamned spirit. Or was she next to me the whole time? She leads me a little way from the group, and we find a nice resting spot in the cool grass to lie down on.

I hiccup three times in a row, and that sets both of us off laughing.

"In Austin, we'll have so many friends like them," I say, leaning my head against her shoulder, inhaling the sweet smell of her shampoo. It's so much easier to be close to her with the booze burning through me. "Only cool, fun people."

"I was thinking maybe Santa Fe, actually." She twirls a piece of grass around in her fingers, making a little ring to match the one I got her. God, she's so creative. "If that's okay with you? I mean, if we don't like Austin."

Okay? It's more than okay. And *we*. Just the idea of us doing anything, going anywhere—together—makes my throat tighten up and my eyes glisten with happy tears. I sniffle and wipe them from my eyes.

"I'll go anywhere with you," I choke, stifling a sudden sob. Why am I so emotional? The stars above us spin and spin.

Lux giggles, those bells ring-ring-ringing. "Even to prison?"

"Always to prison. Seriously, Lux. I love you. I'll take care of you. Protect you."

Her fingers entwine with mine, and my heart slams into my rib cage again and again. *I love you*, I think. *I've always loved you.*

"I meant what I said," she says. "About you being the only one who understands. You remember last year's Fourth of July? The barbecue my dad threw for me?"

How could I forget? She absolutely loved the star-spangled bandanna I gave her. Had me tie back her hair with it and everything. Hell, she brought it on this very trip. I still remember how it felt when my fingertips grazed the nape of her neck, the caress of her curls. "I seemed happy, I know," she says. "The whole time I felt like I was playing a role: happy daughter, reliable big sister, confident Cool Girl. But all I could think about was my mom, how she'd left early July all those years ago, how much I wished she'd call me, because I knew she knew where I was. Ugh, I'm sorry, I'm drunk. This all sounds so stupid, doesn't it?"

My heart fills until it aches, until it's ready to burst and spill over with what I feel for her. "No. No, it really doesn't, Lux. Nothing you ever say sounds stupid at all."

———

Someone is jackhammering right into my brain.

SLAM. SLAM. SLAM. Now that someone is banging on the door, and with every pound of their fist it's like my skull is being cracked. I open my eyes and the dim light instantly hurts. I'm in a different motel room, one I vaguely remember. At first, I panic and the jitterbugs start as the little black dots appear in front of me. I'm thinking the worst, but I relax when I notice Lux curled up at the foot of the couch both of us were asleep on. Arjun and Anika and Zara are passed out, limbs sprawled over and under one another across their king-size bed.

SLAM. SLAM. SLAM.

I wrench myself up and stumble to the door. Clearly, no one else in the Hangover Limbo Room is getting it. My mouth tastes bitter and my throat is bone dry. I'm exhausted, even though I've been sleeping for God knows how long. I peer through the peephole, and the black dots come swarming back.

There's a hog at the door. After all these years, even at a glance I can sniff them out really well.

I open it a crack, the sunlight slamming into my retinas as hard as the hog was knocking. He's monstrously tall, with a thick bushy beard and a no-nonsense look in his eyes. When he sees me in my little shorts and tank top, he grunts, like, *figures.*

"Checkout time was three hours ago, little lady," he says with a *tsk.*

I swallow back some of the bile that crawls up my throat. The sight of him makes me want to puke. Maybe it's "hair of the dog," or whatever it is my daddy used to say when he woke up bleary-eyed and bloodshot after a heavy round of drinking.

"You hear me? Y'all need to get your stuff and get a move on!" he snaps. He yanks open the door and peeks inside like we're a bunch of criminals or drug lords hiding rubies and co-caine. "You're all getting charged double if you ain't out of here in thirty!"

The triplets moan and curse and rub the sleep from their eyes, annoyed at being woken up like this. Who could blame them?

I want to tell this hog it's not fair, that this isn't even my room, but my throat is so dry and everything hurts. Then the glittering sapphire of Arjun's bracelets flashes before me as he reaches out and grabs hold of the door, pulling it back so it's halfway closed. The hog flinches and takes a few steps back.

"Hello, sir," Arjun says, his voice calm, friendly, body language open. He flashes the hog a winning smile.

"Get the fuck out of our room!" It's one of the sisters. The other shushes her and they both break into a fit of giggles. I hear Lux's laugh among them.

Arjun ignores them, trying to block the hog's view of them as best he can. "We do apologize. Last night we requested a wake-up call from the office, but it seems they never called." The hog scowls, taking him in, taking all of us in.

"This isn't the Ritz, kid. You have one of those Apple smartphones, don't you?" His voice drips with sarcasm. "You're responsible for waking yourself up well before two o'clock in the goddamned afternoon. Checkout time is eleven."

"We don't," I pipe up. My voice has found its way back in. "I don't have a smartphone, at least. I smashed mine on the side of the highway the other day. Well, me and my friend did. Got sick of it. Was nothing but a nuisance. Kind of freeing, to be honest."

Arjun suppresses a smirk as best he can. The hog's head swivels between the two of us, like one of the cheesy, clueless villains in those old *Looney Tunes* cartoons, the ones who know they've just been undermined but can't quite figure out how. He shoves his meaty hog finger right in my face. "Thirty minutes! And when you check out, you're all paying extra."

"Have a blessed day!" Arjun calls as the hog stomps off. He waits a beat, then slams the door shut. "Asshole. Nice going with that phone story, Trixie. Creative."

"It's true. We really did smash our phones."

Arjun gives me this half-smile like he can't tell if I'm kidding or not, then reaches over to ruffle my hair like I'm one of his sisters. Damn, I barely know this guy but I'm really gonna miss him. And I'm gonna have to give him my Instagram account handle, even though I barely ever use it, and probably never will log back in again.

Even though we'll most definitely never, ever see one another again.

———

After we say goodbye to the triplets, Lux and I brush our teeth, pop some aspirin, then quickly pack up our shit and throw it in the trunk. I grab the motel keys then head to the front office, aim, and throw them hard as I can. They bang as they hit the front door, then clatter to the ground. The hog I saw earlier is in there on the computer. His head jolts up like a startled prairie dog's.

Lux and I give him the finger. We run off.

It feels good to speed off into the warmth of the day, our favorite songs blasting, Lux trying her best to read the giant paper map, her bare feet up on the dash. We're back in the zone, in our element, even though I'm tired and aching and dying for a nap, and my head feels like it's being cut through with a hacksaw.

The roadside diner where we stop for brunch smells like fresh coffee and Pine-Sol. It's miles from the main highway, down an old battered country road flanked by apple trees, hungry bees, and flies buzzing and swirling in the sweet air of the late afternoon. I suggested we eat at Cracker Barrel, but Lux insisted we drive down the mystery road and explore, and then the perfect spot came into view like a mirage.

This place is nothing like Blue Bottle, and everything feels much cleaner and fresher than Middlesville. It may as well exist inside a dream. And the diner is nothing like the one back home with all the hogs.

Never again, I think. *Never going back.*

Lux and I sprinkle powdered sugar over our brunches: french toast with blueberries and heaps of whipped cream for me, pancakes stacked high and oozing with syrup and butter for her. Warm, dappled sunlight fills our little booth, the seats red plastic, glittering like in those old diners from the '50s. Johnny Cash plays on an old jukebox near the bar. The music helps with my hangover, which has already subsided considerably.

Lux smacks her lips and licks her fingers. I toss a sugar packet at her and she smirks. It's so damn nice to be here with her, bathing in the afternoon sunlight, enjoying a moment of peace. Like we're two normal girls having an ordinary breakfast at an ordinary diner. We can sit and eat and pretend like nothing bad has happened, if only for a little while.

"You're gross," I tease. "Can't you eat like a *civilized* lady?"

She clears her throat dramatically, folds her big paper napkin on her lap, and holds her glass of Diet Coke with one pinky out. "Better, my dear?" she asks in her most hoity-toity voice.

"Very proper, *dah-ling.* Very proper indeed."

We snort and giggle a little too loudly. An older man reading a newspaper in a corner booth shoots us an irritated look. I reach my fork over to grab a bite of her pancakes and she pulls her dish away from me, slapping my hand with her knife.

"Ow!"

"Manners, *dah-ling,* manners! You must ask a lady before you doth take a nibble of her confections."

I grin and sip my coffee. Black and bitter, just how I like it best. "I don't think that's entirely accurate, historically, grammatically, or otherwise. But I'll let it slide."

There are so many more things I want to say to her, so many things I wish I were brave enough to ask.

Like: Was last night real or just a dazzling hallucination? Did I imagine the energy radiating between us, the crackling sparks of chemistry? Was it the alcohol and the weed, or did that love I feel for her really get reflected right back at me?

But without the liquor and the weed, the weight of small silences feels far heavier, and my thoughts race and spin around in my head. There's no hiding from them like when I was drunk and high. I'm sharply aware of how everything feels, every sensation, from the sticky plastic seats beneath my bare thighs to the way Lux's expression changes as she ponders over thoughts I desperately wish I had access to. Every time she chews her lip or shifts her gaze from me as I speak, the wings on the anxiety monster in my belly flap a little harder.

I catch a glimpse of the hickeys on Lux's neck, still there, turning blueberry-blue. A storm of sounds and images flashes through my memory: his hands wrapped around her waist. Holding her against the wall. Hurting her. He used his teeth and tongue and lips to suck her neck and grip her arms so tight she cried out in pain. His sour beer breath in my face, his eyes taunting me. What would he have done if I hadn't come in the room? What if I had stayed with the bartender a little longer, or joined the sorority girls wearing leis, stomping out line dances in their cowboy boots?

He would've—

Nope. My stomach turns to ice. *No. I'm not doing it. Not thinking about it.* I stab my french toast with my fork, then let it clank back onto the plate. I've lost my fucking appetite.

No wonder my daddy liked drinking so much. It was an escape from the doldrums and boredom, but also the hypervigilance. That must run in our family, too.

"You okay, Trix?" Lux asks, cocking her head at me. I shrug. "You're barely drinking that, and I know you love your caffeine." She snatches my coffee mug and takes a long sip, then pushes it back to me. "Yuck. I'll stick to soda."

She's trying to get me to smile, and it works, a little. If I hadn't come in the room—if he had managed to do what he wanted to do to her—would she be able to smile now? Would she be able to smile ever again? "I'm totally fine," I lie. It's a struggle to fake a smile, to stop myself from vomiting onto the checkered floor tiles. "I'm thinking about what we'll do today."

For a moment she hesitates, like she can tell I'm lying, covering something up. But then she flashes me a wicked grin and takes a long slug of Diet Coke. "Let's do more shopping first!"

I think of the cash we have, the big heap of it, and figure, why not? What's one more splurge?

She holds up her glass to my coffee mug in a toast, and I clink mine against hers. "Deal."

"To the best days ahead."

Blueberry-blue bruises. His lips on her neck, claws scratching her skin.

"Sure," I say. "They'll be absolutely wild."

⸻

There's no shopping center for miles.

We keep stopping to stretch or get gas or cheap food. Mostly, I complain about the crick in my neck, the tightness bunching up in my shoulders. Lux listens and makes sympathetic noises and takes pictures of everything she sees. I don't know how she still has film in her camera, or how she seems to keep finding beauty in all these ugly, mundane little details.

Every town or rest stop we pass is tiny and unenticing. No more cool country roads with cozy, hidden diners. It's all just Starbucks and Arby's and McDonald's, over and over again, and lots of flat farmland. Without phones, we can't exactly google what's in the area.

Call West Virginia the boonies all you like, but at least it didn't normally take forever and a day to find the nearest mall or outlet store. At least you could always get to another state, or were within driving distance of a big city.

I'm so goddamned exhausted. Time blurs together once more, a continuum of empty Diet Coke cans, engine fumes, rolling roads, and paper maps. The smell of sunscreen and Lux's shampoo. Acres and acres of flat nothing, occasionally broken up by little towns and gas stations and farms and roadside markets.

They don't tell you about road lag in driver's ed. How those long, meandering hours behind the wheel, eyes glued to the horizon, muscles locked into position . . . all of it can cause serious fatigue, aches and pains throughout the body. I let Lux drive now and then, but she hasn't had enough time to practice and we can't risk getting pulled over. Not like me. I've been driving stick since I was thirteen, practicing in my daddy's old truck on Blue Bottle's winding back roads and old dirt paths.

I'm so bored and tired I want to scream.

It doesn't help that it's slow going, even when we do start to see slightly more interesting things. Lux keeps finding something new to photograph that otherwise looks dull as dishwater to me: a roadside attraction, a farmers market, a reportedly haunted cotton gin. The world's largest inflatable banana. Who knew the Midwest had so many marvels? And the shopping, once we discover the little plazas and malls. Lux *loves* her shopping. She buys trinkets and jewelry from a local craft fair, nail polish and mini-skirts and crop tops from the strip mall. We spend the first night in the car, waking up the next morning feeling grimy and hot and in desperate need of a shower. It's hard to sleep comfortably in my hatchback, and it gets hot as hell in there. If I roll the windows down, mosquitoes start biting. I wish I could sprawl out, curl up against a cool pillow. But we need to start saving our money. The next night we barely sleep at all. We stay up drinking more of our liquor and running drunkenly through a mega-Walmart, screaming with laughter under harsh fluorescent lights until someone kicks us out for being too rowdy. We laugh all the way back to my hatchback and hit the road. After being stuck in a car all day and night, Walmart feels like fucking Disneyland.

Two days of doing nothing have breezed by, and we're still somewhere in Missouri.

I miss the diner. I miss work. Shit, I even miss school. This is no vacation like I thought it would be, no all-American road trip full of adventure and heart, our hair flapping in the wind, big white perfect-teeth smiles and lots of laughter like those carefree girls in the music videos. This is purgatory, played to a soundtrack of pop music.

I wonder what's been happening on the news since the incident. If they've found my fingerprints on the knife, even though they wouldn't be able to identify them since I've never been arrested.

And what happened to the boy I stabbed? Did he remember it? Did he say anything to a cop or detective? Is he in a coma or is he awake? Can he even physically *speak* anymore, after the way I stabbed him? My palms sweat and my throat starts to ache. I have to shake my head hard and concentrate on the road.

I wonder all the time if they have any suspects. It kills me not to know, not to have even a clue what's going on. I want my phone back so bad. I stuff the thoughts deep down where they can't get to me.

"You remember that show *Brat Camp*?" Lux asks, breaking through the storm cloud in my mind. She's munching on a giant bag of Chex Mix, sipping her fourth can of Diet Coke, and it's only two p.m. We're passing through a national forest, someplace named after an old railroad manufacturer. I count the catalpas and buckeyes and red maples. Daddy knew the names of all the trees. Used to hoist me up on his big shoulders and carry me through the groves, pointing and making me repeat each name like a prayer.

"Trix?"

"Mmm."

"*Brat Camp*? We used to watch it on YouTube at my house, remember?" I don't, but I nod anyway, desperate to go back to my daydream about trees and Daddy. "It was that documentary show about those 'bad kids' who are difficult. Like, some of them were on drugs, or hard partiers, or had lots of tattoos . . . or were . . . gay. Queer." Lux gulps her soda pop, like those last two words were difficult to get down. "Anyway, their parents had them sent to these awful camps called 'residential treatment facilities,' obviously against their will, where they took away all their piercings and music and books and nice possessions and basically made them work on a farm all day, or go camping and hiking for weeks, sleeping out in the bitter cold. Brutal shit. Not like a vacation. *Survivor* but without the prize money, I guess.

"It was supposed to set them straight or something. Make them realize the importance of life or whatever. All of them were, like, professionally kidnapped in the middle of the night and dragged there scared and crying. Can you believe that's legal? You can pay someone to fucking *kidnap* your kid! And some of them stayed for *years*, because their parents paid for these places. Sounds like a massive scam, if you ask me. Anyway, they had 'counselors'—but I mean, who would work a place like that?— and they'd do these weird endurance things, and—"

"Lux." My voice comes out harder and meaner than I intended. I wish I could park right here and run and climb the trees. Lie in the grass. Work on my tan. Anything but be in this fucking car. "Please get to the point."

She doesn't flinch, just licks the salt off her fingers, used to my moodiness by now. If there's anything Lux Leesburg is good at, it's talking my damn ear off. She sighs and rolls down the window a little, letting in the summer breeze and wasting my precious AC. "I don't know, I guess my question is, if that happened to you, like, if you were taken away from your home in the middle of the night against your will and forced to go there, what would you do?"

I don't even have to think about it. "I'd run," I say. "I'd go off and live in the woods or something. Fuck that shit. No one could make me stay in kiddie prison."

Lux nods and taps her fingernails against the passenger window. She repainted them pastel pink last night after we drunkenly spent more money on some overpriced manicure kit from Walmart. They almost match her hair. "But what if they caught you? Like, what if there was nowhere to run or go? Sometimes these places are out in the middle of the desert."

I rub my eyes, tired after endless miles of highway and so little sleep. "I don't know, Lux," I groan.

"Do you think, even if it wasn't great there, maybe you'd . . . give it a chance?" I glance at her for a few seconds before focusing back on the road.

"What are you getting at? I don't even know why we're talking about this."

"I don't know, like . . . maybe . . . and I know those places are awful and definitely should not exist. But do you think that maybe it'd be almost cathartic to, like, stay and try to change? Take the time to work on yourself? Or even, I don't know, think about what you could've done differently? How you could've prevented things from getting so off-track. I mean, there's got to be a reason those kids ended up there. Their lives weren't exactly good at home, you know?"

A slow, sick wave of dread crawls through my stomach, piling on top of my irritability. I really don't like where this is going. I sharply swerve around another driver and Lux gasps a little as the car jerks her around. "No," I mumble, and it comes out weaker, less sure. "I'd still leave."

Lux is quiet for a long time, watching the road. Finally, she says, right to the window: "I think, maybe, if it were me, I'd stay a while. I'd even listen and think about what they told me, take some of it in."

"You're telling me that you feel *bad* about who you are?" I snap. I don't mean to snap at her, but there it is. The sureness is back in my voice. "What, Lux, you really believe all that shit? You think you have to feel fucking guilty and be a martyr? No, fuck that. I'm not apologizing for who I am or what I've done, and certainly not at some scam kiddie prison that wants to be a church, where they try to *pray the gay away.*" Lux winces. "There's *nothing* wrong with me."

But deep down, in my core, something uncomfortable stays lodged and stuck.

"You're really getting defensive, Trix," Lux says, biting her newly pink nails. She twists the orange-pink ring around and around on her finger.

"I'm *not* getting defensive!"

"Don't yell at me," she says quietly.

Suddenly it's like all the anger and irritability is knocked right out of me, seeing the puppy-dog hurt on her face. "Shit. I'm sorry. Really, I'm so sorry, Lux. I didn't mean to yell at you. This conversation is . . . I guess it's really upsetting me."

She doesn't respond. I flick on the radio and we listen awkwardly to an evangelical church sermon. I want to change it so bad, but I feel uncomfortably fragile. Like the second I touch the dial we'll both unravel and everything will fall apart.

After five minutes or so, Lux says so softly it's like I imagined it, "I really can't believe you don't feel guilty about anything you've ever done."

I switch the channel. I pretend like I didn't hear her.

———

Right before we hit Oklahoma, my hatchback blows a tire. We spend at least three hours on the side of the road, me struggling to change it with the spare in my trunk, Lux taking more photos of God knows what—it all remains so visually monotonous out here. Judy always used to change the tire for me, and now I'm sweating so hard I smell bad, and Lux and I are hungry and cranky, so we make another stop at a strip mall one town over, get hot wings and too-sweet lemonade that improves my mood a tad. In Blue Bottle, you've got to drive at least an hour for anything decent that isn't diner food or pizza. The wings are absolutely delicious, but I can feel the hole burning right through our dwindling pile of cash, and I say nothing as Lux—who I handed a twenty to earlier in spite of my better judgment—buys more trinkets and baubles we don't fucking need from a gift shop.

No matter how much I try to calm down my mind, I still feel this simmering resentment toward Lux for what she said earlier. What the fuck was that conversation anyway?

There's nothing wrong with me.

———

We got real lucky the night I stabbed the hog.

Most places won't rent us a room without ID. Lux told me she'd been able to sweet-talk the receptionist somehow, convince them she was in town to visit Pinesborough State's campus. She's always been way better at talking to adults than me. She has this way with them.

So far, we've been sleeping in the car night after night, and dealing with all that comes with it. But lately, we can't stand it anymore. There's a point at which a person breaks and needs a damn shower and a real bed.

Lux and I spend the next few days navigating the highway while making stops now and then at various motels we see. We try at least ten places, and each time, managers scoff and turn us away. *Sorry, girls, no ID, no service.* One guy even rolls his eyes at us, even though it's one of the scummiest places I've ever seen in my life and you honestly would have to pay me to stay there. I start to tell him as much as Lux drags me out of the place.

"*Don't*, Trixie," she says. "It'll only make it worse. When did you last eat?"

"Christ, I don't remember." The night I stabbed the hog feels like a faraway dream. I rub my sore, tired eyes.

"Okay, then let's get some food. Trixie, don't look at me like that. I know when you're hangry."

I sigh. She's right. "Fine, fine. I could definitely eat a whole horse now that I think about it."

She wrinkles her nose and smirks. "But why would you want to?" We lock eyes and then burst into laughter. She takes my hand in hers and I feel my insides soften. "Come on, I saw a Chinese place up the road."

As we devour a mouthwatering buffet of egg rolls and sweet and sour noodles, I resign myself to days of misery ahead, sleeping in the car. That's when she spots it: a glowing yellow star sign across the highway. She insists we check it out.

I want to protest but bite my tongue, feeling bad about how I've been treating her lately, how snappy I've been. To my shock, we get ourselves a room no question, and a pretty nice one, too, facing a quiet courtyard. All the front desk clerk seems to be interested in is our cash.

Go figure.

Now finally, here we are, and in a weird way, it's kind of romantic, me and Lux together, lying on a real bed with comfortable pillows. The room smells clean, the sheets are fresh, and as luck would have it, they only had a king-size bed available. Now we're together, side by side, my stomach fluttering at the thought of spending the night sleeping next to her. Between the delicious meal and the newfound luxury, an exhausted sense of peace finally begins to settle into my bones. I'm starting to think we could stay here forever and make a new life for ourselves in this accommodating room.

I watch the way her stomach moves up and down as she breathes. It's so beautiful, so soothing. She smells like mint from the gum she's been chewing.

I reach out and push a strand of her fading bubblegum hair behind her ear. Lux smiles warmly, reaching out to me in return. Our hands clasp and we lie like that for a while, fingers interlocked, just breathing. Whatever resentment I've been feeling toward her has long since been buried. Her dimpled smile and her laugh full of bells and the way she half frowns at herself in the mirror as she brushes out her curls each night . . . these are all reasons I love her. Without the confinement of the car, I can just be, just drink her in. Right now, all I feel is love.

There it is again, that spark between us. The crackling energy, like warmth from a roaring fire. I wish I could read her thoughts through the way she blinks and glances around and smiles at me with her beautiful eyes.

I could die like this, I think.

"Trixie," she murmurs.

"Yeah?"

"You know where I really want to go?"

"Hmm."

"The ocean. I've always wanted to see it."

There's this longing in her voice, a sweet kind of sadness.

"We can go," I say brightly. "We can go west instead of south to Austin, stop in Santa Fe like you suggested, then keep on driving. We'll be there in no time. We can see whatever you want to see."

She smiles warmly. "I'd love to do that."

The ocean. I went once as a little girl when Daddy took me to South Carolina to visit family. I remember the frothy waves lapping up the shore, the tiny creatures fighting against the current and burrowing back into the sand with each ebb and flow of the water. The sun was hot and bright but felt so good, like a big warm blanket or a hug, the air salty and sweet. I'll never forget that smell in the air. It smelled like heaven.

I run a finger down Lux's arm and she shivers ever so slightly. A blush reddens her cheeks, and she turns from me for a moment as if embarrassed. My heart goes *slam, slam, slam* like a sledgehammer. Can she read my mind? What if I'm imagining everything, reading too much into every gaze, every time our skin brushes against each other's? Every time I catch sight of my reflection in her eyes? I hope not, because I really like what I see. Lux makes me want to be softer, kinder, gentler. More thoughtful. She makes me want to be a better person.

"The ocean feels a lot like the sand at the lake, only less muddy, less rocky," I say. "I remember it was powder soft. Warm from the sun like fresh-baked bread."

"Mmm," she says. "Tell me more about it." She slips her eyes closed. The rising and falling of her chest has slowed. I want to kiss the freckles on her eyelids, trace her lashes with my lips.

I swallow back some of the longing that's been burning up

the back of my throat. I try to remember the ocean as best I can for her. For us. "It stretches on and on forever, into the horizon," I say in a near whisper. "It's so goddamned blue, and everything is so clean there, so calm. The movies don't do it justice."

She grins. "I want to photograph it all. The waves. The seashells. The way the sun looks over the horizon. Promise me we'll see it soon, Trixie." She catches my finger in hers, wrapping it in a pinky swear. "Do you promise?"

God, I want to. I want to promise so bad, and I want to mean it. I want to lie with her on the sand in the warm sun, the ocean waves crashing against our bodies.

But I don't want to hurt her.

I pinky swear.

"I promise."

⸺

Two nights pass before we finally check out of that perfect motel. Sleeping in a real bed was too luxurious to resist for a little longer. The days were long and indulgent, full of TV show binges and makeshift karaoke with our hairbrushes as microphones, like the kinds we used to have as kids. We only went outside to grab fast food and check on my car.

But it's been getting pricey. We need to get a move on.

The motel clerk recommends us a Laundromat in town to use, since I'm running clean out of underwear and there are only so many clothes we can buy. We watch our shirts and socks and shorts tumble in the washing machine and then the dryer, but still, I ignore my bloodstained yellow shirt, leaving it rolled up and tucked down at the bottom of my duffel. Whenever I see it, my stomach gives a sickening lurch, but I can't seem to get rid of it.

By noon we hit the road again, refreshed from so much sleep,

but then Lux wants to stop for lunch at this place called Dino-
Land, which I'm convinced is the weirdest roadside attraction
in all of Oklahoma. We end up there all damn day, Lux taking
photo after photo, me working on a terrible sunburn.

DinoLand is basically a tourist trap some rich guy did up
on a big vacant lot, filled with plastic dinosaur statues, their
paint faded and peeling in the hot sun. A diamondback snake
slithers across a T. rex footprint in the sand. Lux and I sip root
beer and eat hot dogs and potato chips, our feet dangling from a
velociraptor-shaped bench doused in neon yellow paint.

"I wonder how people find this strange little park out in the
middle of nowhere," I say. "A billboard? An ad online? What
kind of sad person runs this joint? Bet it's a real weirdo who's into
anime porn or whatever. Obsessed with dinosaurs but like, in a
really *wrong* kind of way."

Lux gets on her knees to get a good photo of a massive stego-
saurus painted in red, white, and blue stars. How patriotic. "Uh-
huh," she says, barely listening to me. She walks over to get one
of a lopsided triceratops with a big goofy grin on its face.

"Dinosaurs grinned? Who knew?" I nudge her with my foot,
angling to make her look at me. Smile. Something.

In the gift shop, exhausted moms push strollers through rows
of dinosaur stickers, sweatshirts, and stuffed animals as their kids
whine for ice cream. I know I shouldn't—because we've found
yet another cool spot and we're on vacation and I should be present here and now—but I really can't stop thinking about Mama.

I wonder what Mama is doing. If she's eating. I wonder if Judy
has had any trouble getting her to eat her veggies. She likes them
best cut up, not whole. I wish I could text Judy that right now. My
thumb tingles at the absence of my phone. Without it I feel even
more alone. More vulnerable.

I shut my eyes tight, willing myself not to go there.

It's so hard, but I manage to keep my smile plastered on for Lux, my excitement as high as it can go. Even though I should probably tell her we need to be cautious now. Things cost money and money goes fast, like Mama always used to say. Mama always made me save my spare change, count my earnings, and budget every week. But Lux is beaming and glowing . . . and that's what matters, isn't it? She hasn't said a word about the night I stabbed the hog. The night everything went to hell. *We'll figure it out*, I reassure myself. Whenever I sense her mood is beginning to dip, I crack a joke, or do something silly to make her laugh.

But then she grabs my arm and shakes it excitedly and goes: "Let's stock up on souvenirs! I want one of those inflatable T. rexes that glow in the dark! And maybe a new tank top!"

I'm starting to feel like her mom. "We can't . . . really do that, Lux. We got to be conservative with our cash."

She blinks and shakes her head like she doesn't understand. "How much do we have?"

"We have, like, maybe $800 left," I mumble.

An awkward silence lingers between us. Lux pulls away and chews her nailbeds. I follow her outside, where we plop down on a bench covered in dino footprints.

"I mean, it's fine," I say quickly. "We'll make more. We'll find a way."

"Mmm," she says, maybe thinking of the last few exorbitant expenses, on what's turned into some sort of all-inclusive road trip: giant ice teas at a strip mall, that big breakfast at Waffle House, $50 to fill up the tank with gas. Clothes and jewelry and sunscreen and sandals. Trinkets and baubles. Motel rooms and unlimited buffet breakfasts. Little things and big things, here and there. *Cha-ching. Cha-ching. Cha-ching.*

"We could email Judy," I offer. "Ask her to wire some to us."

Lux winces and I instantly feel bad for reminding her of the past, of home. She still doesn't respond, just stares at her Keds and kicks a stray bottle cap across the dirt.

"If we keep driving straight tonight, or through the night, we'll get through Oklahoma no problem." I try to keep my voice bright and perky, but even I can hear it waver. "We'll be in Austin in no time."

Lux fumbles with her camera, clicking the lens cap back into place. Once again, I've said the wrong thing, I can feel it. I flush with anxiety.

"Or Santa Fe," I add desperately. "You said maybe you wanted to go to Santa Fe?"

She squints hard, like she doesn't know what the hell I'm talking about. "I'm gonna go to the bathroom," she mutters. Lux hops off the bench and heads back inside the shop, hands deep in the pockets of her new jean shorts.

Fuck. I shouldn't have told her about the money. I should've kept it to myself, let her think we still had plenty. Let her believe in the fantasy for one more night.

But the truth is, it's less than $800. More like $743.66. I've been re-counting and cringing, praying each time my math is wrong. How the hell did more than a grand go so fast in just a few days? It's ridiculous, damn near impossible. But it also kind of makes perfect sense the more I think about it. Lux and I've never had this much money in our lives. *Of course* we had no idea what to do with a windfall. It makes me panicky. Ashamed. I'm supposed to be taking care of us, keeping us safe.

Mosquitoes nip at my legs and arms and I swat them off as best I can. This place is full of trash cans, dropped ice cream cones, and half-eaten food. By dusk it'll be buzzing with insects, and two girls with bare summer legs will be looking pretty damn tasty. We should get a move on, get on the road again. Drive straight through the night.

But I'm bone tired and everything aches: neck, back, shoulders. Who knew looking at fake fucking dinosaurs all day could wipe you out so good? Or maybe it's all the tension I've been holding in, letting it fester inside every muscle. We need to save money, but damn it, I don't want to sleep in the car tonight instead of drive it. *Shit.*

A little kid screams bloody murder when her dad tries to buckle her into her stroller. The place is closing soon, clearing out fast of all the families and clusters of drunk, rowdy teenagers smoking weed.

Across the highway I spy another motel, but I'm so damn sick of motels and the car, living out of my duffel bag with the T-shirt stained with the hog's blood.

Kind of getting sick of this trip. It doesn't feel like a vacation anymore.

Will it always be like this? I wonder. What exactly *do* we do when the money runs out? There's no way we can really live off tips and tiny wages. It was hard enough in Blue Bottle, where groceries were cheap and rent was fairly low, and I could get canned goods from church and the food banks, free lunches at school. Recycle bottles for quick cash. How much harder will it be in a new city with no lease, no social security cards, nothing to our names?

A few minutes later, Lux exits the other side of the gift shop where the bathroom is located. She hasn't bought anything else, so that's good, but she leans up against the concrete wall and stands there with her arms crossed, staring into the horizon.

I get off the bench and walk over, unsettled that she hasn't been speaking to me. She isn't looking for me, either.

"Lux?"

She turns to me as I approach, her expression so hard and ferocious it just about pins me to the ground.

"Are you . . . fucking . . . kidding me?"

I blink at her.

"Do you think I'm a joke, Trixie?" Her words come out sharp, like icicles. Shards of glass against my skin. "Like, actually, *a joke?*"

My mouth feels glued shut, but I manage to mutter: "No, of course not."

"THEN WHY DID YOU WAIT SO LONG TO TELL ME WE WERE RUNNING LOW ON MONEY?" Her shout echoes across DinoLand, parents and teens alike turning to gawk at us. I wince. I don't want to have this conversation here, out in the open. Not in front of all these people. I try to take her hand and pull her toward the parking lot so we can get in my car and go, *now*, but she yanks it back, pulling me close to her instead, so close I can feel heat radiating off her skin that isn't just from the sun. She's burning mad.

She lowers her voice, but it's almost worse than the shouting, because it's laced with raw hurt: "You really don't take me seriously, Trixie. I'm just some ditzy Manic Pixie Bubblegum Girl to you."

I watch her stalk off to where my car is parked in the shade, heart thudding in my chest, feeling the stares of the other patrons and the park attendants, all of the whispers and murmurs.

I find Lux facing the passenger side of the car, her arms crossed, one foot propped up against the front wheel. She doesn't turn when I approach. Doesn't look at me.

"Lux, I'm so sorry," I try. "You were right. I should have told you about the money situation earlier. I should've been honest with you the whole time."

She hangs her head and traces lines in the dirt with the toe of her sneaker. "Yes, you should have."

"And I should tell you all important things right away. I shouldn't assume you can't handle it."

She scoffs, like, *Duh, Trixie,* but otherwise says nothing.

"And . . . ugh, you are *not* a joke. I would punch anyone in the face who ever called you that." That gets a muffled snicker from her, but I keep going, because I know she needs more: "And you are definitely not a . . . what was it? Manic sugar dream girl?"

Suddenly we both burst out laughing and can't stop. She finally faces me, and her eyes are red like she's been crying. Damn. I can't believe I somehow made her cry. Made her feel so unimportant to me. Relationships are so fragile, even when you're this close.

I see a flicker of it again, the way the light seemed to change against Lux's face in the motel room the morning after I killed the hog. I can hold both of these images in my mind simultaneously: the Lux I thought I saw through a sparkling filter, and the Lux I've begun to truly see. They flip back and forth at random sometimes, dizzying and mesmerizing, like an optical illusion. But now I know which version of Lux was really the illusion all along, and she called me on it.

I open my mouth to apologize again, but she loops her arm through mine and gives me a quick kiss on the cheek that makes my knees damn near buckle under me and lets me know that for now, I'm forgiven. We get back in the car and I let her blast whatever music she wants. We leave DinoLand in the dust.

It'll be fine, I tell myself. *The money will work itself out. Our friendship will work itself out. Everything will fall into place.*

As long as we're together.

———

The big blue Oklahoma sky hangs over us like a dome. It's peaceful here, quiet and still, and the air smells fresher than it did in Middlesville.

We're not so far from Blue Bottle that we couldn't still turn back and go home. My insides have been churning since we left the theme park, threatening to make me puke again. It's a struggle to remember to inhale and exhale.

As I drive through a maze of cornfields, Lux continues to snap more photos with her '89 Canon, deep in concentration, like everything she sees is utterly hypnotic. I wonder what it's like to have that artist's brain. How the world looks through the camera's eye. When those pictures get developed—if they ever do—will they capture everything about how this spring feels? The taste of Diet Coke, the smell of Lux's shampoo, the way her skin feels when it accidentally brushes up against mine?

Will the pictures show me in my shorts and yellow T-shirt, the one I wore the night I stabbed the hog? The Before shirt, on the Before girl, back when it was clean of blood and hog insides?

Because the girl in the photo won't be me. Not exactly. The Before girl is trapped in the camera, trapped in time, in my clothes, with my hair, a hard, haunted face bright with my smile.

A new room. A new night. A new scummy motel on the northern edge of Oklahoma. We were going to sleep in the car tonight, but the ache in my back spread to my head. I desperately need a bed again, if only for tonight, especially if I'm going to drive all day tomorrow, and thank God, Lux managed to work her magic again with the woman at the front desk. Make it $658 now after paying for the room. We'll have to eat granola bars for breakfast and maybe skimp on lunch the next few days . . .

Lux gets in the shower and I make a big mistake. I turn on the TV, flipping through the channels. Absently. Like one does.

I cry out and my hands quickly fly to my mouth.

No.

This isn't happening.

This can't be happening.

This is a dream.

A very, very bad dream.

———

Lux races out of the bathroom, hair dripping wet, towel barely hanging around her torso. She finds me hyperventilating on the bed, eyes fixated on the screen.

She says my name and shakes my shoulder, asks me frantically what happened, what's wrong. I just point.

"A shocking new development in the story of an attack at a West Virginia college bar Friday evening: the victim of a fatal assault has been identified as twenty-year-old Bryce Grimaldi, son of local Pinesborough State University president, Weston Grimaldi. He was found brutally stabbed in the women's bathroom of the bar.

"Officials say that Bryce was discovered at approximately 12:35 a.m., estimated to be about twenty minutes after his attack by an unknown assailant, in what appears to be a random act of violence. He was quickly rushed to a nearby hospital, where he was pronounced dead at 1:30 a.m.

"While police are still searching for Bryce's attacker, witnesses claim to have seen two young, likely female suspects fleeing the scene about twenty minutes prior to his discovery. Surveillance footage from outside of the bar confirms that two people appear to make a dash for their car—which has so far been identified as a copper hatchback—around

that same time, though the license plate is not fully visible in the footage.

   "Local authorities are asking citizens to be on the lookout for a copper hatchback, possibly driving southbound . . ."

My stomach plummets. My fingers and toes tingle and then go completely numb. No. This can't be happening. *No.* This isn't real. This is a nightmare, and when I wake up, everything will be all right.

Weston Grimaldi is not only very wealthy, he's incredibly well known, and very much revered where we're from. He comes from old money. Blood money.

Lux shakes beside me, eyes locked on the TV screen.

The segment cuts to a news commentator, a woman with lush curls dressed in a blue suede suit. She looks like something out of a fever dream. The rings on her fingers sparkle in the harsh studio lighting. She stares deeply into the lens of the camera, like she's looking right at us, here in this room that won't stop tilting and spinning and spinning, the stale air choking the life out of me.

The woman in the blue suede suit blurs and the room tilts, but I still hear her clear as day, her voice a loud ringing in my ears.

I've heard the stories about the Grimaldis all my life, like those commercial jingles you barely pay any attention to, but are somehow lodged in your brain all the same. Where most men are hogs, bumbling through life, Grimaldi men are snakes with sharp fangs. They succeed. They hunt. They bite hard. They bite together.

Weston Grimaldi is the president of Pinesborough State University. His father attended, as did his father's father, and on and on. Time is an endless loop and breathing is now impossible.

Through generations they made the school a national football success, a famed institute of bioresearch and chemical engineering. A sparkling byproduct of the good old American dream. I shut my eyes so tight I see stars.

I just killed his son.

———

I don't remember everything about Him, about the Dark Place.

But I do remember the kind smile, fangs sharpened to a fine point like the blade of a knife. Soft blue eyes made of razor blades. The offer to see the hogs in the pen behind his trailer. Me saying yes. Me following him inside and letting the door close behind me . . .

I remember Daddy was asleep at the time, knocked out cold from a night of hard drinking. And Mama was at work, maybe at the diner, or the supermarket, or wherever her job was then.

I remember vaguely that it was his wife who found us. Or a neighbor. Someone did, and then there were the cops and then screams. My screams, maybe, or the sharp squeals of the hogs outside. A clash of the two, a frenzy of yelling and static noise.

The rest is mostly fuzzy around the edges.

Did he even have a wife?

Why did I ever trust him?

Because he was a neighbor. And he liked to talk to me. And he made feel me less lonely.

If only I hadn't been that stupid little girl. If only I hadn't followed him inside.

Shoulda.

Woulda.

Coulda.

The music in my hatchback plays soft and low, my hands grip-ping the wheel so tight that the ache in my head travels down to my jaw. I grind my teeth together. Bone on bone. Lux stares out the window in silence. I know she's thinking about her dad, that he's probably been calling. I imagine him dialing and re-dialing into the ether, into the smashed pieces of the cell phone he bought her, now scattered around the highway like nuclear debris.

I can't tell if she's crying, but every now and then I hear her throat hitch, so I reach out and gently rest my fingers on her hand. She grips them in return and squeezes one, two, three pulses. It makes my stomach clench, knowing that I was the one who caused all this pain.

Obviously, we aren't driving along the interstate. Not any-more. Too many cop cars. Way too risky.

We're heading out west on back roads and local highways if we can find them. We've agreed to go farther than anyplace like Santa Fe. We'll drive straight until we hit the Pacific Ocean.

Though I don't know what the fuck we're supposed to do once we get there. Will things even be safer? Should we drive north to Canada or south to Mexico? Attempt to cross the border on either end? My head spins with options. All I know is that I'd scale a mountain to keep Lux safe.

But I know this is no fantasy world where we can buy new IDs, choose new avatars, and press restart, be who we really want to be. This is no daydream.

We are in the true nightmare.

River Creek Public Library is made of weathered red brick. It makes me think of a historic college campus, like something that might exist at Pinesborough State. The interior is clean and quaint. It's nothing like the one in Blue Bottle: no kids running around screaming and hollering, no loud shuffling from card games or sounds of kids' Nintendo Switches bleeping and blooping. It's quiet, save for the *click-clack* of typing and the occasional throat clearing. The patrons are mostly older, retirement aged and gray haired. A few look up when we come in.

Lux grabs my hand and whispers a little too loudly: "We have an hour before they close." A librarian shoots us a sharp look. She's young and, I note to myself, pretty hot.

We choose a desktop computer in the back row, far enough away from most of the patrons and the librarian that we can chat in relative peace.

"Shit, Lux, we're *everywhere*."

We're a trending story on Google News, Twitter, and practically every other media outlet, though so far, no one knows our names. We're "the unnamed female killers." People apparently saw two girls run outside around the time of the stabbing. We watch the blurry footage of us making a run from the bar that night, and while it makes my blood go ice cold to see, it's a relief that neither of our faces is even remotely recognizable.

Except for Lux's bubblegum-pink hair, which flashes in the streetlights for just a nanosecond.

The frat hog is trending, too, under the hashtag #Bryce-Grimaldi. Many remember him and mourn his death, or at least pretend to, sending their crying and heartbroken emojis laced with #ThoughtsAndPrayers. I get my earbuds out of my pocket so Lux and I can listen to the video clips: there's one of Weston Grimaldi from this morning, devastated and teary eyed, his wife beside him as they speak to the student body of Pinesborough

State University about "this terrible, terrible tragedy." Weston's navy suit is sharp, paired with cuff links that gleam gold. They stand at a podium in Alumni Plaza, where graduation is usually held when the weather is nice enough. My throat goes dry. That's where the top kids from our high school go. That's where Lux might've been someday—in that audience full of wide-eyed students—studying in their world-class photography program.

Weston is tall and handsome in a rough sort of way. He booms into the mic, promising justice for his son, an honor roll student, an athlete, a scholar, a gentleman. A proud member of Delta Delta Chi fraternity. Weston sniffles loudly and wipes his nose on his sleeve—an uncharacteristically hoglike move made by a snake of a man, and then, there it is: the flash of murder in his eyes, those baby-blue eyes turning black. His mouth twists, his chin trembles, and he slams his fist down hard on the podium.

His wife flinches beside him. She's very thin, with long, wispy curls of gray and lip injections that make her look like Janice from The Muppets. I almost feel kinda bad for her until she grabs the mic from her snake husband and hisses, "There *will* be justice for Bryce! These lies and accusations against our son are part of an unfounded, hateful conspiracy against our family!"

There's an uproar among the students in attendance. The news crew catches it all: the expressions of bewilderment and horror mixed in with those of fury and rage. Someone screams, "KILL THE SLUTS!" or maybe I imagine it. It's hard to hear over the din.

The police chief speaks next. He promises to find those responsible for this horrible crime.

In one video on a news website, a reporter stands before the school's quad. It's flooded with hundreds of people, mostly students from what I can tell. The news ticker reads: MURDER OF

UNIVERSITY PRESIDENT'S SON SPARKS CAMPUS-WIDE PROTESTS OVER ALLEGED SEXUAL ASSAULT COVER-UPS. The camera focuses in on two students facing off—a girl in a snapback with long, gorgeous braids, and a weasely white boy in a Delta Delta Chi sweatshirt—arguing in each other's faces. On either side, students rally and shout behind them.

"Jesus," Lux breathes. "This is wild. When did this happen?"

I check the timestamp on the video. My fingers shake as my mouse hovers over the digits. "Early this morning, after Weston spoke." I click around for updates, check Twitter and countless user timelines.

There's a sharp divide between those who believe Bryce deserves justice and those who demand justice for his victims. *Victims*. It doesn't shock me that he's hurt other girls and done this many times before. They're referred to as "alleged victims" on all the news sites. *Alleged*. I think of Lux pinned up against the cold bathroom wall, bruises on her arms, terror in her eyes.

If we had gone to the police, would she be another tick mark added to the roster?

Turns out the girl in the snapback is the president of the school's Intersectional Feminist Union. Her Twitter bio reads: "Black Femme Lives Matter." Her name is Nezekiah Wallace. She's trending all over social media, too, a lot of the comments so ugly and racist I can barely stand to read them. It makes me long for my knife again, to stab anyone who would be such a sick, racist fuck.

"You may say you should never celebrate someone's death, but I certainly celebrate the death of #BryceGrimaldi if it means he can never hurt another person again," she writes.

The replies to her tweet are a hellfire nightmare, though support is mixed in.

The weaselly boy who was standing strong against the crowd? That's the president of Bryce's fraternity, Delta Delta Chi. Luckily, he didn't hurt Nezekiah or any other student this morning. There was no physical violence.

At least, not yet.

I feel a sudden wave of revulsion toward myself. Here are these girls speaking up, speaking out. Telling off the bullies and trolls to their faces. Girls who are way more underestimated than Lux and I could ever be, who have the odds stacked against them based on what they look like. How they wear their hair. The color of their skin. They're girls way more likely to get harassed by the cops, or even killed, and the cops would easily get away with it and protect one another from any repercussions. Girls and students who are treated lower than dirt by racist and sexist scum simply because they exist. But they are facing down the hogs one by one all the same, even though it puts them at unfathomable risk, the kind of risk that white girls like Lux and me will never have to face.

What are Lux and I even doing besides running away?

All this is happening so dizzyingly fast. What have I done? What have I started?

One rogue tweet links us to a forum, where an anonymous message board called the Pynk Ladies is filled with dozens of posts. Posts about the frat hog.

"Oh, my fucking God!" Lux hisses.

"*Shh!* Read these."

A year ago, Bryce Grimaldi cornered me at a frat party and shoved his hands down my pants. My sorority sisters stopped it before it went too far. I reported it to campus police, but they did nothing. His frat did nothing. They didn't outright say I was lying for attention, but they didn't not say it, either.

I heard whispers that all the Greeks thought I was a whore for the rest of the semester. I transferred quickly after.

Pinesborough State is a JOKE and will do anything to cover up sexual assault on their campus, especially when it involves the university president's precious baby boy. I know for a fact Bryce has assaulted at least three girls from my freshman dorm.

This is so damn surreal. I keep scrolling and clicking, Lux and I slack-jawed and bewildered.

There's a lone dissenter on the forum. Someone who calls themselves NotLikeTheOtherGirls.

I click the link tagged in their profile before Lux can stop me.

We're on another forum now, one filled with cringy memes the doofus guys in our school would surely love, Pepe the Frog and some anti-Semitic nonsense and the like. The people here are talking about us, too, the mystery girls who stabbed Bryce Grimaldi in the dive bar and then vanished into the night.

Only they aren't calling us "girls."

Bryce was a class act. A true brother of Delta Delta Chi. May he rest in peace, and may the police find those rancid cunts as soon as possible.

I'd gladly shove my dick down their throats and skull-fuck them to death.

And they say *we're* the violent ones? Please. Here you go, ladies, proof that you're the irrational, inferior sex.

Hope those sluts get the death penalty.

"No. Way."

"Yes way, Lux," I whisper. "Welcome to the dark side of the internet."

"Dark side of humanity is more like it."

I can't stop scrolling. Lux grabs my wrist, as if bracing herself for the impact of the next few posts.

> Some sad little girls on Pynk Ladies think they're hot shit, crying wolf about how Bryce raped them at a frat party. Boo-hoo, he wouldn't fuck you fat whores even if you paid him.

> Bet it was someone from Chi Sigma. Those girls are the true cum dumpsters of Pinesborough State. Beat as fuck, too.

> Oink-oink, she's a Chi Sig Pig!

The anger that's slowly been simmering inside of me gives over to a bubbling, white-hot-lava rage, souring my mouth and scouring my insides. There're other feelings there, too, so intense I could vomit. It's hard to pluck them out and pull them apart, but I decide on a few: horror, hurt, *fear.*

Shit like this is why I trust no man. You can't ever tell who's a hog or not just by looking at their face. Better to assume they all are.

A friendly voice comes over the loudspeaker, making both of us jump: "Good evening. The River Creek Public Library is closing in ten minutes. We will reopen tomorrow at nine. Thank you, and have a good night."

I quickly make an account on the hog forum.

> We don't regret it, you misogynistic motherfuckers. All rapists must die, and Bryce Grimaldi was a rapist. We're coming for you next.

I post it at 6:53 p.m. under the name TheTroubleGirls.

"Holy shit, Trix!" Lux gasps. "You just leveled up in badass!"

"Girls, please settle down!" the hot librarian scolds, but I can barely hear her. I'm grinning so hard, the bubbling anger morphing into something else, taking on a new shape. It's a feeling I think I really fucking like.

It feels kinda like power.

This is what they think of us. This is who we are now, at least to the hundreds or thousands who've read the stories and seen the videos since last night. We have some support, at least from students of Pinesborough State who knew Bryce or knew enough to avoid him, but is it enough? Surely no cop would ever hear us out, let alone believe our story or feel sorry for us in any way. Not after what I just posted.

But maybe they never would've to begin with. Maybe it doesn't even matter.

How long do we have until they finally find us?

The countdown clock ticks in time to the pounding of my heart.

Oklahoma rain is so much different than it is in Blue Bottle.

It's angrier, meaner. At first, the sky is pregnant with big, fat rainclouds. Then there's this spark of lightning, and the clouds shatter and break open. Cold rain comes down like shards of broken glass. Lux and I make a mad dash for my hatchback.

Lux fumbles with the paper map in an attempt to find out which scenic route goes "west." Without a clearly marked national map of all the back roads in various states, it's hard to say which route would be best. It's even harder than you'd think without being on the interstate. Plus, there's the goddamned razor-sharp rain. Big fat drops beat down on the windshield as my shitty wipers try to clear them away.

"We need to get rid of this clunker," she says.

"Um, no, Lux, we are not getting rid of Delilah."

"Yes, we are. It's copper-colored. Stands out like a sore thumb." She raises an eyebrow. "You named your car?"

"Doesn't everyone?" I blush and pretend I didn't think of it late last night while we were on the road, like it's always been her name. "Don't look at me like it's weird or I invented the concept."

She rolls her eyes. Her lips are painted with a pale peach gloss today. They look so damn kissable, which is probably a real fucked-up thought to have in the middle of this mess. "It's just not really a car I see as worth naming," she says absently.

"Are you kidding? The clunkers are the only ones *worth* naming! Like, what kind of douchebag names their Lamborghini?"

"What kind of douchebag *owns* a Lamborghini?"

"Um, don't lie and say you wouldn't."

Lux tosses back her hair. "Excuse me, I'm anticapitalist!"

"Not with those Keds."

Lux smirks and gives me the finger. I stick out my tongue at her and start backing out of the parking space. She points to the next road for me to take. I'm about to turn when something—no, someone—catches my eye, and I quickly screech to a halt on the side of the road.

"What the hell, Trix?"

It's a woman, early to midtwenties, if I had to guess. She stands alone outside the library, one thumb looped around the strap of a backpack, the other pointed upward in a hitchhiking gesture.

She's looking right at me. Staring, a plea in her gaze. She looks tired as hell, her posture slouched. She smiles a little when she notices that I see her, and for some reason it makes me ache deep in my gut.

"That weirdo is staring at us," Lux observes.

I can't stop. No way. Not for anyone. We have to keep moving west and get there as fast as we can, especially if we want to see the ocean. It's a pipe dream, I know. But I can't shake it, can't stop thinking: *What if we* did *make it there?*

The woman smiles and waves at me. A friendly smile. Okay, so maybe she *is* a weirdo, but maybe she also genuinely needs some help. I swallow hard, thinking briefly of Mama, of the spaghetti she tried to boil in the bathwater.

I turn off the engine and open my door.

Lux freaks. "Trixie, what the hell are you doing? It's pouring out there!"

I can't say for sure what pulls me to this woman. She probably just needs a ride in this cold spring rain. Maybe it's her stance, the attitude radiating off her that screams: *I'm friendly but don't fuck with me.* Maybe it's the acid-washed jeans she somehow makes look cool, or the steel-toed boots. Maybe that's why I invite her into my car and the torn fabric of our lives.

Her smile is like honey, warm and sweet as I approach her and join her under the little canopy the library's roof provides, relief etched across her face.

"Hi there! Where you looking to go?" I ask.

"Hey!" She raises her voice so I can hear her over the rain. "Honestly shocked you stopped at all." She wears brown leather riding gloves. They make her fingers look extra-long. Remind me a bit of claws. *Maybe she's a rancher,* I think, *a farmhand of some sort.* "I'm not too picky about where I end up, but getting out of here is the main objective." She winks at me, like we're in on some shared secret. "Anywhere you can drive me to is much appreciated, long as it's far away from this raining shithole. I can chip in for gas, too, and food and lodging, if need be."

She's plain looking, someone who could easily blend in anywhere, her skin tanned and leathery from the sun. A long gash of a scar slices down her right cheek. Her body is long, lean, and gangly, her dark hair fastened into a tight bun with a rubber band. She reminds me of a lizard. *If the sun were out*, I think, *I could see her scales.*

"I'm Trixie. I'd love to offer you a ride, but um, I need to check in with my—"

"—girlfriend?" she finishes.

A little sparkler goes off in my belly as my cheeks catch fire. She probably means "girlfriend" how most adults mean it. Friend, who is a girl. But she's really not that much more of an adult than Lux and me, and there's something in this woman's devious smile—and yes, maybe it's the boots, too—that tells me she meant it the other way.

I look over at Lux, who glares at me like I've lost my marbles. Thunder booms, and the rain licks at my arms and thighs. "She'll be fine," I say. "Hop in and we'll figure it out. Long as you're not a serial killer."

The lizard woman puts up three fingers, mischief dancing in her eyes. "Scout's honor." Her sky-blue eyes make me think of winter in Blue Bottle, and I feel a twinge of longing for home.

We hurry inside the car, the woman tossing her backpack in like she's been waiting for us all day and we finally hurried up and came. Water drips everywhere, and her boots cake mud on my floor. "Nice ride," she says, and I can't tell if she's being sarcastic.

Lux stares at me and mouths: *What the fuck, Trixie?* I shrug and rev the engine.

"We'll drive you wherever," I say. "We're on our way west-ward."

"Thank you kindly."

"I'm sorry, but who exactly *are* you?" Lux snaps, spinning around in her seat to face her.

"What did you say your name was?" I ask before Lux can go off on her.

The woman smirks, clearly amused. "I didn't," she says. She takes a pack of Kools from her backpack and smacks it hard against her gloved palm. "Call me Lizzie."

Lizard, I think. *Lizard Lizzie.*

———

"Is there anything more beautiful than an American motel at midnight?" asks our new passenger.

Lux goes, "Uh-huh . . ." She's got her knees pulled up to her chest, sulking in the front seat. Clearly, she has no interest in this mystery hitchhiker, and I can't say I blame her. I'm starting to regret letting the lizard in the car myself.

Lizzie could out-talk Lux Leesburg any day of the week.

"The monuments and great statues aren't what make this country beautiful," Lizzie goes on, voice filled with reverence. She leans her head out the half-open window, puffing Kool smoke out into the rain. It's lightened considerably since we left River Creek. "They're the facade, not the heart of it."

"Sure," Lux says, deadpan. "You should roll the window up. It's getting really cold and damp in here."

"It wasn't until the 1920s that the American highway system was developed," Lizzie goes on as if Lux's voice is merely com-ing from the radio. "Motels started becoming popular in the '60s, when people began to travel long distances by highway.

And because they sprang up in the '60s, a lot of them got things like atomic bombs and spaceships for decoration."

"Huh?" Lux says.

"The Cold War?" I prompt. "Come on, Lux, I know we haven't finished high school, but surely you've paid attention in at least *one* history class."

"I know what the Cold War is, *Trixie*. But why would a motel have an atomic bomb on its sign? Wouldn't that scare away customers?"

"This is a very, very strange country," Lizzie says. "Flip on that radio for me, will you? I need some music." Lux rolls her eyes. I shrug and obey. As if by magic, it's "Hotel California" by the Eagles. I've heard it about a million and one times growing up, but never before has it sounded so menacing.

Turns out Lizzie is a drifter, a chronic couch surfer. She owns an old Android phone that's at least four years old, the screen cracked with spiderwebs, always dinging out mysterious text messages. Her last place fell through—something about her friend getting evicted for having an exotic pet—and there's this whole saga behind it that I mostly tune out. She not only talks a lot, she smokes like a damn chimney and is starting to stink up Delilah even with the window down. But she has a phone with GPS and a good sense of which back roads to use, she doesn't ask questions about where we're going and why, and she can read the paper maps better than either of us could dream of. She also offers to pay for our next motel room and gas, which eases Lux's sulking a bit. Lord knows we gotta conserve our dwindling cash pile from here on out. Plus, Lizzie is well over eighteen. No more making up lies and scrambling to get motel rooms.

And for reasons I can't quite put my finger on, even though Lizzie never shuts up and smells like an ashtray, I really fucking like her.

The Carnival is a seedy hunk of peeling white wood illuminated by a pink neon VACANCY sign. Christmas lights are strung haphazardly around the trunks of gnarled palm trees, leaves lazily skimming the water of the murky pool that flanks its side. A woman in a ratty bathrobe grills by the water.

I think I'm starting to see what Lizzie was babbling about in the car. There's an odd beauty to this place, like it exists in a mirror world, a liminal space where time is slowed down and nothing exists or matters except for rainy puddles in the concrete and a humming soda machine by the main office. It reminds me of the Motel Grandeur back in Middlesville, and I long for that simple night with Arjun and his sisters. Back before we knew the frat hog was dead, before everything went straight to hell.

Lizzie retires early for the night, giving us a grunt and salute as she stalks off to her room, the one that she insisted on having all to herself.

"What do you think she wants from us?" Lux asks. We drag our duffel bags inside and toss them onto the double beds of our own room. There are heavy curtains that smell of mothballs and cigarette holes in the carpet. But it's relatively quiet, and for now, we're safe.

I hope.

I shrug and pull off my sweaty T-shirt, the fabric clinging to my skin. I have one clean one left and I'm not sleeping in the sweaty one. All this money we spent, the laundry we did, and my dumb ass didn't think to buy more T-shirts. "I guess this is her way of thanking us for the ride."

Lux flops down on her bed and sighs. The cheap coil mattress squeaks and she winces. "Yeah but like, *why*? If she has money for a motel, why didn't she just call a cab or get a bus ticket or something? Why does she hitchhike everywhere? Seems risky." She turns on her side and scratches at the peeling paint on the wall.

"Maybe she likes the risk," I say defensively, though why I'm so defensive of the lizard lady, I'm not quite sure. I pull on my last clean shirt, a plain black cotton tee with no graphic design, no cool logo. God, I'm boring. "She's a drifter, remember? She likes adventure. Is it really any different from what we've been doing so far? Any riskier?"

Lux keeps scratching away, peeling off thin layers of cheap paint. Maybe she's thinking of all the cash we've burned through so far, the nights of drinking and fooling around that faded into hazy hungover days. The strangers we met. The strangers we trusted, if only for the moment.

"Well, we need to be extra careful now," she says evenly. "Especially considering our circumstances. Honestly, we should probably ditch her tomorrow. Who knows what she's really after?"

I nod like I agree, because I honestly do, and we have every reason to be suspicious of this strange lizard woman. I lie down next to Lux on her bed, enjoying the cool AC on my skin. Our skin is so close I can feel the energy vibrating between us. My insides tingle.

"What is that?" I ask.

Lux blinks at me in surprise, like I've woken her up from a strange dream. The paint on the wall has transformed into something more than just peels and scratches. "It's nothing." She shakes her head and bites her lip, like I've witnessed something deeply private.

But it is something. It's a pattern. I inch closer to the wall for a better look.

"It's . . . it looks like a fist," I say. "Or a screaming mouth."

Lux snorts. "Like I said, it's nothing, Trix. Just another nervous habit of mine."

I run the tip of my finger across it, feeling the edges and grooves of the mark she's made here, on the walls of the Carnival. The truth is, I see a million different things in this abstract design. A million possibilities.

A sign.

A symbol.

But Lux is somewhere else, somewhere far away from me. Her eyes are focused on the ceiling, some other pattern only she can see. She mumbles to herself, her lips pursing and moving ever so slightly. I reach out my hand for hers. Our fingers brush together, and for a fleeting moment I think she's going to hold my hand and squeeze my fingers . . . but she doesn't.

Instead she pulls away, groans, and sits upright, her back to me. She stretches and sighs. "I'm gonna wash my hair," she mutters, going to the bathroom and shutting the door.

My cheeks flush and my stomach burns. Did I do something wrong? Does she *know*? Can she feel the way I look at her, the way I long for her? The way I can't stop seeing beauty in everything she does, even little marks on the wall? Does it make her uncomfortable?

It must. I should stop being so obvious with my physical affection, I think, staring once more at the scratches and paint peels. I can't place a name to this cocktail of emotions.

I hop off her bed and lie down on my own, letting the room settle around me, listening to the people next door bicker, their nagging voices rising and falling. *She's your best friend, not your girlfriend.* This bed is far less comfortable, the sharp coils from the mattress poking up into my spine. *Maybe it all means absolutely nothing. Maybe there are no signs or symbols in this world at all, just things we desperately want to see.*

The stick-and-poke hummingbird on my wrist itches and burns. I still don't know why I chose a hummingbird, other than that I thought Judy's little sketch was pretty. Maybe it means something more. If Mama were still her old self, she'd have killed me for getting a tattoo so young, or maybe at all. She certainly would've gone after Judy like a rabid dog for giving it to me.

Mama.

It's been so long since I've heard her voice, felt her cool hands touching my forehead whenever I was sick. When she looks at me, does she recognize me anymore? Does she know she's losing her mind?

No. Looked *at me, not* looks. *It's over. It's all over. I'll never have to see her again.*

The thought brings both guilt and palpable relief, two familiar feelings that knot themselves into a pretty bow. I may be the world's worst daughter.

The shower turns off and Lux steps out of the bathroom wrapped in a ratty motel towel, looking a little more awake and alive.

"I have an idea," she says, voice bouncy and eyes bright. "We can transform. It will only take a few hours."

"Transform? Into what, Power Rangers? Teenage Mutant Ninja Turtles?"

She shares a smirk with me and we both giggle. There's that rush again in my belly. Can she feel it too? "No, really. Look. I took these from the Walmart. I didn't tell you but I . . . I did steal them." She hangs her head for a moment like she's ashamed, then reaches into the giant pocket of her camera bag and reveals something wrapped in grocery plastic. "I think we should do it. To protect ourselves."

Insatiably curious, I follow her into the bathroom. Lux unwraps two cheap boxes from the plastic bag and places them on the sink like an offering. Both feature too-smiley airbrushed models, one with hair black as night, and one candy-apple red. I watch her mix the dyes in the plastic bottles that came with the boxes.

"Black or red?" she asks.

I shrug. "Neither. I don't need it."

Does it really matter if I change my hair or not? It's as flat and dull as the Midwest landscape we've been driving through.

Lux sighs, irritated. "*Trix*. Come on. We have to. We'll be safer."

"We'll never be safer. Plus, I blend in everywhere."

"Bullshit," she mumbles. She rolls her eyes and bites at her lip again, lacing her fingers through pink curls that are still sleek and wet from the shower. I realize this may be the last time I ever see them like this. I don't know why—I mean, it's only a fucking fantasy hair color—but it makes me feel unspeakably sad.

"Look, you have a very recognizable face, Trixie Denton. I know you think you're this cartoon character with a closet full of duplicates of the same outfit, but really, you're not."

I laugh. Lux is funny. "You don't have to make me feel better."

She turns and walks over to me, ruffles my coffee-filter hair, then tilts her head to the side, studying my face with such intensity that my cheeks burn as bright as the candy-apple color on the box. "Red," she finally says, placing the box decisively before me on the sink. "Red will suit your eyes and skin. I'll do mine black and then help you with yours." She grins. "Red is your color. You'll be gorgeous."

My blush deepens and I turn so she can't see. I clear my throat and swat her away playfully. "Yeah, whatever. We'll be safer, you're right. Just . . . I don't want to look until you're done."

She nods and turns back to the bathroom mirror. "Maybe

you should wash your hair and condition it while I dye mine? We always washed my hair at the salon before we colored it."

I shrug, because truly I have no idea how to do hair. I never cared much about my appearance one way or the other. Never assigned much meaning to my hair beyond keeping its unusual cut, or gave much thought to what color it was or even should be. But right now, it feels vital, my natural color, this thin, dirty hair between my fingertips. Like changing it will change an even bigger piece of me.

But I trust Lux, and I have to trust that this will help make everything feel and be a little more okay.

I pull the shower curtain closed before I start undressing. We still undress behind semi-closed bathroom doors, or with our backs turned to each other while we slip our bras on and off. It's this unspoken rule we have, one that I seem to have with all of my female friends, as if the sight of our naked bodies will shift the carefully constructed illusion of comfort we've built between us.

The showerhead feels like someone is spitting warm water on me, but I knead the shampoo and conditioner through my split ends all the same, a funeral of sorts for my natural color.

Afterward I take a deep breath and wrap myself in a threadbare motel towel. I sit on the bathroom floor, letting Lux's hands rub the red dye through my scalp.

Now our new crummy motel room reeks of ammonia and the pot the people next door have been smoking for hours.

Luckily, the boxes came with plastic gloves, too, and Lux was smart enough to swipe a little box of baking soda into her camera bag along with them. She rubs the baking soda into her long strands and my short ones, saying it'll help with the smell.

When she's finished, she steps back and gives me a once-over, the kind an artist gives their new painting. "Okay. You ready to see, my beautiful Trixie?"

I swallow hard, something pinching between my eyes. Damn. No, I will not cry. I will not panic.

It's just hair.

I stand slowly and spin around to face the mirror. It's like diving into a pool of freezing water.

Holy. Shit.

She was right. I am unrecognizable.

My eyes are brighter somehow, my cheeks redder, mirroring the vibrant new shade. I feel like a lollipop. I hate and love it at once.

We become new girls within the hour: her, Black Licorice Lux, and me, Candy Apple Trixie. "Guess you were right." My voice comes out hushed, full of awe. I watch her remove the plastic gloves and wipe down the sink, which is stained with our new colors. "Makeup really is magic."

"Well, this is hair, not makeup," she says, and she smiles at me when our eyes meet in the bathroom mirror. Was that a flirty smile? Or do I keep seeing what I want to see? "But I guess you could call it makeup for hair. Hmm. I should get a flat iron." I inch closer to her and let our hands brush as she studies her altered reflection in the dirty bathroom mirror. She looks a little older with the black, like fine aged wine. "My curls." She reaches out as if to touch them, but hesitates, as if they're somehow fragile now and she might shatter them with one touch. They're still damp and fairly flat, but once her hair is fully dried, they'll be back to their natural state. Straight hair will change her face, she assures me. We'll definitely get a flat iron and she'll straighten her hair before we go out in public.

"We'll wear makeup whenever we're out," she says. "Sunglasses. Hats." Red lipstick and a smoky eye will fully transform her. Brown eyeshadow and a nude lip for me. Though I know eventually her makeup stock will run out, or will just melt off in the sun.

"We aren't celebrities," I counter. "This isn't some cheesy heist comedy."

"It'll work," she says, her voice solid and sure. "It has to work." I open and close my mouth, not wanting to argue any further.

"Lux." A lump forms in my throat. She turns to face me, our noses just inches from each other. "Thank you. Really. You were right, and it means a lot that you thought of this. Did this for me. For us."

She brushes a strand of my newly red hair behind my ear. I feel her breath on my cheek and the love in her voice and eyes as she says, "I'll always keep you safe, Trixie Denton."

I love you, I want to say, but I can't let the words leave my lips. It's too precarious.

This is treacherous.

I love you. I love you. I love you.

It occurs to me that Lux never reminded me of an animal. Most people have clear animal alters in my mind: Mama is a gentle manatee, Judy is a wily fox, Boss Man is a vulture. Lux is always just Lux.

What am I?

***

That night I sleep fitfully, awakened by every siren, every sudden noise in the hallway or roar of a motorcycle engine on the highway outside. Every grunt and moan from our next-door neighbors having loud sex. When I dream, I dream of our newly dyed hair being lopped off with a bloody version of Judy's knife.

The knife. The knife. I reach for it but it keeps slipping through my fingers like smoke.

I dream of our phones being smashed by monster tires again and again and again, crushing the glass to little shards of ice.

I can feel each of those little shards slicing down my chest, inches away from puncturing my heart. It hurts like it's happening for real.

When I wake up for the millionth time at 4:30 a.m., sweaty and panting, a bird is screaming outside our tiny window. Or maybe it's singing way too loudly. It's hard to tell anymore. I cocoon myself in the heavy motel quilt that smells faintly of stale cigarettes and shut my eyes tight, trying to breathe in, breathe out. The smell of rank marijuana wafts in from the air vents. Ocean breaths, just like Judy taught me, holding one nostril closed at a time while I inhale deep into my belly.

I hope we do get to the ocean.

I hope it swallows me under.

───

By dawn I give up on sleep completely and pad barefoot outside to smoke a cigarette. It's from the pack of Marlboro Lights I brought with me, and until now, I haven't had the urge to smoke, but the smell in the room tempted me bad.

The sky is candy orange-pink like the ring I gave Lux. Fluffy blue clouds crack open and spill yellow light like warm butter or over-easy eggs. My stomach growls ferociously. When was the last time I ate something? We didn't have dinner, just shared a stale bag of chips between us from the humming vending machine after dyeing our hair. There's an old man, shirtless, smoking a pipe in a lounge chair by the motel pool. A trash guy collects the giant bags by the main office and heaves them into his truck before they bake in the sun.

As soon as the cigarette lights, I inhale deeply: cool, soothing menthol. I know it's bad for me, but what does it matter anymore? With each hit I feel my muscles unknot a bit. Lux is still sleeping peacefully inside, or at least that was how she looked when I left the room. She was curled up on her side, her own quilt on the floor from her tossing and turning. Her bare legs stretched out, catlike, black curls falling across her cheeks. There was a small smile on her face as she lay dreaming.

I hope to God they're good, sweet dreams. Better than mine were, fragmented and horrifying.

My fingers twitch longingly for a bright, stimulating screen. I smoke my cig and close my eyes, pretending to type on an imaginary phone.

I check the weather: hot, humid, no chance of a thunderstorm yet. The air smells thick with pollen. Grass and tree, most likely.

I check the traffic: rush hour won't be too bad, seeing as we're out here in the boonies, but we might hit a few bumps along the main highway.

I check the news.

My mind comes up blank.

Then it hits me, like a tornado of images behind my eyelids:

Discovered at approximately 12:35 a.m.

I'm stabbing him right in the gut.

A *random act of violence.*

His hand clamped around Lux's mouth, bruises blooming on her arms.

Rushed to a nearby hospital.

Blood on my yellow shirt. The sharp peal of Lux's scream.

Pronounced dead at 1:30 a.m.

Raw meat where the knife goes in.

I gasp like a fish yanked from the water and snap open my eyes. The cigarette has mostly burned to ash between my fingers, and I can't stop shaking.

Next thing I know I'm pounding on the door to Lizzie's room.

I suggested we all share a room to save money, but she insisted on getting her own for tonight. Said she had to work on some things by herself. God only knows what strange projects Lizzie gets up to when the sun sets.

There's a loud thump of surprise, and thirty seconds or so pass before Lizzie croaks, "Who's there?" and I say my name, loud and clear. She yanks open the door.

It's weird to see her like this, her long black hair down and loose, those silly riding gloves off her hands. She wears a long cotton T-shirt and shorts, and her eyes are puffy with sleep. She looks younger, softer.

"Sorry to wake you," I say, though I'm not sorry at all. "I need your help with something."

She just blinks at me and rubs her face, like she didn't recognize me at first. "What? What'd you do to your hair? You look weird."

I ignore that and explain what I'm thinking. She perks up, like we're seven years old and I've just invited her to spend the day with me at Chuck E. Cheese.

"Give me a minute to throw on a bra and I'll meet you at your car," she says, a wicked grin on her lips. She slams the motel room door right in my face. I don't take it personally, and it makes me grin, too.

I stub out my ashy cigarette and grab my keys from the room, slipping on flip-flops and walking quietly enough so Lux won't wake up. I start Delilah's engine and kill time until Lizzie comes outside. Her hair is tied back up in the rubber hand, but she's got on jeans and a tank top and a big, bulky coat even though it's hot as hell even this early. No gloves. Flip-flops instead of steel-toed boots. She smiles and waves when she sees me, like I'm picking her up for school.

We drive for a bit until we find the nearest Walmart.

"Remember, there's always a blind spot," she says before we head in. "But watch yourself. Loss prevention is a bitch."

I can do this, I tell myself, feeling the chill of the early-morning air on my bare shoulders. *I am Candy Apple Trixie.*

Turns out it's the perfect time of day to shoplift. All the employees are far too sleepy from their late-night shifts, or still waking up for their early-morning ones to pay us any mind. In the car, Lizzie told me how to do everything: Look inconspicuous. Smile politely at the retail workers. Remove the sensor tags with care. Wander around the aisles and pretend to look at stuff before finding a corner to hide from the cameras, then slip toothpaste and T-shirts and deodorant and shorts and snacks deep into the pockets of her big coat.

She leaves the store first, pretending to get a phone call. I spend another fifteen minutes by myself wandering the Walmart, palms sweating, exhilarated. The shitty music they're blaring puts a spring in my step. Candy Apple Trixie can do this. She's done it a hundred times before. Quick and easy. In and out. I buy a cheap tube of peach lipstick—a little present for Lux—nod and smile at the exhausted cashier, then head outside to find my criminal mentor, sweating in the coat's thick fabric.

She's leaning against Delilah, looking proud, like I just was initiated into her gang or something. "Not bad, newbie. No one was following you, either."

"Probably doesn't hurt that I'm a tiny little white girl," I say, sliding off the coat and stuffing it in the backseat. She snorts. I pull the lipstick out of the plastic bag the cashier gave me and wave it around like a trophy. "Made sure to be inconspicuous. Think Lux will like this?"

Lizzie shrugs and hawks spit onto the concrete. "Don't know. Don't wear makeup."

I got myself more T-shirts that aren't stained by hog's blood, and all in all, saved Lux and me well over a hundred dollars. Lizzie and I pull up at a drive-through for a celebratory breakfast. Handing the money over almost feels like paying penance. I make sure to grab a sandwich for Lux. The lizard lady and I drive aimlessly around winding country back roads for a while, blasting soft rock on the radio, Lizzie regaling me with stories about life on the road, the shit she's gotten away with, fables about barefooted, hard-faced women of the Wild West and great frontier . . . and this time, I don't tune her out.

I laugh and listen and sip my iced coffee as we sing along to the radio, and it's like all the tension in my soul has lifted. I feel reenergized, invincible.

But I make a big mistake.

I don't check the fuel gauge.

By the time we get back to the motel parking lot, Delilah's acting weird. Weirder than her usual self. She's sputtering a bit. Fussing like a cranky child. But I've been so distracted by Lizard Lizzie I don't think much of it.

The early morning sun is way too bright. Blinding whiteness slams into my retinas. I shield my eyes with my hand, standing in the scummy lot in my flip-flops and skimpy shorts and T-shirt, clinging to my paper bag filled with breakfast sandwiches oozing grease. I realize that I'm not wearing a bra. The humidity clings to my skin like plastic wrap. But even in the sticky warmth of the air, I feel safe somehow, cocooned. It's peaceful this time of morning, with just the birds trilling and the occasional hum of an engine along the highway. The land is fairly flat here. It's hot, but if we ever reach someplace like Canada, we'll probably appreciate the warmth. A vision flashes before my eyes of Lux and me lounging at a pool inside a shiny Vancouver hotel, looking down on the dazzling city below us.

Time seems to skip and bounce around the edges, slow down and then speed up. It's been like this since the bar, since the stabbing.

Since I killed someone.

I don't deserve Vancouver or hotels or indoor pools.

I don't even deserve the ocean.

Sometimes I feel like I'm outside of my body, floating above it. Watching from above. Now is one of those times.

There's a patch of lawn by the pool that looks perfect for setting a blanket on and sleeping in the sun. I could plop right down there and let myself melt right into the earth, just breathe deep and let go of everything . . .

No, *no*. I shake my head to wake myself up, slap my face a little. I need to go inside and give Lux her breakfast. Lizzie has already headed back to her room to shower. We should all get going.

Back in the room Lux is still curled up in her sheets like a little bug in a nest. Slants of sunlight fall across her like shards of broken glass. I reach out and lightly stroke her new inky black hair. She moans and rolls over, then opens her eyes and smiles.

"Morning, sunshine," she says. I'm so envious of what a morning bird she is, how she's never grumpy like me when she first wakes up. "The red looks really good in natural lighting." I turn so she can't see my little smile and duly reddening cheeks. Her morning voice is so groggy and cute. She eyes the greasy paper bag in my hand. "I see there's room service here at this lavish accommodation. Smells like bacon if I'm not mistaken."

"That rhymes." I laugh and sit down on the bed beside her, setting the bag on her nightstand. "Bacon *and* eggs. And I made them add sharp cheddar, since I know you don't like it mild. Surprised they had it at a drive-through, but it seems like this part of Oklahoma isn't so backward after all."

Lux stretches and purrs, almost catlike. "Nothing but the best service around here. What time is it?"

"Quarter to nine. Listen, the room's been paid for, so I was thinking we should get going now, get a head start."

She wrinkles her nose. "Can we ditch that weirdo today?" Lux sits up on her elbows. The slanting sunlight seems to slice through her face, illuminating her chestnut-colored eyes.

"I mean, I don't know, Lux. I feel kinda bad we're . . . ditching her all of a sudden. Especially since she paid for the rooms."

And helped me shoplift a shit ton of stuff for us. I was planning on telling her, since she stole stuff too, but right now I weirdly feel guilty. Like it's different if it's me. I got us into this mess, after all.

Lux blinks at me. "I thought you agreed we shouldn't trust her."

I shrug and look down at her pillowcase, pulling at the loose threads. All of the things I stole for us flash through my mind. "I mean, we shouldn't, but we're going that way anyway, you know? We might as well give her a ride?"

She gives me a long, hard look, then finally lets out a sigh. "I don't understand you."

"What do you mean?"

"You keep saying you want to keep us safe. Get out west as quickly as possible. But you're so impulsive, picking up creepy hitchhikers—"

"—*one* creepy hitchhiker. And she didn't seem creepy at first."

"No? Not even when she started lighting up in your car and rambling about nothing, like, mere seconds after you let her inside?" She groans. "You really don't think Lizzie could be dangerous? Like, at the very least, she's *not* a potential problem for us?" She widens her eyes at me, daring me to say yes.

I think of the Tower card the bartender flashed before me that fateful night, the flames bursting from the window. *You always have a choice*, she said. And I chose to stab the hog.

I chew at my lip and realize as I say it: "She reminds me a little of Judy."

Lux's expression softens. "You miss her a lot, don't you?" She inches closer to me, her bare shoulder so inviting. If I were a braver girl, I'd relax my head against it. Her curls would feel so good against my sunburned neck. "We can talk about her. About everything."

"I don't want to talk about it." I shake my head. "Really," I lie. "I'm fine."

Lux leans in so close my stomach does a somersault. Her gaze locks onto mine. For just a moment, time itself stops. The world is still and silent.

There's something burning she wants to say. I can feel it. But she closes her eyes and says something else, something that feels less like the truth: "Okay, Trixie. I trust you."

———

Shit. Fuck.

The engine won't start.

I looked at the stupid map, decided on the route for today. Packed all our stuff and loaded it into the car. I was so ready for us to get the hell out of here. And now the engine won't *start*.

Delilah's well below a quarter tank of gas. She's near empty. I should've checked. I should've *fucking* checked this morning.

I try one more time to rev her engine, sweating bullets without the AC on, then hear a horrible, loud bang.

This can't be happening. No, no, no, *no*.

I already know. Judy warned me this might happen when she sold me this piece of garbage.

The engine is blown.

"FUCK!" I scream. "FUCK!" I slam my fist against the wheel again and again, not caring that it's honking like mad. I want to tear Delilah apart from the inside out, tear apart this whole rotting little town we're stuck in. I want to smash something. I punch the dashboard hard and it flies open, old CD jewel cases and registration papers flying everywhere. Some are mine, some are Judy's, some are from the owner before.

I want to scream until my throat bleeds.

A shadow slides across my vision, blocking out some of the searing sunlight as Lizard Lizzie slithers in front of my passenger window. She's back to being dressed in full weirdo attire, leather riding gloves and all. But for the first time, she looks mildly alarmed.

"W-what the fuck happened?" she stammers.

I shut my eyes tight and wipe away as many tears as I can, trying to steady my shaky breath. "Just a little car trouble," I mutter.

"Damn! The car's leaking oil like a factory spill!" She recoils from the ground like it's covered in blood. "*Car trouble*. Understatement of the century. Christ."

I step back out into the humidity. Lux stands a few feet away from us, mouth hanging open. Lizzie gives Delilah a good whap on the hood with her leather-gloved hand. "Car trouble indeed," she mutters.

I clear my throat and say, "Could try a jumpstart." My voice is all croaky from my crying and screaming, like a bullfrog on steroids. I know it's useless, but I don't know what else to say. I want her to go away now. All the bravado and pride I felt this morning has leaked out of me with the rest of Delilah's fluids.

What was I thinking, stealing shit from a Walmart when we're already on the run? And I wasn't even wearing makeup or a hat or sunglasses. Careless. I didn't think. Lux was right. We should get out and go now. I want to grab her and sprout giant wings and fly us both up, away and over this disgusting parking lot and out of this decaying little nowhere town.

"I'll check under the hood," Lizzie says, but I hear the doubt in her voice.

I glance over at Lux, mouthing, *She's dead.*

Lux's eyes widen even more as she mouths back, *Oh. Fuck.* We run toward each other and I collapse into her waiting hug. Some of the tears spill out onto her only clean pink tank top. "Oh, Trix," she murmurs, stroking my hair. Her fingers are cool from being inside. It feels so good on my scalp. "I'm so sorry."

Lizard Lizzie gives Delilah's engine a thorough once- or twice-over before somehow determining we should at least try a jumper cable, like I said. No shit. Lux stands with me in the parking lot, biting her fingernails to shreds as the harsh sun beats down, threatening to melt us all down to nothing. It's way too warm and it's only getting worse. I can feel it coming. The jitters. I don't even want to stay too close to Lux anymore. Sweat drips from my face and down my back, my skin sizzles, and I curse myself for not putting on more sunscreen. The air smells of burning asphalt and gasoline and rubber. All I want to do is crawl back inside Delilah, crank up the AC, and speed out of here with Lux, but we can't. We're stuck.

She's really, truly dead.

———

Over the last few hours, we've become quite the spectacle in the parking lot. Lizzie's asked each and every person we've seen if they can help somehow, but they all just shrug or shake their head, avoiding us, skittering away like rats fleeing a damn glue trap. Lizzie refuses to give up, keeps fussing over the car like it's a video game level that she won't acknowledge she can't beat.

I swallow down the giant lump hardening in my throat. I won't cry. No. I won't cry over a car. She's just a car. No, *it's* just a car.

Only . . . it's *my* car. My means of freedom. My only link left to Blue Bottle and Mama and Judy . . . besides Lux. I feel like tearing out my hair. Collapsing on the hot concrete and crying until I can't feel anything anymore. But I have to hold it together. Lux stands by my side, leaning against me, gently stroking my arm as if to say, *It's all right.* A motel employee gives us false notes of encouragement, wants us to call AAA. Ha, as if I have a membership to AAA.

I could call Judy on Lizzie's phone, tell her to come get us. But this isn't fair. It's too early.

Maybe this is game over.

No, it can't be. Not yet.

"We could have the motel call us a cab," I murmur into Lux's ear. I lick the salty sweat beading on my lip. All I know is, I feel like someone's stuck an ice pick between my eyes, and my skin is inflamed and turning red. I need to get out of this heat and soon. We could have gone into the motel office to wait it out, but they're closed now for lunch. Who closes for lunch? "We have some money left. Or maybe we could take a bus."

Lux balks. "To where? California? Like that wouldn't cost us two arms and a leg!" Her voice is tight, high and urgent, and she's talking a mile a minute. "Can we borrow someone's phone? Call a cab and then hop out and ditch it or something?"

My phone. My car. Both dead. Maybe this is the penance I deserve to pay for killing someone in cold blood. God's way of punishing us. This was all a mistake, trying to run from that night. Sooner or later, we were bound to get fucked in some way.

"I can't leave Delilah," I say. My voice cracks under the weight of my words.

Lux rubs my arm. Her palm is warm now, sweaty. "Someone will tow her and we'll . . . come back for her."

We both know this isn't true. We're never coming back here.

I look over at my leaking hatchback baby, with her broken back windows and huge dent in the front bumper from the time I was learning to drive and doing it so, so badly.

"We need a car," I say firmly. I will not cry. I will *not* fucking cry. "We could hitchhike," I sputter. Lux grunts and goes, "*Seriously?*"

Lizzie slithers over.

"Well, she is certainly fucked," she says. She slaps her gloved hands together, the leather making that unmissable *smack*. How is she not burning up in those things, in those heavy boots and jeans? I don't see a single drop of sweat on her. It's like the heat invigorates her. "But we aren't fucked. There are always options when you're stranded out in the wilderness. Sometimes you gotta make your own luck."

"Options?" Lux asks, deadpan once again. "*Luck?*"

"Sure." Lizzie sucks her teeth. "No use crying over spilled oil."

"That was my car!" I snap. "My only car. *Our* only car."

Lizzie chuckles. Our eyes meet and it's like she's looking right through me, like Lux isn't even there. "Time to put on our big-girl pants and make something out of this mess. And I do need to get going." Her scar widens as she smiles, big and wide, showing her fangs. "Come with me, Trixie. I'll help you."

I was fourteen the first time Mama forgot my name.

We were sitting in a Cracker Barrel having lunch, Mama drinking her usual sweet tea, me with my lukewarm mug of black coffee, when the waitress rolled up on us for a refill.

"Oh, your daughter is a *dish!*" she gushed. "What's her name?"

Mama's face softened and she opened her mouth. I sat there, waiting, giving the waitress a patient smile. Then Mama's face furrowed in confusion. "Uh . . . well," she stammered. I thought she was only playing at first, and I tossed my paper napkin at her, but then I saw in her eyes that something was wrong.

"Mama?"

The waitress kept glancing nervously between us. Mama just continued to stare at me, the frown turning to a look of sheer horror, and it was like the whole world was made of Jell-O and squirming and swirling at the edges. The waitress made up some excuse to go tend to another customer, even though it was noon and empty as anything in there, but at that point she'd faded back into the background like TV static.

I grabbed Mama's hand and shook it.

"*Mama!*"

She blinked rapidly and then finally gave a little laugh. "Sorry, honey. I must've had a little zone-out for a minute. You know I get spacey when my blood sugar's low." I glanced at her plate. She'd eaten nearly all of her food. Something deep inside of me was coming unglued, and these ugly feelings were emerging, dark and stormy and scared, but I shoved them back deep, deep down.

"Are you sure you're okay?"

Mama reached over to stroke my cheek. "Yes, yes, love, I'm okay. I'm perfectly okay." She sounded unsure, and she still hadn't said my name. But no, she was fine. I convinced myself it had been only a moment, a weird little glitch in the matrix of her mind, and we continued eating our lunch and chatting about this and that, the dark and stormy feelings wriggling in my belly the whole while, threatening to crawl right out of my mouth and slither out into the world.

What the three of us do next is almost unthinkable in its sheer stupidity.

You would think that after stabbing a hog boy and leaving him to squeal and bleed to death on the dirty floor of a dive bar bathroom, this would be nothing for me. Easy-peasy. A slice of Mama's pumpkin cheesecake. Nothing that would bother me more than a mere passing thought, aside from a maybe a now-and-then kind of regret.

You would think.

Maybe it's the heat. That might be what drives me to it, in part at least, makes me agree to something so outright foolish. I've heard before that the heat's enough to make anyone go bonkers. Folks see mirages in the worst of it, shimmering hallucinations conjured by their dehydrated minds.

We're going to steal a car. Someone's baby. Someone's own Delilah.

It was Lizzie's idea, of course. *Borrowing*, she called it. A *loan*. She assured us that the plan would run smoothly, so long as we followed her lead every step of the way. *"Let me do the talking, girls, and the thinking. You do the acting."*

It's ridiculous. It's preposterous.

It's somehow the only thing we can do.

When I balked and tried to argue, Lizzie shot me this look that seared right through me and said, *It's not like this is your first time being a criminal. Like you didn't just steal from a whole goddamned corporate megastore.*

I'll never forget the way Lux flinched, her mouth forming an O of something similar to surprise, but not quite. Her eyes flickered to me and I could read the questions on her face: *When? Why?* Maybe *How?* I shrugged. What could I say?

I mean, she'd stolen things, too.

Up until this point, I thought maybe, just maybe, the lizard lady truly had no idea who we were. Now I have no doubt in my mind she's onto us. She's no dummy. She's not just a drifter, either.

She knows we're on the run.

The funny thing is, I kind of don't give a shit right now. And it's not just the harsh climate, but Delilah's untimely death, that's clouded my judgment. That and the homicide I committed. And the intense pangs of hunger. The desperation buzzing inside me like a dying mosquito.

The three of us walk farther up the shoulder of the highway, deeper into the muggy, humid air that reeks of sweat and engine fumes. Somewhere not too far from here, a lawnmower whirs to life. To think there are people in their houses around here having lunch, playing with their little kids, going about their ordinary days while Lux and Lizard Lizzie and I walk to the nearest rest stop or roadside attraction we see to find a car to steal. When did my life turn into a cheesy thriller? My duffel grows heavier with each step I take, and I can tell that Lux is starting to struggle with hers, too.

We're so going to prison.

Every time I glance over at Lux, she refuses to look at me.

Lizard Lizzie walks in front of us with a brisk air of confidence. Still not a drop of sweat on her. She whistles the same tune over and over, something folksy and vaguely familiar. I start to hum along, ignoring the sweat dripping down my face and the nasty wetness pooling underneath my already dirty bra.

Can't go back.

Won't go back.

Lux isn't doing well. She walks with her shoulders down, clearly tired of hauling her duffel weighed down with her bulky camera bag and bundle of dirty clothes. She doesn't say much, and whenever Lizzie cracks a joke, the notes in the bells of her laugh ring sharp and off-key.

But what am I supposed to do? I'm exhausted, too, my head aches, and my body hurts everywhere. I'm so hungry and hot. All I want is a nice cold shower. A good meal. A car with air-conditioning.

And that's what we're getting. *This is lunacy,* I tell myself, over and over. *Lord, please let us get a ride. Get us a ride.*

After walking for nearly an hour, we find a sprawling shopping plaza parking lot and settle on a sunflower-yellow sedan.

I argue that the car is conspicuously bright—a potential magnet for cops—but Lizzie shrugs me off. She says it's so dented around the bumper that no one will miss it enough to put up a fuss. Plus, it's old enough that it doesn't have a fancy security system we have to get through, maybe a midnineties model. Perfect for hot-wiring. Bonus points: it's parked alone in the shade out behind a dumpster, behind the plaza, far out of view from the road and the peeping windows of the stores.

But first, we hit up the plaza's hardware store, cold air-conditioning hitting me like a slap in the face as we walk inside. It smells like cedar chips and oil and plastic, and it's almost as bright as it was outdoors, all harsh fluorescent lighting. Lizzie whistles while she shops, knowing exactly where to go, down the long aisles as country music plays from the speakers. She buys a long metal rod and a wooden block that she'll use to wedge open the car door. Lux and I buy bottles of water and gourmet lollipops, like this is any other day on our vacation from purgatory, like we both aren't shaking with fear now that we'll be adding another crime to our rap sheet.

Lizzie is a natural. It's like I'm watching someone play *Grand Theft Auto*, the way she seamlessly pops open the driver's side door with the metal rod and the block. It takes her all of two minutes to break in.

Lux and I stand there in the shade, watching in awe, lollipops hanging from our half-open mouths. Lizzie sighs with pleasure and slaps her leathered hands together.

"Now what?" Lux asks, giving Lizzie a pointed side-eye. Her mouth is full of caramel apple so it sounds more like: "*Maw-wha?*"

Lizzie puts a finger to her lips and plops right into the driver's seat, unzipping her backpack. "Now we get out the screwdriver," she mutters. "And the wrench. But first we remove the steering column, then we find the wires." She unearths a pack of gum from her bag and pops a piece in her mouth. "You girls hang around over there and stand watch, all right? Don't stay too close to me. If you see anyone, whistle loud. I got to concentrate for a bit. Let's just say if I snip the wrong wire, it'll be Bad News Bears for you and game over for me."

Yep, definitely a seasoned criminal.

Lux rolls her eyes and pops the candy out of her mouth.

"This is weird, huh?" she asks.

"Enjoying a lollipop and sweating my ass off in bumfuck, Oklahoma, while a stranger is busy hot-wiring us a car? Nah, I'd say it's a pretty dreary day."

She frowns. "No, weird like scary weird. Surreal. I can't believe we're doing this, Trixie. I thought . . . I mean I wanted to . . . you know what, never mind."

"No, Lux, tell me. We tell each other everything, remember?"

She presses her lips together and squeezes her eyes shut, like she's holding back tears. "I don't want to, I swear, but I . . . want to go home." She lets out a breath as she says the last part, like she's been holding it in forever.

I grab her hand and grasp it tight, clearing my throat and the tears lodged there. "I know, Lux," I say softly. I can't lie and I say I want to go home, too, but I do know, or can guess how she feels. I think of her dad, who must be worried sick about her. Her little brother, who must miss her fiercely. The life she's left behind and all but given up, all because I killed a hog in her honor. I swallow hard. "Do you want to go home anyway?"

Storm clouds rain across Lux's vision. I see it then, the way her face sets firmly into place, decisively. "No way." She shakes her head, her black curls going *swish-swish*. "We're never going back."

Never going back.

Never going back.

———

The carjacking takes Lizzie all of fifteen minutes, then we're good to go.

She's so confident behind the wheel of the stolen sunflower sedan. I sit, for once, in the passenger seat, no longer the captain of my ship or this mission. It feels funny, this strange new car, not my Delilah. I miss the way her wheel feels between my hands, the nights I slept in her with Lux. She's in the back with the bags, knees to her chest, eating the other gourmet lollipop I didn't have the stomach for. The glassy look in her eyes tells me she's been silently crying.

We pass a Donut Palace and a dairy farm. Big brown cows graze in the grass, tails flicking away the flies. I fight the urge to say "cows," like Lux and I usually do. It feels wrong in front of Lizzie, and especially right now. Everything here is green and brown and dusty, the buildings short and squat and simple, the land flat as a pancake.

Lizzie's a shit driver. She slows for a red two seconds too late, then jerks to a stop so hard I'm glad I'm wearing my seat belt. Cars honk like crazy when she sways into their lanes. But hell, she knows how to work the gear shift. She says she'll teach me tomorrow how to turn the engine on and off without electrocuting my whole damn self. *She fucking better,* is all I can think, because I'm getting nauseous just sitting here. And I'm so agitated, waiting for my turn to drive. Every now and then, I sneak a glance back at Lux to make sure she's okay, but her face looks haunted every time. It makes me even itchier. Even angrier. More restless.

The lizard may have stolen this car for us, but she's damn sure not keeping it.

We're somewhere in northern Texas tonight, all of us exhausted from a day spent stealing a car. Truth be told, I've lost track of where we've gone or where we should be going. I'm just so damn tired and car-lagged, plus a little carsick from Lizzie's bad driving. When we stop at a McDonald's for dinner, I open the backseat door for Lux and help her out. She's as tired and frazzled as I am, leaning her hip into mine as she loops an arm around my waist, and I certainly don't resist.

After chicken nuggets and salads with wilted leaves, Lizzie insists that we stay in this run-down place called the Dingo. Weirdly, she seems to know the front desk clerk. They're all chatty and chummy with each other. Lux and I pay for our own room when Lizzie offers, and, inexplicably, she sulks off to hers across the hall and slams the door. She already has control of the damn wheel. What else does she want?

I stand outside our room to smoke my first cig in what's felt like forever. I hesitate for a moment, the little nicotine stick beckoning me, taunting and teasing me. Then I cave like I did the other night. I figure I owe it to myself to enjoy at least a few puffs, especially considering the circumstances.

A little while later, a truck pulls up and a gray-haired hog emerges, knocking on Lizzie's door. He grins big and wide when she lets him in. Now I know why she needs her own room, and how she gets all her money, aside from pickpocketing distracted tourists and day-trippers like I've seen her doing. But tonight, she's not my problem. Lux and I finish what's left of our white rum from Middlesville. We put on our matching Day-Glo bikinis for the first time since we bought then—hers hot pink, mine neon green—and dive headfirst into the tiny motel pool.

It isn't heated, but the water is still warm from the sun and feels luxurious after a day in the car. I hold my breath underwater and see how long I can stay at the bottom before I start to get light-headed, eyes open, enjoying the silence, the wobbly stillness here.

I should borrow Lizzie's phone or go to the front desk and call Judy.

I can't stop this ticker tape of a thought, this broken record that keeps skip-skip-skipping through my mind.

I should at least find out about Mama.

No, no, *no*. I can't do that, can't go there.

Not can't.

Won't.

At least, not yet.

I force myself to come up for air, my bubble of stillness broken. The sounds of the night come rushing back: crickets whispering from the tall grass and trees, going *shh-shh-shh* like they're singing us some distorted lullaby. The occasional whirr of a semitruck on the highway, down the hill from the motel. A big dog's throaty barks.

Lux splashes me. I splash her back. She smirks. She wants to play. I'm game, but first I decide to play it cool. I pretend to ignore her and float on my back, waiting a while. The sugar stars glimmer and wink down at me.

She splashes me again, harder this time. "Why do you love to hurt me?" I pout. It sounds like an invitation.

Her voice is soft when she says, "You're fun to hurt, I guess."

I keep my eyes glued to the stars, those infinite galaxies painted above us. Sometimes I hate staring at them for too long. It gives me crazy vertigo. "This must be what it feels like to float in space, you know?" I say. "I wish I could go to space."

I feel her swim toward me, her presence right behind my head. My heart quickens. Her voice is low, like a purr: "First take me to the ocean, Trixie Denton."

I don't know if I can ever keep that promise. But right now, more than anything, I want something real and true.

Lux begins to tread slow circles around me, a hot pink shark in a scummy motel pool. I mimic her movements until we're both caught in this strange kind of water dance.

It's been running through my head like a marquee, pulsing through my chest. I should blurt it out. Let it out. I should—

Tell her something true.

"You could go to the cops, you know." It's a relief to let the words I've been holding back tumble out of me. "You could turn me in and go home."

Lux stops swimming midstroke and blinks at me. "What? Why would I?"

Is her heart beating as fast and hard as mine? The look of shock on her face is so pure and raw, and it gives me a drop of courage.

I take a deep breath and continue. "Because you hate all this, I know you do, and it was me who did it, Lux. It was *me* who killed him. You did nothing wrong, other than help me flee the scene and get out of those horrible bloodstained clothes. You're innocent. You can still go home. Start over. See the ocean now, if you wanted to, without me and everything I've done weighing you down."

"Where is this coming from, Trix?" Lux asks softly, gently. She's not mad. Just confused. Maybe a little hurt.

I swallow back the burning tears. "You'll get sick of me eventually. Tired of my bullshit. You'll . . . you know. You'll leave."

The crickets fade and the world goes still for a moment as we draw closer and closer together, two magnets unable to resist the pull. Then her chest is up against mine and my hands are on her shoulders. Our foreheads press together and we're breathing the same air, in and out, sharing lungs. Breathing but breathless.

Lux gently cradles my cheek in her hand. "Oh God, I would *never* leave you." She says it fiercely. "We're in this together. It's you and me till the end. Don't you know that by now? I *love* you, Trixie."

The way she says it . . . it's not the way you'd say it to your best friend.

My breath catches in my throat. I can't stop it now.

"Lux . . . can . . . can I—?"

She gives a gasp of approval and presses her lips to mine, like she's been waiting years for me to ask her.

I react instinctively, grabbing the back of her neck and pulling her in to kiss her back, hard. She opens her mouth. Our tongues meet, and right now I am so goddamned hungry for her. I've been starving all my life. Her lips taste like luxury: soft, sensual, sweet. Energy crackles between us, sparks of static and electricity. We kiss and kiss until she bites my lower lip and comes up for air.

"Whoa" is all I manage.

"Yeah."

"Yeah?" I'm panting. "That's all you've got to say. *Yeah?*"

She waits a beat. "Yeah." And then: "Shit. I've always loved you, Trixie."

I gape at her, unable to process anything that's happened in the last sixty seconds.

She rolls her eyes and smirks, slicking back some of my hair. "I always knew you'd be hot in red. Geez, you're so clueless sometimes."

She giggles and I laugh too and then we kiss some more. Her hands snake down to my waist, and then our stomachs touch, pressing close against each other in the shallow end of the pool.

<hr>

There are Confederate flags all over the Dingo.

Some are stickers pressed against the glass of a mirror, or wrapped around the sharp edge of a desk. There are fabric flags as well, proudly draped across navy blue walls. I don't know how many were put there by the staff or the owners or anyone who was passing through, who wanted to leave their mark on this place and let themselves be known.

There were Confederate flags in West Virginia, too. Bumper stickers on the backs of hogs' Jeeps and Harley-Davidsons. They

said, LIVE FREE AND DIE A REBEL. They said, IF THIS FLAG
OFFENDS YOU, STUDY AMERICAN HISTORY. As if I hadn't. As if I
didn't know what that fucking flag implied.

The bumper stickers read, THE SOUTH WAS RIGHT. Now I can
almost hear them whisper it through these walls: *Slavery wasn't
that bad.* And: *Honestly, we wish it were still around.*

So much hatred here in this dingy little place, with these
hateful flags that symbolize the legacy of a violently racist nation.

I think of the symbol Lux was scratching into the wall back at
the last motel. Or the symbol I imposed on what she scratched.

We need a symbol. We deserve one. A good symbol.

It sparks in my mind's eye: a Venus symbol, engulfed in
flames. Burning like a supernova hurtling through space.
Through time.

Like us. Like our love.

Burn it down.

Together, we are on fire.

Together, we are freedom.

I follow Lux back into the room.

Into the shower, where we continue to kiss and wash the chlorine from our hair with the cheap motel soap and shampoo.

She takes off my bikini top. I take off hers.

Semidry, we're in the bed closest to the AC unit. She kisses
me everywhere. Behind my earlobe, on my lips, down my stomach, between my thighs . . .

I don't know what I'm doing or what to do, so I let her lead,
just follow my senses and let these natural urges I've had for years
take over. We fumble and giggle at first, because this is new and

awkward and strange, and then something clicks into place. We've found our rhythm.

I can't believe this is happening. She's here, in my arms, between my fingers. Lux. *My* Lux. Now it's real and true and we're both here, together. Utterly electrified.

I kiss her everywhere my lips can reach, her skin smelling faintly of chlorine.

What we do to each other between those motel sheets is aggressive and hot. Animalistic.

It feels like nirvana.

Or whatever the fuck that's supposed to feel like.

———

I must have dozed off, because there are razor blades in my stomach, and they jolt me awake.

The room is pitch black, the fan whirring. Lux sleeps peacefully on her stomach, her bare back glistening in the moonlight that pours in from the open window. We forgot to close the heavy curtains. Not that anyone would've seen us.

I groan and make a mad dash for the bathroom. I'm cramping so bad, and when I get on the toilet to pee I see the blood leaking out of me.

Great. Just great. The well-timed period strikes again.

Blood. Gushing out.

Stop it, Trixie.

Raw meat where the knife goes in.

I shudder and try to shake the thoughts from my mind. *Go away, go away.* My heart is thumping and I feel so sick. In the mirror, I get a full glimpse of how run-down I really am: the dark circles under my eyes, the droopiness of my face. How much have I even been sleeping? I can feel it in my bones, this deep-seated exhaustion.

Back in the room, I fumble around in my duffel for a tampon, but after I go back in the bathroom to insert it, I see the blood again and it whips me around right back to that night.

Meat and flesh.

Blood pouring onto my yellow shirt, like ketchup on mustard.

I lift the lid of the toilet seat and puke my guts out. By the time I'm done, my abs are shaking and my mouth is full of metal and bile.

I killed someone.

I fucking killed someone in cold blood.

It wasn't even self-defense. Sure, I was protecting my very best friend in the whole wide world. I was protecting the love of my life. And yes, he probably (most definitely) deserved it. But I could've gone and gotten help. I could've screamed. I could've done anything but stab him.

I brush my teeth, trying hard to rinse the taste of vomit from my mouth, then slip on a sports bra and a pair of cotton shorts. I need some air. Motel key in my pocket, I take one last look at Lux in bed. Her hair is extra wavy from the pool water, tousled around her head. There's a smile on her face. She looks so serene. So . . . peaceful.

Outside, mosquitoes hum and swarm around the sickly yellow lights of the motel pool. It's humid out here, a relief from the chilly room. It smells like freshly mown grass and summer. It must be around two a.m., or so my internal clock tells me.

Lizard Lizzie sits on one of the pool chairs, reclined, scribbling something in a little black notebook with one hand, a cigarette in the other. She wears her leather gloves and a cowboy hat. I enter through the gate and take a seat in the chair beside her.

"My daddy used to smoke those."

Her mouth turns up in a grin but her eyes stay glued to her notebook. "So did mine," she mutters.

"Where you from, anyway?"

Lizzie chuckles to herself and takes a long drag from her cig. "Nowhere you've been." Her eyes meet mine, and there's a devilish glint to them. Something oddly seductive there. "Then again, maybe you have. You girls seem to get around."

I want to fire back, *So do you*, but instead I cough and go, "What's that supposed to mean?"

There's this pointed look she gives me like, *It means whatever you want it to mean, sweetheart.* She takes another long, deep drag and goes on like she didn't just say something shady. "Nice night, isn't it?"

I shrug. "Reasonably warm. I like it."

She offers me her cigarette.

When I inhale that sweet, familiar hit of nicotine I relax a little, closing my eyes. Lizard Lizzie chuckles again.

I raise an eyebrow at her. Something in the way she just laughed at me makes me feel raw, exposed. Picked on. "What?" I ask, all bristly. "You want it back or something?"

She waves a hand at me and chuckles again, then reaches into her pocket and pulls another from the pack. "Oh honey, I've got plenty." She lights it and takes a drag. "You keep that one. You seem to be enjoying it."

Having the cigarette between my fingers and the nicotine in my lungs gives me a sudden boost of confidence. "What are you writing?"

Her lips purse together into a scowl. Her voice comes out hard and mean. "None of your business."

"Oh."

She shakes her head. "Sorry. Reflex. I'm a bit . . . I'm kind of a private person. Don't share much with strangers."

"You still consider me a stranger?"

Lizzie studies me for a long while, then goes back to her scribbling, the cigarette perched between her fingers. "I'd say so. Though you're a kind stranger. Put up well enough with my rambling and ranting in the car all day."

It's kind of shocking to hear her say something so self-aware. I decide to take advantage. "Why did you insist on paying for our rooms again tonight?"

She shrugs and keeps her head down, inhales again. "Dani's a cheapskate who up-charges tourists. If she thought I was with you, she'd have given us a good group discount."

"Dani? The front desk lady? Okay, you do know her."

A smirk plays on Lizzie's lips, making the scar on her cheek flicker like the tongue of a rattlesnake. "Good friend. Old friend, in fact."

"You come here a lot," I say, realizing. I take a long, smooth inhale, let the smoke trickle out of my lips and into the night. "You cycle through places, don't you? You don't just go somewhere once. You're kind of like a fish. You migrate back and forth."

She laughs a little and taps some of her ashes out against the side of her pool chair. "A fish, huh? I don't like to be stuck in one place too long, no. Had more than enough of that as a kid." Some haunting memory clouds her face for a beat, but she quickly shakes it off. "But I do have my favorite places."

"I feel you," I say. "I always wanted to leave my town. Travel. See the world. I guess I can't really do that now, though."

She frowns. "Why not?"

Shit. I clear my throat and think fast. "I uh, have a sick mama at home I got to take care of. Responsibilities. This is kind of a . . . an escape." The razor blades slice down my belly again as I say all of this out loud. "Lux and I we—we both needed this trip."

Lizzie seems to consider this for a moment. "And you're just 'going west'? No real destination in mind? When do you intend to go back?"

I wince. I know she probably doesn't mean to, but now I feel like I'm being interrogated. These are all fair questions, but they're ones I've been avoiding. Ones I'd hoped I'd never have to answer to anyone, let alone myself. Ones that Lux and I have put off discussing concretely.

"Not sure," I say finally. "When the time is right."

She nods like she understands and shows me what she's been drawing, not writing, I realize. "Like it?" she asks, all bright and childlike, like she really cares about my opinion.

I lean in closer to see. It's a sketch of a little bird, not too different from the stick-and-poke hummingbird on my wrist. Only its wings are being clipped with scissors, and it's squawking and bleeding and crying. My blood chills.

"It's nice," I say weakly. Lizzie pouts a little like I wounded her, so I add: "It's great. You're really talented."

That fluffs her feathers and she smiles. "Thanks. I'm real proud of it." She crushes the tip of her cigarette onto the concrete, stubs it out with her bare toe. "Though you don't have to lie, you know. If you don't actually like it. You can tell me if you don't."

I feel that sinking in my stomach I always get when I'm caught fibbing. "Oh" is all I can say.

"I value honesty above all else. In fact, I hate liars." She hawks and spits onto the ground, making me jump a little in my seat. Something callous reaches her face, turns her back into a lizard, coiled and ready to spring. "I really fucking hate liars."

I walk back to my room—*our* room—feeling shuddery, antsy. I try to picture it, but the image makes no sense: Lux and me in a courtroom, awaiting our fates, then shipped off to separate juvenile detention facilities, locked away for years, while Mama withers away and dies and Judy shakes her head like she's sad, sad, sad. It can't happen. It won't happen.

Lux and me dead in a ditch somewhere, gunned down by the pigs like in the final scene of *Bonnie and Clyde*.

It can't end like this.

It can't.

It won't.

One way or another, we have to get to the coast. Or maybe . . . if we can, we should head north and go to Canada. South to Mexico.

I don't know which move is right.

I don't know, *I don't know*, God, I'm so fucking scared.

I'm still cramping badly in the morning, but Lux is here. In bed with me. She kisses me awake on both eyelids, and I feel all warm and slushy inside, knowing what we did last night.

I'm not sure yet what we are, exactly, what this means, but for now, especially amid all this chaos, I want to enjoy every minute of it.

The Dingo has a little breakfast area with cold cereal, pastries, and slices of cheese and fruit. We sit together and hold hands across the table while we eat, me drinking my coffee, her enjoying a Pepsi from the vending machine because they were out of her favorite soda pop.

"You keep drinking those at the same rate, one day you'll start peeing and won't be able to stop until your body's clean out of fluids," I say in between bites of my blueberry muffin. It's extra sugary, just how I like it. Reminds me of the ones Judy used to bring me during my lunch breaks.

"You're disgusting."

"But you love that about me."

She blushes and plays with the ends of her curls. I think I blush, too.

"Lizzie said she'd show me how to turn the car on and off without electrocuting myself this morning." At the mention of Lizzie's name, Lux's brow furrows. "I think she's still asleep. We should get on the road soon. Discuss which route is best, where we're headed. Probably get the gas tank filled and—"

"I have a sinking feeling about this car."

I put down my muffin. "Oh yeah?"

I think back to last night, the conversation Lizzie and I had out by the pool. How the tail end of it made me all shivery, almost made the jitters come on.

Lux nods and fiddles with the tab of her soda-pop can. She hasn't really eaten anything, I realize. "Like you said, potential cop magnet. And, well, the owners are bound to be looking for it, aren't they? I don't trust what she said."

"Are you not hungry?" I get up and rummage through the little breakfast platters, suddenly restless, extra jittery. "We can grab an egg sandwich at a deli if you aren't feeling any of this stuff."

"Trix. Did you hear me?"

"We'll change the plates," I say absently, as if that's some simple, easy solution. "We'll find a junkyard around here and have Lizzie swap them out. Shouldn't be too much of a task."

"And what if we get pulled over?" Lux stares down into her nearly empty can like it's a hole she wants to crawl into and hide inside. "What then, Trix? You have your license, sure. And maybe the registration's in the dash, but it won't match. And I mean, the ignition is obviously fucked with."

I shake my head, frustrated suddenly, like these things weren't true or possible until Lux uttered them aloud. "We won't get pulled over," I say firmly. I pop a mini muffin in my mouth and hand one to Lux. "We'll always go below or at the speed limit. No fancy driving. Avoid the main highways as much as possible, like we've been doing."

She chews at her lip, hesitating, then accepts my muffin, nibbling at the edges and picking at the crumbs, but never taking a big, full bite.

⸻

I wish for the millionth time today that I had access to the internet.

I wish I could read today's headlines, or even briefly check my weather app or see what new TV show is airing tonight. Which new movies they'll be showing at the Blue Bottle AMC. It's hard to imagine people at home are going on as normal, doing things like buying groceries, walking their dogs, picking their kids up from school. Everything that I used to find utterly boring about living in Blue Bottle sounds tantalizing right now.

I wonder endlessly what the rest of the world is saying about us now, what they're saying about Bryce and his family and the whole mess I created with Judy's knife. How much they know about who we are.

The internet could be mostly in Bryce's favor, full of sympathy and love for the murdered son of a prominent family. They might also be enraged, disgusted, like those horrible comments we read in the library. Hoping the worst for us. Justice and no mercy.

Without my phone screen to stare at all day and fuss over, I'm more alert, more awake and focused on the here and now.

But that only makes it so much harder.

⸻

Turns out swapping the plates was a pretty good idea. Lizzie knows the area, so she has a good guess where someone might have left a few abandoned cars. We're in luck: there are Michigan plates on an old abandoned gray Nissan, or what's left of it, rotting behind an old tire factory. Lux takes plenty of photos of the giant cement building with smashed windows, getting on her knees and crouching down for all sorts of different angles.

I turn to Lizzie, hard at work refurbishing our stolen car. "Make your own luck, huh?"

She unscrews the old plates and puts on the new ones as best she can with her limited tools. Grunts and tells me to hand her a wrench or something from her backpack. She's being weird as hell this morning. Maybe she slept funny, or didn't sleep much at all. Maybe she had more of those mysterious visitors. Not that I judge her for it or anything. We all gotta make our money somehow.

Whatever. While she works, Lux and I sprawl out in the thick grass. We swat at gnats and mosquitoes and pore over a new paper map the motel gave us, trying to find the best route across this part of the state. Sure, Lizzie has her phone and her GPS, but I've come to like the paper map, the way it feels solid and sure in my hands, the veins and arteries of roads and highways scattered across it, leaving me dizzy and even more confused than I was the last time I glanced at it.

Why is reading a map so hard?

As I squint and trace the road we're on, I have to back up. This doesn't make sense. Weren't we just here the other day?

Am I wrong, or did we go south instead of west?

"Can you do my back?" Lux asks. Today she wears a banana-yellow tank top from home that reads SATAN IS MY SUGAR DADDY in hot pink bubble lettering. Clothes she'd never dare to wear in front of her father. As far as he knows, Lux mainly sports slouchy T-shirts and appropriately fitted tanks. She wears the good stuff underneath when we go out.

Lux brings her tank top straps down, revealing her freckled shoulders. I itch at my mosquito bites and crawl over to her.

The map can wait.

We've been putting sunscreen on the hard-to-reach parts of each other since we were little kids, but now, it feels so damn different. Touching her feels intimate. I flush hot all over as I rub the warm cream across her bare skin, and she sighs and relaxes into my hands. My throat goes dry. The sunshine is a big, warm hug, but suddenly I feel restricted, like swallowing is a little difficult.

Touching her out in the open like this scares me, even though there's no one around as far as I can see besides the lizard lady. But what if someone walks by, happens upon us? Would they be able to read the way I feel for her in the movement of my hands across her skin? I imagine faceless people floating by, frowning, shaking their heads. Saying words like *dyke* and *queers* under their breath, words that always made me nervous when kids at school threw them around carelessly, unaware of how volatile they were. How much they hurt when they almost hit me.

Why do I care so much, anyway?

I try my best to ignore the thoughts, but they keep on coming one after another. Shit. I pull away from Lux and mumble some excuse about having to go find a place to pee since Lizzie is taking forever. Lux raises an eyebrow but says nothing. I wade into a patch of overgrown weeds, enjoying the moment to myself.

Isn't this what you wanted? The voice rises and swells suddenly from some hidden cave inside of me. *Now you have her and you still aren't satisfied.*

I shake my head so violently I get a little head rush. No, no. I can't think like this. We have to focus on where we're going next, and the map, and the car . . .

I sigh and stand just as Lizzie swears so loudly they can probably hear her two counties over. She waves her hand around like she's accidentally hurt herself. She sees me watching and shoots me a dirty look before going back to putting a new rear plate on the sunflower sedan.

What the hell was that about?

Lux is studying the map when I return, chewing at her cuticles like she always does when she's particularly flustered. My shadow falls over her as I move closer, and she smiles up at me, some of the tension in her face breaking away.

"She almost done?" Lux asks.

I shrug. "I hope so. I'm ready to get out of here."

Lux nods slowly, like she's trying to understand my sudden impatience. "Okay. Well, I think I've found a route we can take that should get us to New Mexico in about a day." She traces a line across the paper map and grins to herself, clearly pleased with her work. "There's some stuff I'd like to stop and see, actually, if we go this way. And maybe we could even see the Grand Canyon after, don't you think? There are some things I wouldn't mind risking prison for."

She says it like it's a joke, but nothing about it feels funny.

"What about the ocean?" I ask. "We can drive through New Mexico, but I thought we agreed to get there as quickly as possible. As far as we can get from West Virginia."

She tears apart a tiny blade of grass, face falling, like a kid who's been reminded that Disney World isn't happening this year. "Oh, right."

"Let me see this route."

I kneel down and study the map with her, following her finger as it goes over each road line. Something is off. "Wait. Are you *sure* that's the right way to New Mexico?" I ask.

Lux. scoffs. "Uh, yeah, Trixie. Look, that's the interstate. See how it goes like this?"

"But it circles back." I retrace the route and try to show her. Part of me wants to bite my tongue, let her think she's right and live in blissful ignorance, but there's a stubborn part of me, too.

Lux slaps the map out straight. "Look. *Here.* This is the way we have to go. Do you see? *That* way would get us lost."

"But we already passed . . ." I let my voice trail off, not wanting to admit it out loud. It would be easier to just agree with her and not argue, but I can't risk it. I promised Lux I'd be honest with her. I promised I'd tell her when things feel wrong. I take a deep breath and steady my voice. "We already passed Milestone, Lux. Didn't we? I remember seeing a sign for it yesterday."

"No, I don't remember that. I thought we were in Sundance. Or . . ." She goes back over her own directions, a muddied look crossing her face.

Shit.

What town even *is* this? Why haven't I—*we*—been paying closer attention?

The road lines blur in and out of my vision as the cruel spring sun continues its beatdown with unrelenting force. Summer is coming, and fast. It's only going to get hotter, especially as we get farther west. I suddenly feel light-headed, woozy. What if Lux is right? What if I'm wrong?

What if we're *both* wrong?

Why the fuck did I ever trust Lizzie?

I curse myself a million times. I should've known better. Why was I so foolish and careless?

Suddenly the lizard woman whoops and hollers so loud I nearly jump out of my skin. "I GOT IT!" She smacks her gloved hands together, laughs, and takes a step back from the car to examine her handiwork. "No one will ever notice a thing."

"Sure," Lux says. "No one will notice the fucked-up wiring if they pull us over. Or the lack of valid registration."

But Lizzie doesn't seem to hear her. She starts humming and pacing around the car, and it makes the hairs on the back of my neck tickle.

"Well," she says after a while, "you girls do need to hit the road now, don't you?"

Lux and I exchange a strange, nervous look.

———

We're back on the road, Lizzie behind the wheel again. According to her we're headed westward, but I no longer believe her. I don't trust the clipped way she says "yes" when I dare to ask if she's sure, or the strange way she mutters under her breath, the radio drowning out her words. Road signs pass us by, ones I recognize from looking at the map, and it clicks into place: Lizzie's been steering us wrong for days, and she damn well knows it.

We need to get away from her as soon as possible. My wind whirls, trying to reason a way out. An alternate solution.

It makes me antsy all over, like my skin is popping with itches I can't scratch. We stopped fifteen minutes ago "for gas"—really, Lizzie stopped to siphon gas from other cars at a depressing little shopping plaza. She finally showed us how to do it, said we should probably learn sooner rather than later if we wanted to be "financially viable." You can only do a little bit at a time, and you have to blow directly into a plastic tube to increase the air pressure inside the other car's tank. Without an air pump, it's exhausting work, especially when it's a billion degrees outside and humid. But even outlaws on the run need to learn to budget well.

The stolen car's overall wiring is predictably dodgy, so it's pretty warm in here. Sweat pools between my breasts and trickles down my back. I feel bad for Lux, who is trapped in the back with Lizzie's bulging backpack, a place the tepid air has an even harder time reaching. To make matters worse, Lizzie is blaring some awful, mindless song. It almost sounds like Christian rock, now that I listen closely. It's way too corny to be anything punk.

"You okay over there?" Lizzie asks me with a smug smile. She knows I'm not okay, knows damn well that I hate every second of this, not being in the driver's seat. She probably even knows I know we're going south instead of west, further down into the belly of Texas. I'd go with Lux in the back, but I need to keep my eyes on the road. At least up here I'm somewhat in control.

Or I can try to believe that I am, and I can try to think of a plan. Maybe at the next stop we can grab our stuff out of the trunk and just run and hitchhike. No, that's too dangerous. We could get picked up by another lizard lady, or someone much worse. Maybe we can find a bus somehow (too many people), or steal another car. No, that makes no sense. That's impossible. Pretty soon my anxious mind starts shooting nothing but blanks.

I stare out the window. We pass at least a dozen signs advertising a fresh produce stand in bright bold font: POTATOES! CHERRIES! STRAWBERRIES! There're little paintings of happy peaches and dancing watermelons on some of them. If I weren't so nervous, I might want to stop and check it out. Let Lux take some pictures.

But neither of us are in any mood for picture taking.

My heart aches for Delilah, for the days before she died, before we found out the frat hog was dead. We were really living in ignorant bliss.

Lizzie turns down the music and grunts. "You know, I saw something funny on the news this morning." She sucks her teeth. "Most of the news these days is the same old, same old. Same dying planet. Same depressing shit. But this, man, *this* was a *real* good segment, actually made me sit up and pay attention for once." I watch her lock eyes with Lux in the rearview mirror, a grin forming across her scaly lips. I turn to see that Lux and I are thinking the same thing, and we're both terrified.

"They have good stories sometimes, some unsolved *mysteries*, you know?" Lizzie stretches out the word *mysteries* like it's some cool new slang she just learned. "You two like true crime? No? You both sure are quiet today, and after I did something so nice for both of you. And taught you a new skill, to boot. I haven't even really gotten a proper thank-you. It's important to say thank you, especially to friends who do big favors for ya. Don't you think?"

"Thanks," Lux murmurs. She clears her throat and tries again, but her voice is as flat as the land that rolls and stretches out before us. "No, really, thank you so much. We have a new ride now, thanks to you. And plenty of gas in the car."

Lizzie snorts. Surely she can detect the sarcasm.

I watch the ranches and long stretches of barren land whizz past us and wonder if this is what it's like for those dumb teens at that awful point in the horror movie when they know they've made the wrong decision and are about to be driven off somewhere to be slaughtered like cattle, but there's not a goddamned thing they can do about it.

"A buddy of mine stays at a river town this time of year, does commercial fishing and all that," Lizzie goes on. She sucks her teeth again and it makes me jump in my seat. "He should have room for us on his houseboat, if you don't mind the mosquitoes. Vicious little critters. They do like to bite."

"No, thanks." It surprises me to hear my own voice leap right out of my throat, but there you go. "We don't do houseboats. We'll get ourselves our own accommodation."

"Yeah," Lux says. "That sounds good. Thanks, though. Again. Thanks for *all* your help."

Lizzie snaps off the music entirely and Lux gives a little gasp. The scar on her face flashes in the sunlight, and the road rumbles beneath us, foreign new tires crunching gravel. "My buddy is in the force, you know," she says darkly. "But he does like to keep up to date on the national news. Especially big stories with potential big payoffs."

We could jump out now, but then we wouldn't have our duffel bags—which are stuffed in the trunk along with our money—or a ride. You can be damn sure I took the money out of Delilah's dashboard. I stuffed it deep inside the folds of the bloody yellow shirt. The one with the hog's blood.

"Payoffs? I don't know what you're talking about," Lux says carefully.

Lizzie turns the wheel sharply and Lux squeals. Suddenly we're on a winding country road that seems to grow narrower with every mile.

I know Lux knows that I know she was right about this lizard from the get-go, and I was careless, and maybe this is game over now. I can try my best to fix this. I owe that to her.

I slaughtered a hog. I can handle a lizard.

Lizzie grinds her teeth. "I'm no dummy!" she spits. Like, actual spittle goes flying at the windshield.

"Never said you were," I counter.

"But you were thinking it. Weren't you?" She swivels around to glare at Lux in the back. "I know *you* were, especially. You never liked me."

Lux's mouth flops open and closed like a fish.

"Leave her alone!" I holler. "It doesn't really matter what we think of you. In fact, I really liked you before you turned out to be a raging bitch!"

Lizzie puffs out her cheeks. They grow bright red. She narrows her eyes. Her scales dance in the light. Now I can see them clear as day.

She starts to tremble, but eventually exhales hard, like she's remembering I'm not worth getting all revved up about.

"I told you, Trixie, I hate liars." She says it slowly, in a guttural growl, like I'm a little kid who doesn't understand. She grips the steering wheel so tight her claws turn white. "And you lied to me. Both of you did."

"We did what we had to do. Surely you can understand that."

"How's that?"

Lux stays silent in the back. She holds herself with both arms, rocking back and forth.

"Okay, sure," I say. "Maybe Lux *was* thinking you're not the brightest." I know for sure that behind me her mouth just fell open. "But I know you *are* bright, because if you weren't, you'd think turning us in to the local cops or feds or whoever for some measly reward would solve your issues. But you and I both know how much they'd love to hear my side of the story. You know, the sad tale of the minor who was kidnapped with her sweet little friend and forced into a life of crime by a con artist. I'm sure the feds would be tickled to hear all about the car you jacked, too. The people at motels you pickpocket and the Walmart you showed me how to rob. Maybe you even told us to stab that boy back in West Virginia."

My tongue stops cold as I realize what I've done.

Lizzie looks so smug she might burst into confetti. Lux shrinks further into the backseat.

"So, you admit you did stab him?" Her voice is cool, full of amusement. She chuckles, takes out her pack of Kool cigarettes and pops one in her mouth, lighting up. She parks on the side of the road, turns off the car, and rolls down the windows, the sweet smell of manure mingling with the gentle hush of cicadas. It makes me miss dusk in Blue Bottle. The sun will be out for a few more hours, but evening is coming fast.

"If you knew what he did to me," Lux says in a small voice, "you would've stabbed him, too."

Lizzie blanches. The slash of scar across her cheek sinks in as her lizard skin relaxes. Her whole demeanor changes, maybe softens. "He . . ." She swallows hard after cutting herself off before doing it once more. I always marvel at people who do that. It's like they're holding back what they really want to say without realizing they're doing it. "If you . . ."

Lizard Lizzie pauses a long while before speaking. She offers me a cigarette, but I decline even though I'm dying for one right about now. When Lizzie offers one to Lux, she spits, "Go fuck yourself."

Lizzie closes her eyes and shakes her head. She smacks her face a little, like she's mad at some obvious error she made. The stolen sedan stinks up with the smell of tobacco.

I notice Lizzie looking at me, at my wrist where the little hummingbird stick-and-poke tattoo Judy did is etched on my skin forever. I think of the drawing she showed me the other night, of the little bird crying and bleeding as its wings were snipped off with scissors. The image is now seared into my brain, ready to haunt every dream.

I'm not sure how I know for absolute certain in that moment, but I do. Lux, Lizzie, and I . . . we are all interlinked. We are all part of the same sad, never-ending fucking story.

Lizzie clears her throat before she finally speaks. Her voice comes out gruff and wobbly, like an actor reciting lines they've barely memorized. "Listen, I like you, kid," she says to me. "Not so sure about your girlfriend here." She wags her cigarette toward the back with disdain, as if Lux were nothing more than a pesky mosquito. "But you, you have spunk. Grit. I did put the pieces together, did weigh my options today, did consider turning both of you in. And it could work out in my favor, no matter what fairy tale either of you comes up with." She taps her ashes out the open window. "But the thing is, when I was your age, I got into some deep shit myself. I don't know if the things I did were right or wrong, or if that even exists in the grand scheme of it all, but I made it out of the swamp one way or another. And I ended up like this." She grimaces and chews at her talons . . . her nails. Suddenly, she looks a little less like a lizard to me, a lot more like a human.

"You two aren't evil," Lizzie continues. "Lousy criminals, for sure. And not innocent, no, but whatever happened back in West Virginia with you stabbing that boy or whatever it is you did, well, I can't fathom one damn good reason either of you would do it for anything other than self-defense. I mean, quite frankly, neither of you has the chutzpah to be a true cold-blooded killer. I just can't see it." She chuckles again and leans back in her seat, pondering the sky. "I guess what I'm saying is . . . I . . . believe you."

I stare down at my dirty sneakers. It wasn't self-defense, not really. I was defending the girl I love, but I didn't have to stab him. I didn't have to leave him to die, rapist hog or not.

Not that Lizzie has to know any of that. Not that it matters anymore. What's done is done, I tell myself, and I don't feel a damn bit guilty.

"You aren't evil, either," I say. "I've learned a lot from you, too." I'm sucking up hard, because, truly, I don't know this woman from a can of paint. For all I know, maybe she is a serial killer. Maybe she would hide corpses in the trunk of this stolen car. Our corpses. But I need to get her to ease up, to let Lux and me go in peace.

To my disbelief, she does more than that.

She gifts us the sunflower sedan.

All she wants in exchange is fifty dollars from our waning cash pool and a ride to the closest tourist stop where she can try to find another ride. "Wherever you girls are going, frankly, it's nowhere I want to be, especially not when they catch up to you," Lizzie grunts, stepping out of the car she stole for us. She adjusts her leather gloves, heaves her backpack up on one shoulder, and gives us a salute. "Just remember, girls: Be smarter. This only ends one of two ways."

I stare after her as she stalks toward the Chili's off the side of the highway. Parents wrangle a gaggle of toddlers in the shade by their minivan. Lizzie eyes them for a moment, as if considering her prey, then seems to decide against it. One last time, I watch her scar flicker across her cheek as she grins and spits a wad onto the hot concrete, then disappears inside.

And just like that, the lizard has slithered away and the car is mine. Ours. Mine and Lux's, because now all that matters is us.

I name her Razor Blade.

"Fucking *finally*!" Lux hops into the front seat, leans it back as far as it goes, and props her bare feet up on the dash, back where they belong. I start the engine the way Lizzie taught me, put the car in reverse, and back out of the spot we pulled into, relieved but deeply unsettled. Still shaky. I'm uneasy behind the wheel with all its exposed wiring, and without Lizard Lizzie in here with us, babbling away and smoking and making little observations every minute, it feels strangely empty and quiet.

I flip the radio back on and switch to a good station.

I realize I'm also sad for little things like Lux's phone and all the music she had on it, and in our rush to abandon Delilah, I left behind my beloved CD collection.

Things will never be the same. I can try to forget for a while, get lost in Lux's lips and arms, but the pain sits there, waiting for me, lodged inside my heart.

"*So* relieved she's gone for good," Lux says. She pops a piece of bubble gum in her mouth and chews noisily, cranking up the radio. "I swear something was truly off about her. Mentally, that is."

I bite the inside of my lip. "Don't say that."

"Why?" Lux snaps. She's still heated with me for the whole damn ordeal, I can tell, and honestly she has every right to be.

"You know she's more than a little bonkers," Lux argues. "I mean, I just about thought she was planning on killing us and leaving our bodies out for the coyotes back there."

Lux blows a big pink bubble. Usually, I'd reach over and poke it, let it pop and deflate. But I keep my hands firmly on the wheel, concentrating on the road ahead of me. This road to nowhere.

"Anyway, she was Bad News Bears," Lux goes on. "Though you did call her the lizard lady, didn't you? Yeah, she was a no-good, spineless lizard. The kind you run right over."

"Lizards have spines," I say softly.

Lux pops her gum. I merge us back onto the highway as carefully as I can, because we don't know which back roads to use anymore. Not without a good map or Lizzie's GPS.

"I have some thoughts on where we should go," I say. "I know you want to see the ocean, and I'm still taking you to California if that's what you want, but there might be better options. So far, we've been more focused on the journey, not the destination. You know?"

Lux sighs and presses her cheek to the dirty passenger window. I catch a glimpse of her reflection, spot the tears in her eyes, trickling down her cheeks.

It just about destroys me.

"I was thinking Canada," I say, trying to brighten my tone. "Maybe we'd be safer there? Because—"

"We'd never make it past the border and you know that."

I merge lanes to avoid colliding with a semitruck. It hits me now, how leaving the country someday has always been my idea. Never Lux's. My half-brained idea for a year abroad morphed into some kind of fantastical vision. A utopia that could maybe save us from the hell we've found ourselves in.

I've pictured shiny Vancouver hotels, mountains caked in snow. Fluffy pancakes drowning in maple syrup. Moose and quaint ski lodges. Miles of lush deciduous forest for us to get lost in.

Something perhaps that reminds me of West Virginia, if only a little. Of home.

It's all a fantasy, I know it. A pipe dream, but why can't I let it go?

I clear my throat, but still my voice cracks. "All I know is," I say, "we have about three hundred and fifty dollars left. Is there a better option? A safer choice? Maybe even Mexico, if not Canada?"

"I want to see the ocean," Lux says, a hitch in her voice that seems to whisper: *You promised me.*

"There's beaches and the ocean in Mexico and Canada, too," I offer weakly, nudging her with my knee, trying to get her to smile. "It might be risky to stay in the country. Don't you think?"

She turns to face me, her eyes red and swollen. "What's not risky anymore?"

Shit. I'm the reason we almost lost everything. I'm the reason she's in this position now, in a stolen car, hundreds of miles from her home and the life she sacrificed to follow me on this journey.

I blink back my own tears. Damn, where did those come from?

"Okay," I say. I spot an exit I recognize from our map, one that'll lead us farther west. "It's settled. I'm taking you there. To California. To the ocean." I owe her that, at least.

I wish I felt nothing. I wish this were all a very bad dream. It's too late, though. We've been in the true nightmare, and there's no waking up. All I need to do is keep us safe, if that's even possible anymore.

A shock of light catches my eye, and it's not someone's high beams. I look down at my wrist where the hummingbird is etched into my skin. For just a split second, I swear: I see it covered in glistening green scales.

The goddamned FBI can try to find us, stop us if they can. It doesn't matter, really, not anymore. Together, Lux and I are a giant, burning supernova, hurtling through space and time at light speed, ready to explode at any moment.

With her by my side, her hand on my knees, her lips on my lips, I can do anything. We can do anything.

I desperately need to believe this.

Because I know, I just know, even as I hold on tight to her and the bliss between us, that our star is burning out. Lizzie was right. Our time is ticking.

Just remember, girls: This only ends one of two ways.

I fill in the rest of Lizzie's sentence in my mind, even hear it in her gruff, scratchy voice: . . . *in prison or in a body bag.*

It's all downhill from here.

There's an email from Judy sitting right in my inbox, taunting me.

My fingers twitch as I hover the cursor above the link, afraid to click on it and just as afraid not to.

I stay paralyzed like that for quite a few minutes.

My heart skipped like a stone across water the second I saw her name.

Lux and I are at a roadside internet café somewhere in the dustbowl of Texas, dolled up in makeup to age us as much as possible. Lux even straightened her curls and put waves in my hair. We're still a little lost from Lizzie looping us around, but now we seem to be headed in the right direction, toward California. I think Lux would like it there, all those palm trees and gorgeous mountains.

Kind of like the ones back in Blue Bottle.

That is, of course, assuming we don't run out of money for gas between here and California. Assuming we can read new maps.

Assuming a lot of things.

The internet service here is fucking horrible. We didn't plan on stopping long. I meant to email Judy to ask her to wire us money through Western Union. Lux and I were supposed to be looking for updates to our story, too, but we found more than we bargained for. A major feminist blog ran a think piece last night on whether or not "alleged rapist" Bryce Grimaldi's death should even be considered a tragedy. Included are dozens of anonymous quotes from other girls, girls who claim to have been harassed and assaulted by him on and off campus at Pinesborough State. Girls who know he's a total creep. Girls who've heard stories, had to console a close friend or sorority sister after the horror he inflicted on them. Girls who've been there with other men and don't need to be told this is all so damn real.

Lux has gone down the virtual rabbit hole. Her foot taps and her legs wiggle as she chews the shredded cuticles on one hand

and navigates the hell that is the internet with a desktop computer mouse in the other.

She wants to print these things so she can read them in depth during the trip, but I argue that we're paying enough per minute as it is to be online. Every second counts. We have to be strategic.

So far, that's fallen apart. We've been in this place for at least thirty minutes, and I'm shuddering to know how much money we're tanking. Still, it's a relief to have access. Who knows when we'll get it again?

I've already read through the seemingly never-ending commentary on the hog forum since I made the first Trouble Girls post back at the library. I've seen everything, from the vicious backlash I've come to expect by now—so violent and horrible it leaves me numb to read—to the waves of support and excitement from our self-declared "fans." But even some of the support—and the mere fact that we have "fans" to begin with—is tinged with an undeniable hint of menace.

We've also discovered our AMBER alerts, the smiling school photos they chose to post like inverted mug shots across the internet. Two beautiful, wholesome Blue Bottle teens. Two nice, normal West Virginia white girls gone missing, the community in shock and fear, especially since it's the same county with a pair of murderers on the loose.

At least for now, they haven't connected the dots. Though of course, Lux's dad is no doubt furious, demanding the cops find her immediately. It's only a matter of time.

Like I said, I was about to email Judy. But then I saw my inbox.

The subject line from Judy's email is simple and written in all-caps: *PLEASE COME HOME, TRIXIE DENTON.*

I breathe in and out, the sick churning dread filling me up, and click it open.

Trixie,

They found the knife.

They found my fingerprints on it from a previous arrest and traced it back to me. I'm not proud of it, but it's true, and I did end up doing my time and paying penance. I advise you do the same, kiddo: Turn yourself in now. We can help you. Get you a lawyer. There're people behind you both.

The cops asked a lot of questions, but so far, I haven't told them anything. I said I lost it. But, honey bunch, they'll ask more questions. I know they will. Because they found your car, abandoned along the interstate in rural Oklahoma. They asked me a lot of questions about that, too. I don't think they believed any of my answers.

It relieved me to know at least it meant you were probably still alive, as much as it made me sick to my stomach that you've been linked to this horrible news.

Trixie, I know that whatever you did, or think you did, you think it's so bad that you can never come back from this, or ever come home. But I want you to know that I love you so much, and so does your mama. She's been asking about you. I'm here for you, missing you like crazy, praying for you every second of every day. I haven't slept this past week. It's been the hardest damn week of my life.

Please come back. Please at least email me and let me know you're okay so I can get a decent night of sleep.

Please at least let me try and help you.

Love always,

Judy

It's a trap, is all I can think. It's a trick. She's waiting, her email and my email wired by the cops, some federal agent waiting in the wings. The second I respond they'll track my location and come and get me. I close the email and log out. Little black dots turn to big, bulging ones that swim before my eyes, and I heave and race to the bathroom where I puke up this morning's egg sandwich into the toilet so hard my insides spasm.

I stay in the bathroom a long while, staring hard at my reflection in the mirror. My new red hair is already a greasy mess and needs another good wash and condition. I've always had acne, but my breakouts are especially bad around my mouth, painful little cysts popping up under my lip and on my chin. My eyes are bloodshot, tired, pools of deep dark beneath them from lack of proper sleep. My health teacher, Mr. Adams, would *tsk-tsk* at me and remind me how the brain doesn't operate at its best on lack of sleep. Especially a teenager's.

I can almost hear his friendly, upbeat voice now, reverberating across the classroom: *This is why school should start later and end earlier with far less homework!* He'd always say it with a wag of his finger, and some of my classmates would cheer. *Chronic sleep deprivation is disastrous to the development of a young person's brain!*

The finger wagging and boundless enthusiasm. The way he'd march up and down the classroom, reciting his beliefs on teenage health like they were sermons.

The thought is so funny to me that for some reason I start giggling and I can't stop. I laugh so hard my eyes water. I realize that I miss him. I miss my fucking *health* teacher. I really must be losing it. I have to splash cold water on my face and take deep, long breaths before going back out into the café, nerves only slightly calmed.

She's been asking about you.

It could be true, but it could also be a lie to bait me into replying. Tugging at my little heartstrings and all that. Judy knows my weak spots. Mama probably doesn't remember me anymore, I tell myself. I'm a ghost to her. She might see glimpses of me in Judy's face, or glimpses of her sister, or whoever the hell Willow was.

The few other patrons type and click around, occasionally swearing under their breath at the slow internet speed or a faulty printer. Lux is still at her desk, hunched forward, huddled and focused on whatever is in front of her like she's finishing her college admissions essay and the deadline is in five minutes.

"Did you find anything useful?" she asks quietly. "About us? Anything at all?"

"No," I lie. "Nothing but the usual."

Someone in the very back of the café catches my eye. It's Bryce Grimaldi. Oh my fucking God, it's *him*. He's *here*. A scared, small sound comes out of me.

But then I blink and he's just some hog boy, sitting with his hog friend. *Bryce is dead. Bryce is dead.* I'm so cold and sick all over.

"What is it, Trix?"

"Nothing," I say quickly.

"Wait. Look. They're talking about the protests at Pinesborough."

I lean in closer to read along with her.

Women's marches, women's rights . . . typical feminazi screeching. Half the time, they don't even know what it is they're screaming like banshees about. Women and privileged girls like these are nothing but sheep. If women really wanted equality, their asses would be bleeding on the front line, not just into their expensive little tampons.

"I don't want to look at this, Lux."

"This one guy says that feminism was invented by Marx and his ideas about destroying the family unit." She cackles suddenly, surprising me, and takes a long slug of coffee. Since when did she start drinking coffee? "I can't *believe* this shit!"

"Come on, Lux, let's go."

"And they've posted all these photos of girls at Pinesborough State, too, comparing their bodies and haircuts and clothing styles from freshman year to now, saying some don't even look like the same *species* once they joined the Intersectional Feminist Union." Lux grinds her teeth, clenches her jaw. I turn away from the screen in disgust. I can't look at it anymore. I can't hear any more of this.

The hog boys keep shooting us glances, same as the rest of the people here, but they aren't the same tired, annoyed looks the older patrons have been giving us. When one of the boys sees me looking, he turns and whispers something in his buddy's ear, and they both crack up and flash their raptor eyes at me and smirk and mouth something I can't make out.

I can't be sure, but it looks like: *bitch.* Or *Suck my dick.* I stiffen.

"Oh God, Trixie."

"No more, Lux."

"Trixie. Seriously. Look."

Lux is trembling now, pointing at a new forum post on the screen.

There's a screenshot of her from the surveillance footage of us leaving the Eagle Water Outpost. Someone drew a bright red circle over the flash of her faded pink hair that's visible for just a few seconds, illuminated by the outdoor lights. That someone posted it along with the caption: Any bitch who dyes her hair pink deserves to be raped.

The post has over a thousand likes so far and counting.

I swallow down the bed of nails that just filled my mouth. They pierce my throat and stomach and rip open my intestines.

It's a good thing I puked a few minutes ago, because I'm nearly about to again.

I log back on to the hog forum before I can change my mind. I create a new thread:

> You can threaten us all you want. You can threaten every woman you've ever met with your sneering voice and cold, dead, sociopathic eyes. You can even threaten my girlfriend. But know there are girls like us, waiting in the wings. Girls with knives on their fingers and razor blades for teeth. Girls, like me, who will gut you like a fish the minute you try and lay a hand on one of us ever again.
>
> You won't know who it is until it happens. By then, it'll be too late, the knife too deep in your intestines, the smile too bright on the girl's face. The girl you thought you'd get to hurt and destroy just to get your sad little dick hard.
>
> We could be in your house right now. Behind you. Watching. Waiting for you to strike.
>
> And believe me, if we need to, we will strike again. And again. And again. And again.
>
> Sleep well, motherfuckers.

Posted at 2:35 p.m. under the name TheTroubleGirls.

Lux gapes at the screen.

Big tears fill her eyes as she grabs my hands in hers and asks in a shaking voice, "Am I really your *girlfriend*?"

Your girlfriend. Your girlfriend.

Every emotion tangles together and my heart can't decide whether it wants to slow down or speed up because everything is happening here, now, all at once.

Lux Leesburg is my girlfriend.

Lux Leesburg is one half of the Trouble Girls, and I am the other.

———

I always wonder what kind of girl I would've been, or could be, if my life had been different.

If Mama hadn't gotten sick. If Daddy hadn't died of an overdose. If I hadn't ever met Lux when we were kids, or if I'd never been born in Blue Bottle at all.

If only I'd had a little more money, a little less freedom. If I'd gone to a preppy school, or lived in a shiny city skyscraper, or been the daughter of someone rich and famous.

Would the hogs have come for me all the same? Would I still have ended up a killer, a liar, a thief, a runaway? A grumpy bitch who judges and sneers and makes snide remarks in her mind? A selfish coward?

All I know is, I'd still be me, and I'd still want to love every part of someone just like Lux.

———

I didn't know what the hell a haboob was until I came to northern Texas.

The locals at the diner we stop at the next morning for breakfast call it that, say it's more serious than a dust devil, closer to the ground than a normal dust storm. As far as I can tell, it's this big, choking monster cloud of red-and-brown dirt that crawls across the land for miles and miles. Around the edges of it, the sky is black and gray. Haboobs, we've been told, are birthed by thunderstorms.

As I eat my grilled cheese and pickles, Lux goes outside to

take photos of the monster cloud, absolutely mesmerized. The wind whips at her curls and the sapphire tank top I stole for her from Walmart.

We've been wearing our hats and sunglasses in public: a baseball cap for me and a big floppy one for Lux. I've even let her put more makeup on me, even though I hate the way it feels on my face.

The TV is tuned to the Weather Channel, and the locals are watching like it's the latest football game. Our waitress comes by and refills my coffee. She's around Mama's age, if I had to guess. The nametag on her blouse reads MARY. "Sixty miles per hour, they're predicting," she says with a grimace.

"How long do they last?" I ask.

"Well, about three hours or so, if we're lucky. You should probably stay here and wait it out, though if it comes closer we're gonna turn off the air, maybe shut down the kitchen. You could also drive through it, though . . . I wouldn't recommend it."

"Damn, okay. Thanks." Where are we supposed to go?

The door bangs open and Lux runs in, breathless with excitement. "I got the best photos!" She plants a big kiss on my lips and slides into the booth across from me. An elderly woman behind us makes a disgusted noise and gives a dirty look, but Mary just winks at us and moves on to refill the next person's empty mug of coffee.

I smile at Lux as she chatters away about the amazing shots she captured, half listening, half admiring how cute she looks when she's all riled up. I hate to burst her bubble, but I have to fill her in on the situation: we need to find shelter tonight, and fast.

Preferably free, but no way are we sleeping in the car with a storm brewing. So, I give her the rundown, cringing in anticipation of her mood plummeting again, of the sadness reaching her eyes and the joy leaving her body.

But Lux just nods along to my anxious story before saying, "Oh, that's easy. The Victorian."

"The . . . what?"

"It was on the way over here, that way. Not too far from that big megachurch." She points in a vague direction, and I continue to stare at her like I can't understand a word she's saying. "It was this big, gorgeous red Victorian mansion, just sitting there. No mailbox or anything. Lots of weeds in the front lawn. Looked abandoned. I wanted to stop to get photos, but I was so hungry, I didn't say anything."

She shrugs and takes a big bite of her grilled cheese. I can't help but smile. Thank God for her photographer's eye.

"You're a genius, Lux. We'll try that."

Suddenly I hear our names. It startles me so much I nearly spill hot coffee all over my lap.

Onscreen, the TV is showing the news now: two teen girls gone missing from Sheriff's County, West Virginia, the same county where Bryce Grimaldi was found murdered last week. Police are investigating a possible link, perhaps a serial murderer, though there are rumors online that the girls are responsible.

I don't think, I just throw ten dollars on the table, grab Lux's hand, and dash out of there into the whirling haboob. Luckily, she's got her camera bag strapped around her arm. Wind whips my face and sand scratches my eyes, but we make it to Razor Blade. It takes me a few tries to start her, and Lux keeps pestering me to hurry up, glancing back anxiously at the diner as if some FBI undercover agent will run out and force us to surrender.

Wind and sand smash against the windshield. I drive slow but steady, just a few miles in the direction Lux said, until I see the sprawling red Victorian—impossible to miss in all this desolation—and I park as close as I can to the entrance before

Lux and I make a quick dash through the dust for shelter in its haunted mouth.

———

"They're starting to figure it out." It's Lux who whispers it, her voice small and fragile. "If not now, soon. They'll catch us."

We're standing in what must have been the mansion's foyer. It's dusty and dark in here, and there are holes in the walls and the floors, but we're free from the whipping winds of the big haboob. And it looks like someone else has been here recently. There are little votive and tea candles lining the window ledges. Graffiti art on an old wingback chair in the corner. Someone left a box of matches in a small glass ashtray on a three-legged side table. The match box reads BIG FISH BAR. I go over to examine it.

"Trixie? What are we going to do?" Lux still stands at the entryway, clutching her duffel and camera bag, her floppy hat drooping over her eyes. She sounds like she's on the verge of crying again, but for some reason, I'm lucid and calm. I pick up the box of matches and rub them between my fingers. They're good, sturdy matches. They'll make a nice big flame when I spark them.

I look up at the gorgeous glass chandelier dangling from the ceiling above me, fixated on the way it sways as the haboob smacks the sides of the house. I guess I always assumed they'd put it together, sooner or later, that they'd realize two and two equals murder. Maybe I had some hope they'd assume it was some wild conspiracy theory that these two small-town runaways were responsible for the death of a frat hog, but the forum post I wrote, the timing . . . of course they know. They're starting to figure it out.

Did a part of me want them to know all along?

"Trixie, you're scaring me. Please say something."

I clear my throat, then go over and give Lux a big hug, matches still in my hand. "It's gonna be okay. I swear. They won't find us." I shut my eyes tight because it hurts so bad to lie to her. "And I promise I'm not trying to be scary, we're just in a spooky place. I doubt it's haunted."

I rub her back and she laughs, but it sorta sounds like she wants to cry, too. I think of our supporters, our haters, all the people perched and waiting for another reply, a word, a hint from the infamous Trouble Girls.

The last one I gave them sure was a doozy. Might have been my magnum opus.

As I lead Lux into what used to be the mansion's living room and we settle onto a musty old couch and light some candles, I make a secret vow to give them another one as soon as possible.

———

Upstairs, a lone rocking horse haunts my waking dreams.

This used to be a nursery, I think. The room is massive, empty, and cavernous but for the little brown horse in the center. The wallpaper is faded, happy yellow lemons, and unlike the other rooms we've explored, there's no debris or broken furniture or picture frames leaned up against the walls. No sagging ceiling panels or cobwebs, though there is plenty of dust, covering the wood like nuclear fallout.

"I think she still lives here," Lux says quietly. She's calmer now, holding one of the tea candles.

I nod, assuming she means a ghost or spirit of the child who used to call this home. "Most likely." My voice echoes, bouncing around the room. "It's colder in here, isn't it?" I shiver and rub my arms. "Which is weird, because it's probably the least drafty room in the place."

"She was a frontier woman," Lux says. "I'm sure of it. She was forced to move here with her cruel husband after an arranged marriage, and stay quiet and mind the house, and let him do what he liked with her. She dreamed of cutting off her hair, slitting his throat in the night and riding west to Oregon on her horse with just a shotgun and a satchel. But she never got up the courage, so her soul remained along with her dreams."

I kiss the freckles on Lux's eyelids, thinking of the fables Lizzie told me in the car, of the barefooted, hard-faced Wild West women before us. No doubt their spirits fill every crevice of this mansion, every room that once held their silent suffering and pain.

We've spent the last hour exploring the nooks and crannies of the house, the musty bookshelves and the crumbling gourmet kitchen, the bedrooms and the old-fashioned bathroom with the funny toilet, the downstairs sunroom with its big collapsing striped canopy. There's even a collection of doe-eyed porcelain dolls in one horrible corner. They scare the ever-loving shit out of me.

Of course, Lux takes tons of pictures, her flashbulb going off again and again, leaving spiderweb patterns of light behind my eyelids. The haboob howls and screams and slams against the walls, but inside the Victorian, it feels safe.

Safer, at least.

Lux circles the room a few times, closes her eyes, then sits down across from the big picture windows.

"Okay, you're getting a little too witchy, Lux."

She ignores me. I sit next to her, giving myself a moment to breathe, relax. I grin to myself at how cute she looks, like she's meditating with her candle, or maybe trying to speak to the other side.

I breathe along with her, deeply, in and out. Ocean breaths.

The house rattles and shudders as the haboob rages on. Hopefully it will end soon.

Finally, Lux breaks the quiet. "Do you think most of them think we're cold-blooded killers?"

"Who?"

"Most of the country. Or the world. The people watching the news, reading the stories. Do you think most of them think we're evil sluts and want us dead?"

I don't have the answer, but I grab Lux's hand and hold it tight. "I don't know, but I don't think most people wish death on others, especially when they don't know the full story." I don't know what makes me say this, or if I even believe it myself. It sorta sounds like bullshit, like something patronizing you say to make someone feel better.

Lux shakes her head, annoyed with my answer. Can't blame her. "But they do. It's called groupthink. People want justice, they see a scapegoat for all their anger and pain, and they think punishing the scapegoat will at least bring them some relief." She exhales so sharply dust motes go flying. "I can almost hear their screams in the wind, Trix. Can you? It's like: *Kill the sluts. Kill the sluts.* Over and over again. *Kill the sluts.*"

"Now *you're* starting to scare me."

Lux laughs a little. "Sorry, maybe I'm just exhausted. This whole time I've been so, so exhausted."

"Don't apologize."

"I can't stop thinking about this one tweet I saw." She runs her finger along the floorboards, tracing intricate patterns in the dust on the floor. "I don't know if you saw it, too. It was from this guy who definitely would prefer us dead. But he said something like, if he could get away with it, he would've raped me, too. He would've shown me who's boss." She squeezes her eyes shut, and I rub up and down her arms. "And he would've enjoyed it."

She's right: there's a chill here that isn't in the rest of the house. This room is colder. It's like the spirits are pressing in against us, listening.

"Trixie? Did you hear me? You're staring off into space again."

"I . . . I don't even know how to respond to something like that, Lux," I say feebly. "I'm sorry. I truly don't. I'm all out of words and thoughts."

Lux nods like I just said something profound. Maybe I did. It's hard to think now. "They want us dead. I know they do. Or if not dead, they'd rather have us suffer. Sometimes I don't know which one would be worse: gone forever, every thought and memory and moment you've ever had wiped from total existence, or in constant pain and agony, wishing you didn't exist anymore."

Little black dots dance in front of my vision, making tiny black freckles on her cheeks. I try to picture it, everything I've ever thought and seen and felt: gone. Getting orange snow cones after school from the ice cream man, the way the paper gets clammy as it melts in my hand. Biking down the road to our little house, sweat dripping down my back, and Mama on the porch, waving, waiting with pie and ice cream for me. The way big chunky snowflakes look against a bright red sled in the winter sun, moments before your best friend in the world shoves you down that steep hill and you go flying.

But we're never going back. I'll never see any of it again. Not the ice cream man, or the red sled kept somewhere in our attic, or my house. Somehow, it's the deepest, darkest pit of grief I've ever plunged into, but then Lux speaks and pulls me out of it before I go too far.

"No matter what, Trixie, no matter what happens to us or who comes for us, I can promise you this." She looks right in my eyes. The black dots vanish. All I can see is chestnut. "I won't go out without first burning down everything they ever loved."

I think of the symbol I created for us: the burning Venus. I draw it in the dust on the floor then move closer to Lux and lean my head against her shoulder, collapsing my weight into her. She nuzzles into my neck and kisses the space right below my throat. We fit so well together, two pieces of one unsolvable mess of a puzzle.

Lux sets her tea candle on the floor and whispers something, maybe to the spirits who live here—the woman who dreamed of slitting her cruel husband's throat before riding off to freedom—maybe to God or to herself, asking for answers to questions I don't want to think about. I can't make out exactly what she's saying, but I think I hear the word "free."

"I came up with a symbol for us," I explain. "A Venus symbol, but it's engulfed in flames."

"I love it," Lux says. "I want to spray paint it on every surface."

I pull her down to the dusty floor and kiss her hard and deep. She makes an urgent noise deep in her throat and moves to pull off my shirt. I unhook her bra as she cradles my hips in her hands. I kiss down her stomach, and together, on that dust-coated floor, we make our own kind of haunted love.

And it strikes me, on the floor of this abandoned mouth of a house, during the wildest Texas haboob known to man violent wind crashing against the Victorian again and again like a smashing fist—that right now, I finally have everything I've ever wanted, even though the world is ending all around us.

I wake to dust motes, to harsh sunlight and the smell of stale, old, antique haunted love.

I wake in the cavernous room with Lux curled up asleep on the floor, using her big floppy hat as a pillow; faded, happy yellow lemons on the wall; and the lone rocking horse in the center of the room. Even though everything else around us is dead, I swear, for a second, the horse starts to rock back and forth. Back and forth.

I'm clearly hallucinating. I don't remember falling asleep, or dreaming, really. Just Lux's body up against mine and then empty, never-ending blackness and shivering cold. It's much warmer in here now with the light. I check my new watch, the fake gold one I nabbed from the outlet mall: 8:00 a.m. We really slept for hours and hours. I gently shake Lux awake.

"We should go," I whisper, even though there's no need. Even though where we are now is probably no worse than the next place we'll be.

On the way out, we scour the cabinets in the crumbling kitchen, but they're bare, of course. No rations for us to take with us on this Conestoga wagon of a journey out West.

"You know what's weird?" Lux asks as she shuts the pantry door. "I slept like a log."

"Me, too. I don't even remember falling asleep. Or waking up at all during the night. I don't think that's ever happened to me before."

"What, falling asleep?" Lux teases. She tosses an empty tin can in my direction and I duck to the side before it clatters to the old tiles.

"Not waking up once. Normally, I'm up every few hours. And I remember my dreams."

I follow Lux across the foyer and out into the morning air. It looks so different here in the daylight, with no haboob in sight. Birds chitter and bugs buzz and hum. A lonely tractor rolls down the road. Luckily, Razor Blade is still parked where I left her, though the windshield is caked in dust.

"The storm seasoned her good," Lux says with a smirk. "Let's pop her in the oven."

"You're hungry, aren't you?"

"Famished."

As I wipe off the dust as best I can with the edge of my T-shirt—which smells really funky—I ask Lux what she dreamed about.

Her smirk fades away. "Pigs," she says. "A big grunting, snorting group of them. Some of them had tusks, so I guess you could call them hogs. Isn't that strange?"

―――――――――

"What's one thing you've always hated about yourself?" Lux digs noisily into her bag of cheese puffs and stuffs more into her mouth. "It doesn't have to be physical."

It's only noon and despite the good sleep I got in the Victorian, I'm already road weary, truly ready to pull over, lie down, and let the earth reclaim me.

Driving for hours on end never stops being utterly exhausting.

I run my tongue across my crooked bottom teeth. "I don't like this game."

"Fine." She sucks the cheese dust off her fingers and I give her this look, like *gross*. I love her, but today every little thing she does gets under my skin, starts to irritate me. Just answering her questions feels draining. I want a minute to myself to think and breathe. I guess it's an unfortunate side effect of having her all to myself, 24/7.

Just like I always thought I wanted.

"Okay." She flops her bare feet onto the dashboard of Razor

Blade, and I get a brief pain in my heart, remembering Delilah, the way Lux used to kick up her Keds against her. "I always hated that I never had a sister or anyone to play with."

I turn the music up. Right now, I want to let it run right through me. "How is that something about *yourself*?"

She takes another loud bite of cheese puffs and tosses back her hair. "Because it made an impact on who I *became*."

My back aches from sleeping on the wood floor. It'll cost us at least forty-five dollars, but I figure I can afford to spring for a cheap motel room if we can convince them to let us have it. Our makeup from the day before is smudged to hell, but we have enough to redo it and look at least eighteen. Just for tonight. Then we can resume sleeping in the car.

Cheese dust all over Lux's face. Crumbs in her lap. A mouth that always moves, never stops asking questions, making observations. Chatting about nothing and everything. Did Clyde ever want to kick Bonnie out of the car? Maybe this is what loving Lux is. Loving anyone. Enduring every little tic and quirk until you want to scream.

Maybe what I need is a real meal and a good night's sleep.

"You okay, Trix?"

The look on her face . . . you'd think someone had just asked if they could stab my puppy. I shake my head, feeling guilty for having these thoughts, and squeeze her cheese-dusted hand. I try my best to smile.

"Just tired."

Even though I'm looking at the road, I can feel her frown boring into the side of my head. "No, you're not. I mean, yes, you're tired, sure, but something's up with you. Something's *bothering* you, I should say."

I start this dangerous little game I've been playing with myself while driving: I squeeze my eyes shut for as long as I think I can without veering off the road.

"Trixie. Denton."

"I don't know what the hell we think we're gonna do when we get to California," I blurt out. There. I said it.

Immediately, I regret letting the words slip out of my mouth.

Lux is quiet for a while, watching the slopes of alternating green and brown roll past us. I like this back road we found. It's windy and fun to drive on. The sky is gray today, congested with stuffy clouds. I know I've probably upset her somehow, but deep down, I'm glad she's gone silent.

"We'll . . . finally be free," she says, voice wistful and full of hope. She speaks to the open window, to the cows (which she points to and says "cows"), and grain silos and abandoned windmills. "We'll be safe. We'll actually start a new life, not drive for hours every day and crash when we're exhausted. A stable, solid life. And we'll go see the ocean, like you promised." She swivels to face me. "That is what you promised me, Trixie. Remember?" She sounds like a child when she says it, petulant, terrified I'll take away this thing she wants so badly. When I look over at her face, I see once again the hurt I've caused, ingrained in every pore, in the girl I love and have maybe broken beyond repair.

I want to say, *You're right.* I want to say, *I love you. I'll give you the ocean and I'll give you the world if you want.* I want to say so many things, but right now my tongue feels like it's made of lead, and lifting it to say anything she wants to hear is impossible.

After clearing my throat, I ask her, "Can you check on the map what road we're supposed to turn on at the next intersection?"

I don't turn to see the look on her face. I know it'll look like I just up and slapped her.

I think of her cheek pressed up against the glass the night

Lizzie let us go, the sinking dread sitting between us. The way her eyes were puffy and red from crying.

That feeling of dread. Hopelessness.

I can't feel that again. Can't go there or think of it.

I switch radio stations and crank up the volume.

I've always hated talk shows.

Political pundits. Commentators. Radio hosts and conspiracy theorists. They're all the same. Right or wrong, they raise their voices and yell and claw and fight for screen- and airtime. They claim they care about the issues, and maybe some of them do, but really, I know they just want be on TV. And they never, ever listen to anything anyone else has to say. The more heated the argument, the more of our eyes and ears they can consume. Monsters, really.

I especially hate these assholes on *Morning Accord,* even if one of them seems to be sort of on our side.

Lux can't get enough of this trash. She watches shit like this religiously back home, which is why we've had this terrible talk show on TV in the world's cheapest motel room for the last half hour. The clerk took one look at us in our sunglasses and hats and heavy makeup, as I stood trembling, thinking for *sure* she could read my thoughts, and any minute she'd recognize us and turn us in. Lux spoke in that particular convincing way of hers, like she was utterly bored and couldn't be bothered to wait another second to be helped.

Then, *bam.* Once again, we managed to weasel another room. Lux Leesburg, I've concluded, is a gifted actor, and she seems to have mastered this particular role.

She's in the shower for this bit of the talk show, and while I lie on the bed and watch alone, I admittedly don't change the channel.

This time, it's a debate about the infamous Trouble Girls, the two teen runaways suspected of murder who have confounded a nation. There's certainly plenty of evidence that it probably *was* these girls who were responsible for the death of Bryce Grimaldi—the knife found at the scene, the abandoned car, the surveillance footage from Eagle Water Outpost linked back to the two missing West Virginia girls who disappeared at the same time—both so-called experts can easily agree. Those girls did it. Then there are the protests at Pinesborough State University and the growing tension in every corner of campus. Some donors are pulling their financial support for the president and his university kingdom while others are sending big fat checks to the Grimaldis. The ongoing strife among the Intersectional Feminist Union—which sides with sexual assault survivors who were never heard or supported—the administration, *and* Greek life at large has continued to rise.

"It's clearly a PR nightmare," the first talking head says, this well-dressed dweeb in expensive slacks and a turtleneck. "But more importantly, it speaks to a larger, very distressing witch-hunt narrative this country seems to be clinging to lately." He sits with his legs crossed, adjusting his horn-rimmed glasses, like having a graduate degree makes him a goddamned expert on sexual assault and women.

His opponent, a large man with a far less expensive-looking sweater, slacks, and smaller spectacles, vehemently disagrees. "But a witch hunt for *whom*, exactly? The alleged girl killers, or Bryce Grimaldi and other alleged sexual offenders? For all we know, these girls could be innocent! There could be a missing piece to this story. And even if they were responsible for Mr. Grimaldi's death, we weren't there. We haven't heard their side."

"Which is likely full of lies!" his opponent barks. His hand movements are large and sweeping. *Careful*, I think. *You might smack that brand-new Apple Watch against the wall and break it.* "We have no evidence that Bryce Grimaldi is a sexual offender, but we do have ample evidence that he is dead, and Occam's razor tells me it's these two girls who did it—"

"—oh, give me a break, *Occam's razor*—"

"Yes, Frederick, Occam's razor. And not only did they do it, I know this in my heart: they did it in cold blood. Why else would they have failed to come forward and tell the police what he supposedly did or tried to do? If it indeed was self-defense, don't you think they'd have gone for help the second it happened?"

Even Frederick is dumbstruck for a moment. I feel my lips curl. If I were a wolf, my fangs would be on full display right about now.

In cold blood. I can't argue with that, not completely. But the bit about us going for help . . . I shake my head again and again. No one would've believed us. Not a damn soul.

And this man is proof of why.

"These girls are wildly dangerous," he goes on, crossing one leg over the other and adjusting his sharp green tie. "Most likely psychotic. Their young age doesn't prevent that possibility; we've seen child serial killers and other truants and violent criminals start much younger than seventeen. They left a car abandoned in a parking lot, but somehow, they're still out there, still undetected. That implies a great deal of calculation and premeditation. In fact, another car was reported stolen not even *three miles north* of where the broken-down hatchback was left stranded. No doubt these girls were involved. They may be ruthless, but it's a smart, crafty kind of ruthlessness. Then think of the forum posts about the 'Trouble Girls.' Sure, it could be someone playing an elaborate prank, but I believe the police said they tracked the IP address both times, and both locations seem to be part of some escape route. Is that really a coincidence? How many coincidences can there be before someone says *enough*? Frankly, this all frightens me. It should frighten you, too."

I admit, I puffed up a little at "smart" and "crafty." It was pretty brilliant, what we did, how we got away. How we left all those cops and wild hogs snorting and raving and guessing, rooting around in their pens and squealing in frustration.

And *ruthless*. Yes, I kind of like that. Let them think we're dangerous, that we're coming for them if the hogs dare try to hurt us again.

Those posts, too, I am still proud of.

Frederick sighs deeply. "Listen, while you raise interesting points, again, this is all technically conjecture, most of it based on a loosely connected theory." He removes his glasses and wipes them on his sweater.

"You know what I think? What I really think about all of this, what it really amounts to?" Douche Hog natters, as if he hasn't fucking spoken enough. He steeples his fingers and rests his pig chin on top.

"NO!" I toss a lone Twizzler at the TV screen. Poor Twizzler. It really didn't deserve this. "I *don't*, you fucking pig!"

"I think—though I suspect it is malicious in large part—either way, these girls are doing all of this for attention. I mean, it's working, isn't it?"

Oh. *Fuck* no. My stomach drops ten, thirty stories. My fists curl into balls. I'm ready to punch that fucker in the face and break his nose. The rest of what they both say fades to white noise, the *wah wah wah* of the adults on the old *Peanuts* cartoons, and then all I see is white.

White-hot rage.

I punch the pillows as hard as I can, again and again until I'm breathless.

Fuck that shit.

I pretend the pillow is the heads of the hogs, the heads of every motherfucker in the comments sections who laughed at rape, assault, harassment, violence. Who belittled us, withered us down to nothing, threw shoes and rotten tomatoes at the heads of these sad, sad little girls, performing an elaborate drama for their amusement, all for their mockery.

I pretend the pillow is the head of Bryce Grimaldi's fucking corpse. I punch and punch.

Eventually, I stop and collapse onto my stomach, feeling a little calmer, heat burning through me like a forest fire.

"What were you screaming and banging on about?" Lux comes out of the shower, jet-black hair dripping wet, lustrous and beautiful in this dingy motel room's lamplight. She's wearing a fluffy white towel and nothing else, and the sight of her nearly naked makes my heart reach my throat. I wish we had more time, that our clock wasn't ticking. That we could teleport ourselves to the California ocean right here, right now, and I could hold her body in the crest of the waves and kiss every freckle on her face. I wish I could hear the bells in her laugh at the sights and sounds of the sea, the sand, the big blue beach sky.

She crawls on the bed next to me, letting the towel fall away. She inches closer to me until our faces are nearly touching. I'm angry and turned on and bursting with love all at once.

It's very fucking confusing. I could scream and cry.

"Thought you hated shows like this." She gives my nose one playful poke and goes, "Boop." It makes my blood pressure instantly lower. All I want now is to snuggle her.

I grin, shake my head, and turn off the TV. I can't stand to see these hogs speak another word with their stinky hog breath. Not when I have Lux. All I need is her.

"Come lie with me under the covers," I say with a sigh. "I could use a minute."

Lux happily obliges. The sheets are cool and crisp, the best kind of motel sheets. The AC hums happily, and outside, a friendly dog barks. Children laugh and play on the motel lawn. Enjoying life with their beloved furry friend. A simpler life made up of simpler moments, but I'd trade all of that for the feeling of Lux's skin against mine, her lips on my bare shoulder, my heart in her hands, pumping with blood and love.

Even if it comes with exasperation.

"What did they say about me?" she asks, and I bristle a little, because that's always what she wants to know.

"It wasn't so much about you as it was both of us." I play with a loose thread on the comforter, teasing it out and snapping it off. "This one asshole said that everything we've done has been . . . for attention."

Lux stiffens beside me. "What?"

I nod and repeat it even though I know she heard me perfectly well. "Yup. We're probably malicious, but most important, what we want is attention."

"Attention," she echoes. Color rises to her cheeks. She grips the comforter until her knuckles turn white. "They're saying we risked our fucking lives, left our families, threw everything away, and went on the run for *attention*?!"

"Yes." I could calm her down, tell her it's no big deal and we shouldn't worry about what anyone says, but it feels nice to share this urgent heat with someone.

Besides, I'm so fucking sick of trying to not worry about what other people say. Sometimes, it really hurts.

Lux sputters a bit. "Which means that anyone who's ever been assaulted, if they dare to complain, or stand up for themselves, or say a thing . . . But oh, of *course*, nothing Bryce fucking *Grimaldi* did was for attention!" She slaps the comforter with an open palm. "There's no possible way the scores of trolls who hate our guts and want us dead posted slander and horrifying shit about what they want to do to us was for *attention*! It was us, the girls! Because anything girls do, it's for the attention of men, don't you know? It's for their eyes, their benefit! Nothing we did could possibly be because it was what we wanted to do or say in the moment, regardless of how anyone else thinks or feels. Ugh!" She groans, throws her hands in the air, and sinks back into the pillows.

"Yeah. See why I needed a minute?"

"What are we gonna do?" Lux asks the ceiling. Her eyes turn glassy, her face pained.

I feel bad now for telling her this. I hate seeing her in distress.

"There's nothing we can do." I sound so distant, far away. I feel like I'm floating up on that ceiling, watching us both from above. "They control the story now. It's out of our hands."

"No, fuck that! They can try to spin it all they want, but—"

"It's out of our hands, Lux. Trust me, it pisses me off just as much as it does you."

Lux inhales deeply and closes her eyes, huffing out a defiant breath. "Fine. This just confirms why we never went to the cops. No matter what we do, or what we say, or how we say it, it'll get spun eventually. If we submit, they'll call us weak. If we fight back, they'll try to knock us back down. So really, we might as well do whatever the fuck we want now."

"That's exactly what I was thinking." I press my lips right near her ear, kiss it, and whisper the same words I whispered the night we met Arjun and his sisters, the night of the fireworks: "Let's go light some shit on fire."

We can't stab a herd of hogs, but we can set fire to the things they love. We can leave a message, leave our mark. Let them clean up the ashes we leave behind.

We go hunting that night until we find what we need. Not far from our motel is a tiny Texas town called Peppercorn. It's unlike most towns we've seen in this state so far. Beneath the lush green grass and pretty flowerbeds that adorn the cheerful lawns of sprawling colonials, there lurks something far more sinister, buried deep within the soil.

In town is a shop called the Good Old Boys & Rebels' Store, a little red roadside barn catty-corner to a Taco Bell and a crumbling white church. Peppercorn has more churches per capita than libraries or restaurants or parks. These aren't the same churches we see in most places; they're the fire-and-brimstone kind, the kind that wants girls like us to be taught a lesson. Put in our place. Made an example of.

The kind filled with people who believe girls like us shouldn't be in love, shouldn't be together. That we should burn.

We paint our faces, put on our hats and sunglasses, and duck into a hardware store, where we swipe two canisters of spray paint.

We come upon the perfect house. It's painted a cheerful pink, with gardens of sunflowers out front that remind me of the ones back in Blue Bottle. Colorful pinwheels spin and whirl in the front yard beside a little garden of Confederate flags. Someone has knocked signs into the dirt that read things like: MAKE NORMALCY NORMAL AGAIN and IT'S TIME TO TAKE BACK AMERICA! There's even a big, bright red one that reads in bold white letters: WE SPEAK ENGLISH IN AMERICA. LEARN IT OR GET THE HELL OUT.

The pink house seems to be at war with its neighbor, a sturdy red brick home with an open lawn and a few meek signs of its own. Signs that proudly display the rainbow flag. A PFLAG sign. A sign urging everyone to COME TOGETHER.

All of these signs have been desecrated with thick black spray paint. There are X's across a few. Someone even crossed out the "P" and the "L" in the "PFLAG" sign. It's worse than the ADAM AND EVE, NOT ADAM AND STEVE I've seen on some church signs.

It's so ridiculous it's almost comical. I guess now and then, you find a blemish in the American landscape, a microscopic horror show.

I strike a match and set fire to the Confederate flags, one by one, watching the flames lick the smug fabric until there's nothing left but embers. Lux and I stand there for a moment, holding hands, eyes burning, reveling together in our ritual. We stomp down the offending flags, crushing the wiring under our sneakers. We spray them with our burning Venus symbol. Then we run for the car.

We drive off, ferocious and cleansed from the flames and the smoke and the smell of a burning Confederacy. I find an abandoned lot to park in and we find ourselves in the backseat in a tangle and strip off our clothes, famished for each other. I kiss every inch of Lux's body, grazing her nipples, down her bare belly, down and down . . . listening to her soft moans as my lips leave marks like burns across her skin.

———

Before we left the hardware store, I swiped a hog's unlocked phone right from his pocket while he stood chatting it up too long with the cashier, both of them shooting the shit about what a "pain in the ass" their wives can be. The battery is dying and the service is bad, but I did find this, posted yesterday on a major news site:

> Police now believe that the recent disappearance of two missing
> Sheriff's County, West Virginia, teens is directly linked to the

murder of college student Bryce Grimaldi. Twitter is buzzing with allegations that the teens were responsible for Grimaldi's death, as well as a number of online posts with quotes threatening violence and promising death to those who'd go against them. They've branded themselves "the Trouble Girls" and have become a source of intrigue and controversy across the country and around the world. Let's take a closer look inside this shocking, developing American mystery . . .

The battery dips to 5 percent. I have to be quick. The phone feels heavy and alien in my hands, and they tremble as I log on to the hog forum, ready to make another statement, to give my people the next message they've been craving.

But someone's already done it for me. Dozens of times.

There are so many imitators, so many people pretending to be us, signing their posts "the Trouble Girls," posting death threats and confessions and long manifestos about why all rapists are evil and deserve to have their balls cut off. They may as well have been inked in blood.

It's taken on a life of its own, turned from a dust storm to a raging haboob. A chorus of frenzied voices and pain and fury. It no longer belongs to me.

I drop the phone in the dirt and leave it there to melt.

The rest of northern Texas goes by in a confusing blur, shifting slowly from flat green-and-brown farmland to dry scrub and desert grass. The latest map we stole says that I have to go back on the highway soon, because after a while, it's the only road, and to be frank, I've gotten us lost again more times than I can count trying to navigate shortcuts and roundabouts. Rarely have

I admitted it, though, not wanting to cause Lux any more need-less anxiety.

She hasn't seemed to notice my occasional directional fuck-ups, or if she has, she hasn't mentioned them. She sits stewing in the passenger seat, unusually quiet, lost in her own thoughts. She doesn't take photos or point out cows or anything of inter-est. She didn't even say a word when we drove past Mesquite, then had to circle back for miles until we passed the town again.

As she stews, I think about the Dark Place. About Him. Other times I think about Judy and Mama, and I have to hold in the sobs that threaten to break me open from the inside. Rarely do I consider the hog whom I slaughtered, like it happened in another lifetime, or didn't really happen at all.

Mostly I try to focus on the present moment with Lux. For now, we're enraged, but we're free. We keep the windows rolled down most of the time, letting our hair dance in the breeze. We listen to the latest news bulletins, me clenching my jaw, Lux quietly grimacing. Rarely do we hear about ourselves. It's like out here, in this barren part of Texas, where minutes stretch longer than normal, people have more to think about than two wayward teens who may or may not be murderers.

After studying the map at a rest stop where we devour our last granola bars and don't speak, I finally figure out which road takes me back to the main highway. I swallow down my shame at the hours I wasted getting us turned around, feeling a lot like my daddy, who was always too prideful to ask for directions or admit he was lost.

Hours and hours pass. I'm aching and so hungry I could gobble up roasted roadkill, but I don't want to interrupt these beautiful, rare moments of peace and quiet between us, nothing but the music and the rumble of the road. It hypnotizes me, this highway, helps me forget the men on *Morning Accord*, the chaotic voices online, the images of protesters and frat hogs and Weston Grimaldi's python glare.

"Look," Lux finally says, and I react like it's been five years since I heard another human speak. "New Mexico."

We're one step closer to California. One step closer to the ocean.

I try to picture the things I've never gotten to experience before: towering redwood forests, dazzling cities with rows of colorful houses and miles of traffic. Warm weather year round—or at least, much warmer than in West Virginia if we keep to the southern end of the state.

Or maybe it'll be more of the same endless road. Last night, I dreamed we finally reached the ocean but it was made of plastic, a set piece. I woke up sweating and terrified.

But for now, we've arrived in New Mexico. It's like we've started a brand-new chapter.

I hope we see it through to the end.

You wouldn't know it if not for the big yellow state welcome sign, adorned with cute little red and green chili peppers. The landscape's been desertlike for miles and miles now, and there are no mountains in sight. Not yet. But here we are.

WELCOME TO NEW MEXICO: THE LAND OF ENCHANTMENT.

"I feel it," Lux says quietly. She closes her eyes and breathes deeply. "The enchantment. Do you?"

I nod. Something has shifted since we crossed the state line. A bit of the weight I've been holding for days has lifted. We pull over on the shoulder, as if we need to commemorate this moment. Lux gets out her Canon and snaps photos of the welcome sign. I feel like the desert shrubs and scrub around me: hot, hollowed out. Not lifeless, not exactly. But not lush and green and thriving, either.

I join Lux, stepping out of the car, groaning as I stretch out the kinks in my neck and legs and back as best I can. I feel awful, dehydrated. How long has it been since I've had a sip of water?

It's hot here, but it's good, dry heat. Nothing like humid West Virginia, and I've never seen this kind of land before outside of textbooks and movies. I've never been on a plane, never flown and seen what this star-spangled country looks like from above. It must look strange from a bird's eyes, all this emptiness. No houses. No stores or crowded highways. Not really.

But somehow, right now, I feel strangely at peace. I take Lux's hand. Her face softens into a smile and I lean in and kiss her. For just a moment, everything feels okay again.

We get this grand idea: another photo of us, in front of the sign, just like the one we took the day we left for Fever Lake. The wind is in our hair, and once again, we're captured, frozen in time. Lux and Trixie. Trixie and Lux.

Only in this one, my hands are tangled in her black-licorice curls, my lips pressed against hers, coated in the peach lipstick that I stole for her.

Lux's dad is on TV.

It's mounted on the wall above the bar in this cozy little breakfast nook. The TV, that is. Not Lux's dad. Though the HD screen is so true to life, the camera so focused on his face and the volume cranked up so damn loud, you'd swear he was in the place with us.

Metal clatters as Lux drops her fork.

"If you could say one thing to your daughter right now, what would it be?" It's the voice of some disembodied interviewer. The camera zooms in a little, whoever's running it probably salivating over the footage they're about to get, the news channel ratings it'll surely spike.

Everything about Mr. Leesburg is illuminated in lucid plasma: his chocolate-brown goatee, sun-kissed skin, tired expression lined with wrinkles, and slightly crooked nose. He breathes in and it's a wet sound, like a tongue flapping against gums, though I know he has teeth.

He locks his chestnut eyes on the camera and they fill up with tears. It's spooky, like staring at Lux in the body of a middle-aged man. "I'd say, wherever you are, Lux, please come home, sweetie. We miss you so, so much. Your brother and I both do."

The camera pans to little Milo, who sits beside Mr. Leesburg on their striped living room couch. He glares into the camera lens, as if it's solely responsible for his older sister's disappearance.

"He's gotten so big," Lux whispers, and I say nothing to correct her, even though it's only been a couple weeks, at most. Because Milo does look older, somehow. He still has the same round, chubby cheeks and big blue eyes like his mama, but those eyes have lost a lot of their sparkle, and his cheeks are puffed up big like a chipmunk's. He's clearly pissed. Is he pissed at the camera for being shoved in his face? Is he pissed at me?

Does he believe, somehow, that I took his sister from him? We've colored together and played with magic clay and dinosaurs a few times, sure, but whenever I was at Lux's—which was almost all the time—it was always to get every single drop of time and affection from her that I possibly could. Milo knew I wasn't part of his family, but that I was someone special and different, someone who came and went far too often, constantly begging his sister to come with me and leave the house. Do something fun. I cringe thinking about it now, all those times I dragged Lux away and blew off Milo, acting as if the little guy could take care of himself.

I was so damn selfish. Ever since Lux's mama left, she really did need to be there more often for her brother, and I didn't think about it like that. Not really.

The camera cuts back to Mr. Leesburg. "We're doing everything we can to find you, Luxie. Everything. Whoever's got you, whatever happened to pull you into whatever horrible situation you're in, know that your daddy is looking for you and fighting for you every day. I love you so, so much. Stay strong, baby girl."

Does he think I kidnapped Lux? Forced her into a life of crime and debauchery? It wouldn't be completely untrue.

It's hard to gauge how Lux is feeling. Her face is blank, eyes hidden beneath her cat-eye sunglasses and dark eyeshadow, almost void of emotion, like we're watching the Weather Channel and they're calling for yet more cloudless sunshine. When Milo came onscreen, I thought I spotted a flash of something like a grimace cross her face, but then it was gone as quickly as it'd come.

They show Lux's high school photo again. My eyes dart around the room, but no one seems to be paying much mind to the TV, let alone to who else is sitting in the diner.

Deep breaths. Ocean breaths. The waitress comes over and asks me something about a refill, but it's so hard to focus. Lux says we'll take the check. She shakes my shoulder, like she's trying to shake me awake.

"Trix," she whispers fiercely. "We've got to go."

We do what we've been doing lately for nearly every sit-down meal: dine and dash. It's pretty busy in here this early in the morning. Lots of trucker hogs and some retirees bundled up in sweaters despite the heat. Lux gets up first like she's going outside to smoke or something. I wait a little while, pretending to watch the TV. They've cut to another story, but I can still see the face of Mr. Leesburg, an afterimage forever imprinted in the plasma, tattooed on my brain.

Our waitress is at the register, getting our check. She looks over and smiles at me and I smile back, a massive, familiar pit of guilt lodged in my abdomen. No doubt she thinks I'm a local girl, a normal girl old enough to be in college but who maybe still lives at home, thus this tiny town. A girl having breakfast with her friend on a Sunday, because girls like us don't sleep in too late, not even on the Lord's day.

I reach deep into my pocket and throw at least five bucks on the table, even though I shouldn't, and Lux will be mad, and we've got to stop spending money on shit like eggs and toast when what we really need is gasoline from a pump, not siphoned from another car. I make a beeline for the door, swing it open, and meet Lux outside in the warm sunshine, where she's already sitting pretty in the driver's seat of Razor Blade, one of my lit cigarettes between her lips, having figured out the nutty wiring herself.

"Don't look so surprised," Lux says as I clamber inside. She gives the cigarette a puff and hands it to me, and I accept it like this is a normal thing we do. "Whoever got me into this horrible situation at least helped me learn a few useful things."

She hawks and spits into the red dirt ground, like the way Lizzie used to. She's not quite a lizard, but she's certainly gotten more lizardlike this past week. Both of us have.

Lux revs the engine to life and off we go again.

We drive the rest of the day without eating, get a few hours' terrible sleep in the stolen sunflower, and by noon, we're of course famished again. Lux and I decide to risk it to dine and dash for lunch at this place called Chucky's, which claims to have the best fried chicken west of the Mississippi River. We share a big bowl of the most delicious mac and cheese I've ever tasted.

There's yet another news segment on the flat-screen TV hanging above the bar about the protests on Pinesborough State's campus. They haven't slowed down but simmered to a boil.

A group of sunburned road hogs sits at the bar, chugging whiskeys, shooting the shit and smacking their lips as they scarf down chips and pickles. They wear American flag bandannas and motorcycle jackets. I wish they'd shut up so I could hear the goddamned segment.

I gather enough through visuals: Nezekiah is there again today, leading a march demanding justice for every other girl or female-presenting student who's stepped forward in the last few years with sexual assault or harassment allegations. For everyone who has been ignored or shut down or even blackmailed to keep quiet by the administration. For every girl who's ever dreamed of revenge, or at least, a little bit of justice.

Among the marchers is a stunning girl in a power suit, heels, and a hot pink hijab. Her name is Esther Sharifi. The camera closes in on her face as she is interviewed on behalf of the Intersectional Feminist Union. She frowns at one of the interviewer's questions—no doubt one meant to provoke her and make her look angry and bitter—and retorts with something I can't hear. She uses her hands to explain, trying to stay calm, to appear rational, but it doesn't matter how she says it. They'll eat her up either way. Reshape and reconstruct her sound bites. Distort her truth.

The road hogs whistle and holler at the screen. One waves his meaty fist in the air.

"Oh, be quiet, honeybunch!" he shouts. "Those girls are cold-blooded bitch killers!"

"Should've bombed the shit out of the Middle East when we had the chance!"

An icy shiver runs through me as they cackle and hurl insults. One hog starts singing the national anthem, and the rest join in, a chorus of leathery swine.

"Those girls are braver than us," I mutter to Lux. She swallows hard, nods, and stares down at our half-eaten bowl of mac and cheese. Suddenly nothing in here is remotely appetizing.

Our waiter just watches and chuckles at the frenzied, racist hogs, shaking his head like they're squabbling over a ball game.

"Sundown town," Lux whispers to me. "That's the hell we've found ourselves in." Her eyes shift around the diner, linking me to the visual clues on the wall: Confederate flags, though we've seen plenty before. Framed newspaper clippings detailing the town's "glory days." These are far more telling.

I feel like vomiting up the mac and cheese, like it's been laced with poison. "Are you sure?" I whisper back. I've read about these so-called sundown towns before: highly segregated areas that became "all white" on purpose. Kept that way to this day by intimidation, corrupt local laws, and of course, violence.

She bites her lip, eyes darting back and forth between me and the clippings. She's always been a faster, better reader than me. "Yes."

We sneak out without paying the check. We find where the motorcycles are parked, the expensive Yamahas and Harley-Davidsons. One has a bumper sticker that reads: I LOVE MY HARLEY MORE THAN I LOVE MY WIFE. SHE DOESN'T NAG.

I find a pocketknife from the trunk, one that Lizzie left behind. We take turns slashing holes in all their fucking tires.

With our cans of spray paint, we leave marks of our rage, Lux's version in hot pink, mine in burning red: our Venus symbol engulfed in flames. Lux curses and cackles like Lizzie would, the bells in her laugh clanging off-key. "Fuck 'em," she growls. "Fuck 'em all." I get swept up in it, that ferocious, intoxicating anger. The fleeting feeling of power shooting from the nozzle of a spray can.

Burn it all down.

Burn everything to the fucking ground.

Oh, how I wish we really could.

———

The night it happened, now mostly a blur, police took me in to the station, and Mama came with me. There were bruises on my arms, scratches on my neck. The officers kept asking me all these questions, but everything inside me was frozen solid and my mouth wouldn't work right. I couldn't speak or take their strange, scary tests. I kept shaking my head and counting the floor tiles.

No matter what I said, I somehow knew deep down they wouldn't understand. Wouldn't believe me. Would side with the Bad Man, with Him.

The long drive home from the station was achingly silent. Mama kept making choking noises in the back of her throat, but whenever I looked over at her, she just smiled at me with tears in her eyes. The saddest kind of smile. At home, she ran a hot bath for me, and I tossed the clothes I'd been wearing straight into the trash bin. Mama said nothing. She sat up late with me, stroking my back until I fell asleep. When I woke, I told myself, I would realize it had all been a dream. A nightmare.

Daddy was ready to burn down Blue Bottle. I'd never seen him so mad and scary in my life. He wanted to kill Him, rip His throat out, all kinds of horrible things. Mama said we should press charges. I didn't know what that meant. The police had arrested Him, but since I wouldn't speak to the cops, He was let out. Before we could do a thing about it, the Bad Man up and vanished into the night.

He left behind a successful family pig farm. Didn't even sell it or anything, just left all those pigs alone to die and the house to rot. Animal control had to come in and everything, send the pigs to local rescues or maybe to slaughter. He was gone without a trace.

I never remembered much else about Him, about the Dark Place, but what I could recall, I would slowly try to teach myself to forget.

———

Since Chucky's, Lux and I haven't eaten a thing. Even if we wanted to dine and dash and risk being seen by so many people at once, there're no dine-in places to be found. There hasn't been for miles, and we can't dine and dash at a regular fast-food joint.

Because we're so damn hungry, it's been real slow going, hard for me to focus on the road, and we have to keep making stops to rest or sleep, especially after I swerved while nearly asleep at the wheel and almost hit another car. We're damn lucky we didn't get pulled over. We woke up at three p.m. today in a daze, parked in the sprawling lot of a big-box store. All our dreams were of food.

I never knew hunger could hurt like this. I've got a raging headache, I'm thirsty as hell, and I don't know how much more of this I can take.

I've had disturbing thoughts of walking into the nearest place and tenting my T-shirt with my finger, pretending I have a gun and I am about to hold the place up if they don't give me everything they have. They skip through my mind on repeat as the highway stretches on, more mirages appearing on a horizon we'll never reach.

When I finally admit them to Lux, she just shrugs and says, "Okay. Whatever. Let's try it." I'm so hungry and exhausted I don't have the energy to think of a counterargument.

I find that I no longer care.

———

It's quiet here. Way too quiet. Sad little weeds poke up from cracks in the concrete. Strange minerals glisten between the rocks and strands of Bermuda grass and hollyhocks. The air is thick with the aftertaste of desert rain. There's an odd stirring all around us, like frenzied whispers from a thousand anxious ghosts.

This is the closest place we can find to rob, this big gray warehouse of a drugstore off the dusty, lonely desert highway. I never knew there'd be so many tumbleweeds in New Mexico. The air is hot and dry except for when the occasional storm cloud rolls in. There's this sweet foreign scent of smoke and earth mingling together. It's unlike anything I've ever smelled before.

We stopped immediately when we saw it. I did think it was a shared hallucination at first, even before we stepped out of our stolen sunflower. I felt that shift in the air again. We're the only customers here, far as I can tell, but it sure doesn't feel like it.

Like I said, the ghosts. There are ghosts here. They seem to whisper, *Get out while you can.*

Or maybe they're hunger-induced hallucinations. Both seem totally possible right about now.

Lux reaches her arms to the sky and then down to the dusty ground. It's time to stretch once again from being cramped and cooped up in the car for another two long hours.

"I'm so hungry I could eat a whole cow raw," I whine.

Lux grimaces and makes huge circles with her arms. "Gross. Cows are sweet, gentle animals." She swings her hips side to side, then makes more huge circles with her arms. I copy her, and it does feel good, or at least makes everything hurt a little less, though it doesn't take away the ache in my belly.

"*Fine.* I could eat a whole platter of roadkill. Nuts. Berries. Coniferous vegetables. Whatever. I'm famished!"

"*Cruciferous* vegetables," Lux gently corrects. "That's why we're here." Lux's voice and face harden. I almost see a flash of scales. It terrifies me.

The fluorescent lights inside the drugstore are bright enough to fry an eyeball, and there's a low, dull humming and buzzing coming from the rows and rows of freezers. Soft rock plays from the speakers. The walls are painted a cheery yellow. It almost makes me feel guilty for what I'm about to do.

This can't be that different from swiping spray paint from hardware stores and T-shirts and jewelry from Walmart.

Can it?

Lux glances around furtively, then moves to scour the aisles of candy bars and chips and soda pop. I pretend to flip through magazines and examine the aspirin and motion sickness medicine near the pharmacy aisle. The pharmacy itself is closed. The cashier is a boy around our age, with baby scruff on his face and floppy bangs on his head. He smiles when he sees me, and it almost makes me change my mind.

Lux works the food, no doubt choosing single-serving packets of candy and Chex Mix, bananas, cinnamon buns, bottled water, whatever she can stuff inside her big camera bag. She tears open a bag of chips with her teeth and dumps a bunch into her mouth, a look of pure bliss on her face. The cashier sways uncomfortably but doesn't say anything. He thinks we'll pay for it, no doubt, these two innocent little white girls in hats and glasses and heavy makeup. I ignore the rumbling in my belly and try to pocket the most useful things in the pharmacy aisle, small things I can fit in these shorts with deep pockets: single toothbrushes, tubes of toothpaste and dental floss.

But what we're really after is the money in the register.

Lux can be mean, but I know I can pull off intimidating the best. After I've collected enough little items, I make a beeline for him, my two fingers beneath my T-shirt like I've got a gun under there, just as I imagined I would. His eyebrows arch up and his mouth pops opens in surprise. It isn't the most convincing, my T-shirt finger gun, but I'll fucking make it convincing.

I pretend he's Bryce.

"Open the register," I say in the coldest, blankest voice I can manage. "Or I'll blow your fucking head off. *Now!*"

The boy's hands shoot up in the air. "P-please don't hurt me!" he stammers. He's young, I realize, younger than Lux and me. Maybe fifteen. "Please."

"No one gets hurt if you open the register, take out all the cash, and put it in a nice little plastic bag for me and my friend," I growl.

The boys considers the T-shirt gun, my cold, dead eyes. I'm struggling to keep them that way, all emotion erased from my face. I pretend that I'm in a video game, I'm the main character, and this is the final task before I can unlock the next level.

I hold up my finger gun a little higher and aim it at him. "Move. Now!"

"Okay," he says shakily. "Okay, okay." He opens the register, thumbing through wads of cash, and I can already tell there isn't much in there, not nearly as much as we'd hoped. But right now, we'll take anything.

The big clock on the wall goes *tick-tock, tick-tock*.

"Hurry up!" I snap, because isn't that what the bad guys are supposed to say?

The boy whimpers and holds a wad of cash to his chest. "Please, miss. My family. This is my family's store."

"I don't care whose store it is. More moving, less talking."

For a smidgen of a second I think I see doubt creep across his face. Like maybe I don't want to shoot him, or don't have the guts to, or don't even have a gun at all. For some reason, this makes me even angrier.

"We need this money or we can't pay rent this month," he begs. "It's all we have. Please. I have siblings. Little sisters. Do you have sisters?" He widens his eyes at me like he thinks he knows me, thinks he knows the nice, good girl inside that he can appeal to.

"I thought she told you to shut the fuck up." Lux appears behind me, a pair of sharp scissors in her hand, her voice a low snarl. She aims the scissors at the boy as if she's about to stab him with them, and he flinches. "If we don't feel like wasting a bullet on you, I'll gladly rip open your throat."

Realizing he's outnumbered and one of us is truly armed and possibly truly psychotic, the boy crosses himself as if asking for forgiveness, then takes out every bill from the register, putting it in a little bag for me, tears streaming down his face.

I reach for it, and I see a flash of sheer hatred in his eyes, aimed right between my own like a laser beam.

"This is all we have," he says, doing his best to sound firm, brave. No doubt his daddy would be proud of him right now, the way he's trying his best to man up in a tense moment, uphold the family name and all that. Fight for what belongs to his own.

We run out of there and I take one quick look back as he cradles his face in his arms across the counter in defeat. I know in my heart this isn't just about the money, though rent is no doubt important. Of all people, I'd know that.

No, it's not just money. It's his honor at stake, this great secret shame: he let two relatively unarmed teenage girls hold him up and rob his family of all they have, and did nothing really to try to stop them.

Those had to have been crocodile tears. I keep telling myself they were.

We get in the car and I'm too frazzled to drive, so I let Lux take control, even though she's jerky with the brakes and the stick and nearly backs into a dumpster on the way out. That's when the guilt seeps into every pore, that familiar horror and disbelief at what I've done to another human being.

I carefully open the plastic bag in my lap and run my fingers over the faded bills. *I hope it was worth it,* the bag seems to whisper.

"How much did we get?" Lux asks.

I count the bills over and over, methodically, numbly. "Not nearly enough. Not worth a robbery charge."

"How much, Trix? Just tell me."

"Ninety worthless dollars."

"Shit."

"And most of it's in singles."

"*Shit.*" Lux shakes her head and snaps on the radio. "You're right. Not worth a robbery charge. That fucker must've stiffed us. He did put on a good show, crying and everything. But at least for now we have food."

"Some," I say. Was he really faking? He must've been so scared.

My stomach growls loudly.

I pop open a bag of chips and feed Lux one, then stuff a handful down my throat. They should be the most delicious things I've ever eaten, but I can't really taste them. Still, they soothe that empty, gnawing ache.

". . . after claims from an employee that he was held at gunpoint by two young women on Tuesday. Police are reviewing surveillance footage from around noon, the time of the reported robbery, and have so far confirmed the perpetrators were indeed female, both bearing a clear resemblance to the missing Sheriff's County teens known as 'the Trouble Girls,' although one young woman appears to have dark black hair instead of striking pink, and the other red hair instead of brown . . ."

Siphoning gas from other cars has proven way too risky an enterprise, and much too difficult for us to manage full time. We just end up spending hours in the sun, sweating bullets and burning up, always on the lookout for someone who might recognize us.

Bottom line is it isn't worth the effort anymore. We'd rather fill up the tank all the way so we'll have as much as we need to make it to California. We'd rather buy and ration food and coffee for the long, exhausting days we have left.

No more diners or eat-in places even if we find them, we've decided. We can't risk being seen in public again. We've caused too much damage. The perk of gas stations is they're full of fellow drifters and those just passing through. People who think the news is part of a media conspiracy and all that. They're liminal spaces: places of transition, where time is suspended and waiting. No one is really watching for us. No one cares where we're going or where we've come from. They just want us to pay for the gas, the crummy boiled hot dogs and sticky muffins, maybe a paper or plastic map if we're lost, and get in, get out. The hogs in the gas station convenience stores are mostly the usual sleazebags, too. Lots of tattooed biker types and truckers, though some seem tamer than others. They congregate over instant black coffee and American Spirits and gossip like church ladies about their days driving trucks across the interstates, transporting food and livestock and mail throughout the country. They're the invisible threads that hold it all together, hogs or not. I listen to them carefully every time I'm in line.

It's how I end up hearing about Slate City: I'm getting Lux and me iced teas and blueberry muffins because they're having a two-for-one sale. A potbellied hog in denim overalls leans up against the counter, telling the register guy all about this place that sounds like something out of a road hog's fever dream.

I wait, pretending to scour the magazines on the rack, the old outdated copies of *People* and *Newsweek*. It's funny how if you're real close to a conversation but act like you're absorbed in your book or phone or whatever, people seem to think you can't hear them. They'll say anything like you aren't even there. I stuff a few protein bars in my dirty shorts pockets. Breakfast for the next few days. Probably lunch, too.

This potbellied hog's mumbling and grumbling is markedly different from most road talk I hear, though I almost tuned it out at first. He's making a word salad of sorts, rambling on about "trailer park murders where guys get drugged out and kill entire families." Charming. He says something else about demonic possession and the end of times, but it's hard to understand. The cashier nods, clearly baked out of his mind on something good and strong, and then asks if the hog's going down to Slate City for the night to "load up." The hog perks his ears, practically drools. *Slate City.* Might as well have mentioned the gates of paradise themselves. The two commiserate over the free booze, the free room and board, how it's so welcoming and open and spiritual, and the little cash I have in my pocket weighs heavier than the food I'm juggling in my arms. Christ, money goes fast, even living out in the middle of nowhere. Even after robbing a family drugstore and getting stiffed. Figures.

Then I hear the word that really gets me interested: *gasoline*. Both of them say these people give out free gasoline to anyone in need. Will fill up your tank for you free of charge. Really hospitable folk, these Slate City residents. They feed you well, too. Hearty meals and decent company. It sounds like a hippie commune. Peace and love and all that. I listen a little longer. They don't seem to care that they're wasting my time making me wait as they gab. From what I gather, Slate City is this weird, off-the-grid community of sorts out in the high desert where people live off the land, live free or whatever.

Live free and die a rebel.

Gasoline, food. Hospitality. Good company. That's what Lux and I need. That's what we could use right now. And if this place is as lawless and cut-off as it sounds . . . well, surely they'd have no clue who we are.

"Where is it?" I ask, loud enough so they can hear me over the din of their own squawking.

I don't have my makeup on today. No hat. No sunglasses. It's just me. The cashier and hog both turn to stare, like they didn't expect this little girl in the corner to have a voice. Like I haven't been waiting here for ten fucking minutes. They look at me like they've just seen a dog speak English, but then the cashier composes himself. He clears his throat, flips through the hog's change, and goes: "Couple miles north of here along the interstate. It's off exit twenty-three, past the telephone poles with red string tied to them. You can't miss it."

Word Salad Hog keeps on staring at me. I can't tell if he's grinning or grimacing. His lips tighten and curl at the edges. He runs his fat pink tongue over his teeth. I see now what he sees when he looks at me: bait. Fresh fish.

"Will I get the honor of seeing *you* there, little lady?" he asks, not bothering to hide the suggestion in his voice.

I keep my eyes pinned on Word Salad Hog as I shove my items in front of the cashier and hand him near exact change. I stay rooted and firm as I lean in closer and closer, waiting for the hog to flinch just an *inch*, then say right to his slimy face, "Only in your wildest fucking nightmares."

The look he's giving me now . . . well, it's like the talking dog started doing jumping jacks and playing the banjo. I give him a grin that I hope is filled with as much venom as I can taste in my mouth right now and get the fuck out of the store.

Feels kinda like power.

When I get back to the stolen sunflower, I tell Lux all about Slate City.

She's in the passenger seat, slowly chewing a granola bar like it's her last meal on earth. I hand over her muffin and iced tea and she gulps them down gratefully. These days, she seems to prefer tea and coffee over Diet Coke. It's like Black Licorice Lux's tastes are as dampened and different as her mood.

We're down to thirty-five dollars until California. Thirty-five fucking dollars. Great. Then what? Lux lifts her cat-eye sunglasses to squint at me. "The fuck is Slate City?" she asks. She blows a big pink bubble and waits for me to pop it, and of course, I do. Just like old times. It makes me miss her pink hair. It's like fragments of the old Lux keep crumbling off her, even though I know that her hair isn't really her, and it's all in my head. "I mean, I guess it sounds like a good enough place to get free gas and maybe take some photos," she says with a shrug. "But Jesus, should we really stop? We should be making headway."

I reach out and tuck one of her jet-black curls behind her ear, then lean in and kiss the space between it and her neck. Her ice-queen composure melts a little.

"It's on the way, more or less," I tell her, even though that may or may not be true. I wrap my finger around a curl and twirl it affectionately. Some more of the Lux I know and love radiates back at me. "We may as well see if we can pick up a good meal and some more gas."

The truth is, I've lost track of what we should or shouldn't be doing.

———

Slate City is ugly as sin, but in a way, it's also the most beautiful place I've ever seen.

We find it easily, right off exit twenty-three, down a road where someone's tied red string around the telephone poles. A tickle races up and down my spine.

"Creepy," Lux notes as I park Razor Blade beneath a big desert willow for shade, and I can't say I disagree. "It's like a warning or something."

We glance around furtively. It's quiet here. A little too quiet. The car will be left unlocked, completely unsecure, since we can't lock it or the trunk. That's the thing about driving around in a stolen, hot-wired car: there's no real way to lock it without locking yourself out.

Our duffel bags are tucked away in the back. I drape one of my blankets from home over them in an attempt to hide our stuff and grab our empty gas can. Lux hesitates, gnaws her lip, then takes her Canon out of the backseat and places it gently in its camera bag, slinging it over her shoulder.

"I'm not taking any chances with my baby," she says firmly, like she's talking about a living, breathing child.

I can't help grinning. It's one of the many things I adore about her.

"I'd never let you leave your baby."

She leans in and kisses me. I fall into her lips, this safe, beautiful space where nothing in the world can touch us, and linger for a moment longer.

But I can feel her trembling, hear her heart pounding. She walks close to me, slightly behind. I hold her hand tight, circle my thumb around her palm, trying to let her know I've got her.

But I'm scared as hell, too.

The shriveled desert grass here is littered with tires, rusty barrels, and slabs of wood. It's definitely a camp of some sort, stretched over about a mile and littered with tiny buildings: trailers painted neon colors, makeshift homes and open-air shops cobbled together out of sheet metal and scraps of lumber. The skeleton of an old car leans up against a massive saguaro cactus, its metal shell covered in swooping graffiti.

The air smells of burning sweetness—skunky marijuana that brings me back to motel room nights and standing in the courtyard before school, smoking my cigarette while the Blue Bottle High stoners got blazed all around me—and something sickly sweet and strange, too. A log fire burns in the center of the encampment, thick smoke rising into the clear blue sky.

Maybe we should leave. I think it but I don't say it. Even though an itchy feeling inside is telling me to run, a burning curiosity and the need for free gasoline and food has gotten the better of me. The muffin made my blood sugar crash hard and fast. My stomach grumbles unhappily.

We watch a bearded man drive past in his motorized scooter, decked out in tie-dye, a giant yellow python wrapped around his neck. I gasp when I realize it's real. The man tips his bowl hat when he sees us and we wave back, me shivering because snakes freak me the fuck out. He's missing fingers, and he wears a green patch that reads PROUD ARMY VETERAN.

I wonder if he's killed people. Surely he has. I guess it's only a question of how many.

"*What?*" Lux asks, startled.

I get flustered, realizing that I've mumbled the questions out loud to myself. I shake my head as if that'll shake the thoughts away. "Nothing."

She frowns and grabs me by the elbow, yanking me to a halt. "You sure, Trix? You look like you've just seen a demon."

I sniff the air, catching a whiff again of that strange sweet-and-sour smell. It makes my toes curl and my breath hitch in my throat. Something is wrong here. Something is very wrong.

"I'm fine," I lie. "Let's go."

Lux hesitates a moment. She sighs, like she's disappointed in me. Like I've answered wrong yet again. She takes my hands in hers and squeezes them tight. "I can handle it, Trixie. Just tell me what's up. I'm your girlfriend. Your . . . your partner."

The way she says "partner" makes my stomach bloom with warmth and my face go redder than it currently is from the baking sun.

I just don't know how to explain to her that somehow this strange place already is too much, but I'm drawn to it like a doomed fly to insect tape.

"This p-place . . ." I stutter. "There's something off about it. Maybe I'm being paranoid."

She laces her fingers through mine, eyes softening. "We'll leave if it gets to be too much, okay?" We share this look of recognition, of mutual understanding. The kind of look only best friends can give each other. But now we aren't just best friends, we're something deeper. Stronger. Her assurance calms me down a little. *We need to get the gasoline,* I tell myself. *Food. There's nothing wrong here. Not really.*

Not anything that isn't made up in my head.

Lux and I walk hand in hand along the barely there dirt path. A freckled young woman in a patchwork peasant skirt and blouse stands barefoot by a clothesline, humming and hanging men's trousers and T-shirts speckled with stains. Everything about her is caked with desert dust, from her eyebrows and hairline to her bare toes painted cerulean blue. She's kind of what I pictured when I imagined what this place might be: barefooted hippie commune. Comfy clothes and easy energy. My muscles loosen a bit. The snake we saw is probably harmless.

"Howdy!" The woman gives us a wave like the man in the scooter did. "You guys friends with Crazy Butch?"

Lux and I exchange a look. I hold up the empty gas can Lizzie scavenged for us. "We're here to get some gas, if we can. Just passing through. We don't mean to trouble you or—"

"Oh gosh, I *love* your hair! Love, love, love!" The woman bounds up to Lux like an excited puppy and starts stroking it. Lux flinches like she's dealing with a wild bird pecking at her ear. "Sorry." The woman giggles and takes a step back, covering her mouth with her hands, which are also dotted with freckles. "Sometimes I forget. Things are different here. The way we are with each other. Different, different."

Lux gives her a half smile and shrugs. "It's okay." I protectively step closer to her.

"I'm Phoenix! And it's no trouble. No trouble at all!" I notice she sort of mumbles out of the side of her mouth when she talks. "We share things here. Everything is shared . . ." She hiccups out an awkward little laugh. "But if you want gasoline for your car and some homemade grub, you should go see Ed." She points ahead to a baby-blue trailer in the near distance. "He's real nice. Sorry. Gosh. I don't mean to stare and babble on like this. I just get excited when we have visitors! We don't get 'em that often anymore."

Lux snaps her bubble gum.

Phoenix giggles again, this time giving us a full display of her rotting teeth. *Meth mouth*, Judy called it. I shudder.

"Okay, thanks," Lux says, her voice as flat as the land. "Let's go, Trix."

We continue our walk up the barely there path lined with bright green cacti and desert shrubs, and when Phoenix is out of earshot, I lean in and mutter, "She's definitely on drugs."

"No shit. This whole place gives me the heebie-jeebies, to be honest. Do you think it's safe, what we're doing?"

I shrug. "Nothing we do is safe these days."

"If you get, like, oh-shit-this-is-bad scared, give me the signal, okay?"

I nod. The signal is easy: tugging our right earlobe three times. We used to do it when we were kids and went searching for ghosts in Lux's chilly basement, right after we'd used her Ouija board to try to summon them.

We arrive at Ed's baby-blue trailer, with red-and-white stripes and little stars painted across the side, and I knock on the wooden front door that's replaced whatever metal one used to be there.

A garbled male voice cries out, "Just a second!"

Lux pops her gum again. I crack my knuckles.

I'm expecting some tall, meaty hog, someone muscular, I guess. I don't expect the door to swing open and a very short, bald man wearing eyeglasses to stand before us, peering through his little square frames.

"Can I help you?"

Lux stands all cool and nonchalant, her posture slouched, one hand in the pocket of her stolen white denim shorts. She takes the empty gas can from me and holds it up, as if that explains everything. As if that explains two filthy, sunburned teenage girls in the middle of an off-the-grid encampment in the high desert of New Mexico.

Ed makes an "mmm" sound in his throat, peers at us a moment longer, then says, "Well, come on in then!" before disappearing back inside.

"Should we go?" I whisper to Lux.

Lux stares at me like I've asked if we should set the place on fire. "What else did we come here to do, Trixie?"

It's cramped in the trailer, not much else here besides a pull-out bed, a teeny tiny kitchen, all kinds of unbelievable junk, old records, and boxes spilling over with assorted knickknacks. There's a nice plasma TV propped up in the corner with a crack down the middle, but otherwise it seems to be working just fine. A woman in a tattered bathrobe and bunny slippers is smoking a cigarette, her feet up on a coffee table.

"New recruits?" she asks. When she speaks it sounds like the croak of a bullfrog.

Ed stumbles into the kitchen area and grabs a handful of beers from the Frigidaire. He pops one open with a bottle opener clipped to his belt, letting the cap clatter to the linoleum. "Passersby. You girls need gasoline, yeah? We got some out back in the tank. You're free to help yourselves. Where'd you park?" He hands us two of the ice-cold beers, and I shake my head, but Lux grabs one and takes a long pull.

"Hey," the woman croaks. She waves her cigarette at us, ashes flying every which way. "Ain't you the girls from the TV?"

A whimper escapes my mouth. Lux grabs my wrist reflexively, breaking a bit of her stone-cold character. She doesn't have to tug her earlobe for me to get it. The cramped trailer feels even smaller, like the walls are closing in.

I have no one to blame but myself, really. It was my hog-brained idea to come here. Everything about the ride to hell we've been on this whole time has been my fault.

"Yeah! I think I know what you're talking about!" Ed says, all enthusiastic. He chugs his beer and settles down on a recliner with the stuffing coming out, putting his feet up. His scuffed-up boots are worn through the soles. It reminds me of the kind my daddy used to wear. He never bought new shoes; I never knew if it was because we were dirt poor or he was just stubborn. "You two the cold-blooded fraternity boy killers?"

We could run. We could make it back to the car before anyone thinks to dial 911. Ed studies our shit-scared faces and then bursts out laughing, running a hand over his bald head. "Hey now, relax! We're not gonna hurt ya girls or call the cops or anything. We aren't *snitches* here in Slate City."

He says "snitches" like it's the worst thing you could possibly be.

"Snitches get stitches," croaks the woman, nodding in agreement.

Ed takes another swig of beer. "Frankly, we don't really care what your business is. We're curious, is all. Don't get a lot of outsiders, celebrity ones at that. But yeah, here in Slate, the laws that apply on the outside don't apply in here. This is, like, sacred ground, isn't it?"

We should still run, go now, a full tank of gasoline and a

bellyful of food or not. But I feel Lux relax a little by my side, and I do the same.

"Good to know," Lux says, her voice cracking on the word *good*.

"Seriously, honey, you aren't in danger here. At least not from the cops. We don't fuck with the pigs in Slate City." The woman sticks out her tongue and flips the bird to an imagined officer, and Lux giggles.

The woman winks at her and flips to a news segment, which is, of course, showing our story. Figures. It's more or less a rerun of the same old same old we've been seeing for days, only this time, it's our classmates talking to the cameras about what nice girls we were, how they can't believe we'd ever do something like the media claims. Interviewers stand with stern expressions in front of campus buildings and Sheriff's County "landmarks," looking so damn solemn and serious. Protests are still ongoing at Pinesborough State, though the tension seems to have simmered down. Now it's mostly the Intersectional Feminist Union vs. Bryce's Delta Delta Chi brothers.

I send a silent prayer of gratitude to Nezekiah Wallace and Esther Sharifi. They've amassed more followers on social media, and their latest speeches have gone viral on YouTube. A state school's Intersectional Feminist Union is now known around the country. The university's administration has to cave sooner or later and start to make real change. They have to. I have to at least hope.

"You two are hard to miss," says the croaking woman. "Even though I do see you switched up your hair." She points at Lux's curls with her ashy cigarette and smirks. "It was a nice enough attempt, I'll say. But you've got a pretty face that's hard not to recognize."

I think of our hats and sunglasses and makeup we've been wearing. Did anyone recognize us before and not say anything? How many people did we cross paths with who recognized us all the same, despite our flimsy disguises?

Ed grunts and waves a dismissive hand. "Oh, don't mind her! She watches too much daytime TV. *Anyone* on TV is a damn celebrity to her. Most of the country probably wouldn't recognize either of ya right away in the state you're in, no offense. You two look like you haven't bathed in a few days."

It's true. We haven't.

Suddenly Judy is on television. *My* Judy. Lux gasps. It's like this big wall I've been carefully laying inside me starts to come tumbling down, brick by brick.

It's the weirdest goddamned thing in the world, seeing Judy flattened like this, a mere image on a screen. I have to hold back from reaching my hand out to her. *She's not really here*, I remind myself, but Jesus, I wish she were.

They're interviewing her in front of her little yellow house, even though she usually works this time of day. No doubt Boss Man is back at the diner, cursing her and the day I was born. No doubt the hungry, leering hogs are wondering where their favorite piece of meat is. The girl with the "tricks" up her sleeve. But it's Judy who is in full focus now, standing next to a sharply dressed interviewer who most certainly is not from Sheriff's County.

Judy looks the same as always: beautiful in denim overalls, gray hair tinged with vibrant lavender. She must've washed the color in again recently. But she also looks exhausted, worn out, older, with bags under her eyes and wrinkles forming beneath her mouth, though she'd holler at me for saying that.

"Is it true she has a mother with severe medical issues?" the interviewer asks her.

I gasp. Judy narrows her eyes and gives him *the look* she gave me whenever I suggested I might ditch school to work a full shift that day. "This girl's family is none of your business. You won't be getting any gossip from me."

Hell, so they've found out about Mama. My heart thuds against my ribcage, shame running through me. I haven't kept our secret as well hidden as I thought.

I want to run right into that TV and bear hug her, breathe in her cedar perfume and let her stroke my hair while I cry. Shoot the shit with her after work again, like it's any normal day. Smoke behind the dumpsters at the diner during my too-short break. My eyes burn and my chest sears like it's on fire. Damn. I can't cry, not here. Not with these strangers in this odd little baby-blue trailer out in the middle of nowhere, with red-and-white stripes and stars painted across the side.

Lux gently grips my wrist, grounding me. At least I have her here. I'd crumble without her.

The segment does a weird jump cut, like they edited a bunch out. Judy's posture has changed, and her eyes have narrowed. Shit. "Not only have the girls been linked to the murder of a young man, but they robbed a family store at gunpoint, so we have to conclude that—"

"There's no evidence that was them," Judy cuts in. Her eyebrows furrow. She got them waxed recently, I can tell. They look good. "That's all conjecture."

"Shit, y'all robbed a store *too*?" Ed barks. He sounds impressed.

"Well, I'll be damned!" the woman croaks.

I ignore them both. Judy is still talking, saying things I don't want to hear, things I don't want to know.

"*We have no way of knowing* what we would do if we were in their shoes! We haven't heard from the girls themselves. Just because the Grimaldi family is rich and important doesn't mean we should give them a . . . a goddamned pass!"

Judy's accent is fully out now like it always is when she gets mad. She barely stopped herself from letting slip something way worse than "goddamned," and you can tell whatever it is, it's what she really wanted to say. I cringe as she gestures wildly, her face growing redder by the minute as she defends us and decries the Grimaldis. They're finally getting the footage they no doubt baited her for, all that stuff we didn't get to see. It's not fair. The hog interviewer looks positively tickled. He landed an on-camera outburst that the internet will turn into a segment played over and over on the nightly news before it becomes immortalized as a Twitter meme. Look at this silly redneck woman with the purple hair. Listen to her goofy, tongue-pulled Appalachian accent. Watch her explode like July fireworks in the country sky at the mere mention of the psychotic girl killers from her Podunk hometown. Come one, come all. Enjoy the sideshow. Isn't she fucking ridiculous?

By morning this tirade will be all over the news, the blogs, the forums. Judy will forever be a joke. A laughingstock. A punchline. A silly, poor, know-nothing white-trash woman in overalls. I can't take any more.

"Turn it off!" I yell. "TURN IT OFF!"

Ed and the woman startle. The woman clicks off the TV. A hush falls over the cramped little trailer.

"Trix, are you okay?" Lux drops the empty gas can and gathers me in her arms like I'm a helpless infant.

I can feel Ed's eyes on me. The seat squeaks as he leans farther back in the old recliner.

The croaking woman stands, meanders over, and gives me a gentle kiss on the cheek. It reminds me of Judy and feels nice even though she's a total stranger. Feels loving, somehow. She smells like garlic and tobacco, not cedar perfume, but it's somehow not unpleasant. "Don't you worry, girls," she says gently, placing a hand on each of our shoulders. "Your secrets are safe with us."

"Maybe we should go," I say softly to my sneakers. I don't want to be rude. Which is funny, because I just yelled and screamed at these people in their own home.

"Would you like to stay for dinner?" Ed asks gently. He claps his hands and rubs them together. "Some of the boys are grilling burgers out back. They'll help you get some gasoline. Just let 'em know that Ed sent you."

"That would be just fine, thank you," Lux says with a tight smile. She picks up the empty gas can, grabs my hand, and leads me back out into the fresh desert air, where I can breathe a bit easier.

"Trixie," she says. She doesn't have to say much else. The way she's looking at me, it's like I'm so fragile I could shatter at any moment. She bites her lip. She knows. She can feel it, too, I know she can: the way my heart beats helplessly for Judy, pumps blood through my tired veins and arteries, wanting to run from and run home to her in equal measure.

"I'm so sorry . . ." I choke out.

"You have nothing to be sorry for, Trix."

"We could . . ."

We could, but we won't. She and I both know this. I let more of the ice queen inside of me melt away as she pulls me close to her and kisses my lips, hungry and hard.

Both of our stomachs growl in unison.

The two men who offer us grilled burgers out back aren't hogs. More like strange desert creatures. They slither and snicker, wiggle and hiss their secrets into the open air. One wears a worn-out, over-sized vintage Disneyland T-shirt that hangs off his skinny frame. He whistles a little song to himself after every other sentence.

The other is plumper, covered in piercings and colorful tattoos, his lips painted cherry red. He calls out to people passing by now and then on a mini-megaphone, giving mini-sermons to boot that sound like excerpts from the kind of self-help manual you'd pick up at the grocery store.

These men should scare me more than they do. They're eerie, sure, more than a little off, but I try to remind myself not to judge. Everyone can't be a hog, can they?

Lux and I sit beside the massive gas tank behind Ed's baby-blue trailer, our own plastic gasoline can now full thanks to the generosity of the desert men. They gave us big plastic jugs of fresh water, too, all of it allegedly filtered from one of their in-home systems. Told us to keep them and stay hydrated.

The second I bite into the juicy half-burnt burger and taste the salt and cooked flesh, a rush of euphoria overwhelms me. I never knew food could taste so fucking good. Lux eats hers slowly, savoring every bite of the meat, the cheap, tasteless bun. She sighs contentedly, then sucks the grease off each finger with care and precision. I kiss the burger grease right off her lips, and I feel safe doing it here. No one stares or says a word. The smell of burgers cooking reminds me of the diner. Of home.

After dinner, the two desert men invite us to join them at the center of the encampment for a nighttime "come down," where a big bonfire is roaring. An elderly man sits in the sand, strumming his guitar and singing sad little lullabies. A gaunt woman wearing bright pink fairy wings—the kind you get at a costume shop—runs back and forth, laughing and dancing in the glow of the fire's embers.

The man with the megaphone raises it to his lips and shouts for the whole encampment to hear: "We salute you, girls!"

I freeze and feel Lux go stiff beside me, too.

The elderly man with the guitar smiles and nods. "It really means a lot to us, what you've been doing."

The gaunt woman in the fairy wings pumps her fist in the air and cheers, "Power to the people!"

Writing that angry post on the hog forum and signing it as "the Trouble Girls" feels like it happened a million years ago, like something I did in another time and dimension. From my anger and pain this movement was spawned that's since grown hundreds of arms and limbs. Activists flourished from the core of it and put their bodies on the front lines, and meanwhile, Lux and I just kept driving, kept running, tagging our symbol onto bumper stickers and stoplights and stray Confederate flags.

I don't know if it's guilt I feel, or shame. Like I've shrunk down to the size of a pin when these cheering patrons of Slate City should be making me feel a hundred feet tall.

I want to express all of this to Lux right now, but I can't, because we're surrounded.

Phoenix is here, too. She tears open big bags of marshmallows, seemingly oblivious to the rallying cries of her neighbors. When she spots us, she waves and gives a full smile, revealing all her broken and rotting teeth once more.

I shudder and Lux squeezes my knee, letting me know she can feel that same strange tension, the energy buzzing through a space that doesn't quite feel safe.

"You girls want to make s'mores?" Phoenix asks.

Lux wears her best poker face and so I put mine on as well. She gives Phoenix an equally blank look as she says, "Sure. We'd love to," in a voice just as affectless.

"Oh perfect, perfect!" Phoenix trills. She gets us some long metal rods to roast the marshmallows on. We burn them to a crisp and mash them together with big slabs of chocolate from a little plastic baggie. The chocolate makes my gums tingle when I try a bite.

"What's in these?" I asked, holding up the offending square.

Phoenix giggles and sticks out her tongue. "Special properties," she says. I shoot Lux a look, and we both opt not to include them in ours s'mores, just to be safe.

Phoenix reminds me of a little kid at a cookout or on a camping trip—drug use aside—and it's nice that none of the other people here laugh at her or make comments one way or another.

She seems to sense we won't laugh at her, either, because after a bit she comes over and plops down beside us. "You girls come from the Youth Outreach Center in Burnsville?"

"What's that?" I ask, savoring every bite of a gooey toasted marshmallow.

"It's a shelter for kids like y—Oh. *Sheesh.* Sorry to assume. I spent most of my formative years there, is all." She takes a big bite of the tainted chocolate right from the baggie, some of it sticking to her face. "Really nice people. They accept everyone, no matter their circumstances. And I mean *everyone.*"

Lux flashes her the kind of Lux smile that would put anyone at ease. "You didn't offend, Phoenix. It's a fair question. We're just passing through, really. We're on a road trip."

"Oh!" Phoenix bounces in her seat. "I love road trips! What a grand adventure! I love that. Love that for you two. Listen . . . if you girls want to spend the night here, my camper is open to both of you. I got plenty of blankets and lots of room to stretch out."

Ed also extended us an invitation, though I'm not sure how

we'd squeeze into that little space, or if I trust sleeping in the same place as a strange man. Either way, both options sure beat sleeping in the car.

"We'll think about it," Lux says, smiling at Phoenix like she's talking to an excited little kid.

The sun begins its long, lazy descent. Tainted chocolate and simmering anxiety aside, the night is beautiful, the sky clear and brilliant with a smattering of stars. For the first time in days, I start to relax. I'm no longer hungry, and my muscles loosen and a real smile fills my face.

"We could start our lives here and never look back," Lux says wistfully, as if she can read my mind. She burrows her face in the crook of my neck. I feel hope shimmer through her veins and travel into mine. The air smells of smoke and burnt sugar, filled with peals of strangers' laughter.

My heart aches for home, but I know I can't ever have the home I left behind. Maybe we can have some semblance of home here. Maybe as long as I'm with Lux, I'll always be home.

I try to picture it: Lux and me cleaning out an abandoned old camper or trailer on the edge of Slate City, furnishing it with broken mismatched tables and chairs. Befriending the strange inhabitants here, adopting their rituals and mannerisms. Riding around and kicking up dust on a motorized scooter. Becoming strange desert people ourselves, molding our bodies and hearts hard to fit the harsh landscape, letting go of all the worldly things we think we need. This reminds me of that magical night in Middlesville, when time seemed to stop and give us both a chance to just live and feel human.

"There *is* something enticing about giving up and letting go here," I say to Lux. She looks up at me and frowns.

"Who says we'd be giving up?"

"Well, we were supposed to make it to the ocean . . ."

Lux moves her orange-pink ring around and around on her finger. There's a red rash forming there from how often she does it, or maybe she's allergic to the cheap material. Figures that I would get her jewelry that turns her fingers different colors. I spot the bearded man on the scooter from earlier driving closer to join the fun. He calls out to the group and they call back, the tattooed and pierced man yodeling a happy song on his mini-megaphone.

"Trix, originally we were going to Austin." Lux sounds tired and annoyed, like she's talking to a whiny toddler. "And then maybe Santa Fe, and then finally we decided California. What does it really matter where we end up, as long as we're together?"

I start to say something about how *she* begged me to take her, then think better of it. I nod as if she's right, because I want to be and feel close to her again, and she settles her head back against me. It feels amazing, but already my legs are starting to get that itchy sensation from the inside. I want to get back into Razor Blade and start up the makeshift engine cables and drive us off into forever.

I'm ready to go. Now. Somewhere. Anywhere but Blue Bottle, of course, but somewhere. The farther the better. My legs and heart and lungs are all ready to sprint to the very edge of this fucked-up world before I keep running.

———

Lux and I take turns carrying the heavy gas can back to Razor Blade, where we fill up her hungry belly. We're well fed and watered now, but there's still that weird tension hanging between us, the words left unspoken. The sweat that's been collecting for days under my bra is starting to itch something ferocious. The more I scratch, the redder and itchier it gets, but I can't help myself.

"She hates me," I hear myself say. I'm used to blurting things out now. When you don't have a moment to yourself, you tend to start doing that.

Lux wipes a big bead of sweat from her forehead and chuckles at me. "You mean Judy."

I wait for Lux to reassure me that no, Judy doesn't hate me. She doesn't hate either of us. She loves us and wants more than anything for us to fess up, admit we made a mistake and we want to make amends. Nothing we can't fix.

Only we didn't make a mistake. I stabbed someone, and it felt damn good sticking the knife in his gut and groin. Then we both ran for the hills and left him there to bleed and die, left everyone we knew and loved behind to pick up the pieces of the horrific mess we made. We stole things, robbed a kid who was younger than us in his own family's store. We hid. We never called home, not even to tell our family we're still alive.

Lux stuffs her hands in the pockets of her shorts. They're filthy, covered in oil stains and smeared with red dirt. She kicks a big rock across the sand, and it bounces a few feet away.

"We let her down," she says to the rock. "We really fucked up big time."

My mouth feels like it's stuck together with peanut butter. I take a long swig from one of the water jugs gifted us by one of the desert creatures, but the nasty stuck feeling is still there.

"She'll never forgive me," I manage to say.

"Maybe not." Lux shrugs at the rock, then strolls over and kicks it so hard it goes flying into a big thorny shrub. Little yellow geckos go scuttling every which way. "We can't think about that now. We have to think about ourselves. And what do we think, Trix? Are we staying or going tonight?"

"Mmm."

I take the empty gas can from Lux. I stuff it in the backseat with our duffels and the bags of food and clothing we've accrued while making sure no one's broken in or anything. But the desert willow's branches feel protective, somehow, and the people here don't seem to be the thieving type.

I fill up my lungs with the sweet, dry desert air and lean against Razor Blade's hood. She's sustained her share of dents and bruises since we got her. I'm a bad car mother, even if she is our kidnapped baby. "I guess we can rest awhile." I feel as though I'm floating above my body again, staring down at myself leaning against the sunflower sedan and avoiding eye contact with my girlfriend.

"We should stay the night, at least," she suggests. "If you want to. We don't have to stay forever. I don't know what I was thinking. I mean, I think it'll be fine, and we'll get to eat for free again in the morning. And God, my back is still killing me from the car. Phoenix did say she makes a mean Denver omelet. Don't you think?" She gets close and gently shakes me by the shoulders. "It was your idea to come here, remember?" I finally meet her eyes, see the fear swimming in them. The desperate need for me to take control, to make a decision for the both of us and make it sound sure and solid and true when it comes from my lips.

"We'll stay with Phoenix," I say. It comes out all uneven, unsure, even though I'm doing my best to sound firm. Like I'm reading from a bad script. "Just for tonight. Then we'll keep going and drive straight through to California in the morning, or however long this gas lasts us. We'll make it, Lux. I know we will."

She sighs deeply, softens her grip on my arms, and pulls me in for a hug. Her embrace is so warm, so secure. I could spend an eternity in her arms, even as both of us are sweating all the water from our bodies, melting like snowmen in a place that probably never sees snow.

"Okay," she says. "Okay, that makes sense. Sorry I was hasty earlier, thinking maybe we'd just live here. That's impossible, right?" She laughs, and it warms me to hear the bells. "I'm so overwhelmed by . . . well, everything."

"You don't have to apologize," I say, though the thoughts race through my head anyway: *Does she really mean it, or is she saying it to make me feel better? Deep down, does she blame me for all of this?*

As I stroke her back, I wonder briefly what Judy would think of us being together like this. Did she see it coming? Would she be shocked? Disgusted? Something tells me she wouldn't, even though Judy and I never discussed anything like this before. I try to imagine what she'd do or say if she were here right now, try to picture her like a hologram a few feet behind us, waving and smiling in her diner apron, smoking a cig.

Only try as I might, that imagined hologram won't smile or wave at me. I can't see anything more than Judy, my Judy, with her achingly familiar face, forever stuck with a look of sheer, utter disappointment.

Our arms are so tired and our minds are so busy with wishes and regret, we forget to think to grab our duffel bags.

We forget that things are never truly safe.

⌐───────⌐

Phoenix's camper is much wider and roomier than Ed's. That, at least, she was telling the truth about.

It's set a ways back from Slate City's barely there dirt path, cozied up next to a family of saguaro cacti. She has her own makeshift front yard filled with gnomes and hot pink plastic flamingos. There are a few plump Christmas elves with big, creepy grins on their faces. Holiday lights twinkling red and green are strung up all over. There's even a giant green circular plastic bin, big enough to fit at least three people. It's filled to the brim with cold water from a garden hose: a makeshift pool.

All in all, it's quirky as hell but pretty nice. Reminds me a lot of the trailers in the park I grew up in back in Blue Bottle. We had our own "white trash" pools, too. Every summer, all the neighborhood kids took turns splashing around and having the best time. Even though other kids on TV and in movies had bigger houses and real swimming pools with diving boards and everything, we never thought much of it.

Inside Phoenix's camper, it's cool but not too cold. Lux and I survey the small cooking area and the living room with the cracked leather sofa, cream-colored bookshelves filled with giant textbooks, and figurines of fluffy white dogs and angels. Sad little oil paintings hang from the off-white walls, each stranger than the last: a snake devouring a melon, a man with a tree for a beard, a male dog peeing outside a cozy winter cottage beneath a handful of stars. You can taste the dust in the air, the way it settles into every crevice of the trailer.

There're other rooms down the tiny hall, which presumably is where we'll be staying. Phoenix busies herself in the kitchen, making us a pot of tea in a colorless kettle. Lux and I sit on the sofa and wait to be told what to do. It feels like hundreds of years have gone by since we've been invited to sit in a living room and have tea. I study the dozens of cigarette holes burned into the leather, the big black cardboard box that sits on the coffee table, sealed shut with duct tape.

Lux twists her orange-pink ring around and around on her finger. The rash is already turning a strange purplish brown. I touch her hand gently and hold it close to examine it in mine.

"Why don't you just take it off? It's making your skin sick."

Lux smiles faintly at me, tucking a black curl behind her ear, and says, "Because *you* gave it to me."

I'm trying to think of how to respond or interpret this when the kettle hisses and Phoenix squeals with delight. "Honey or sugar?" she asks. We politely decline both. Shit's probably laced with "special properties," too. She brings over plastic cups filled with hot water and bags of plain Lipton, and we all sit and blow on our tea as she smiles and smiles at us, her rotting black teeth on full display. I do my best not to look away or gag, but I can't stop thinking about how much her teeth must hurt. How disgusting it must feel to eat or drink or exist with a mouth like that. Lux flashes her signature grin in return, but it's not quite enough to mellow the tension bubbling in the room.

Phoenix's eyes land on me. Her rotten smile widens. It's unnerving. I tell myself I won't drink the tea even if it makes me seem rude.

Lux crosses her legs and breaks the ice with, "It was real nice of you to invite us to spend the night, Phoenix. We're pretty tired from sleeping in the car."

Phoenix giggles and taps her long nails against the plastic cup. *Tap-tap-tap.* She does it every few seconds. "No trouble at all, honey. Where did you say you were headed?"

"We didn't." I don't mean for it to come out so sharp, but there it is.

Tap-tap-tap.

Lux clears her throat. "West. We're enjoying a spontaneous road trip to end a long school year."

The mere mention of "school" makes my stomach dip like I'm

on a rollercoaster. Never in a trillion years would I have thought that instead of serving hogs cherry pie and buying clothes and school supplies at the Salvation Army at the end of my junior year, I'd be ready to spend the night in a meth head's camper in the middle of New Mexico.

"And where are you coming *from?*" Phoenix is still smiling, but her bushy brows narrow a little. They remind me of a big fuzzy caterpillar.

"Colorado," Lux says quickly. "We stopped at the Grand Canyon before we came here. It was amazing, wasn't it, Trix?"

Phoenix blinks at us. "The Grand Canyon is hundreds of miles northwest of here in Arizona. Did you drive all the way there and then drive all the way down here?"

Lux flushes. The back of my neck prickles. "Yeah," I say. "We took the scenic route."

Those bushy eyebrows narrow even further. "Why New Mexico? Why stop in the middle of nowhere?"

Lux laughs nervously. I take a sip of the Lipton without thinking and burn my mouth badly. "My mom was born in this state," Lux says airily, like it's no big deal, like our strange route makes perfect sense. "I've always wanted to see it."

Phoenix seems to consider this carefully. "How did you even find out about this place? It isn't the type of spot that tourists tend to know about. Especially not two pretty young girls on a road trip. What are you both, fifteen? Sixteen?"

I'm trying to think up a quick and believable answer when something beeps and vibrates so loud that all three of us startle. Lux yelps as my hot tea spills onto her bare legs. "Shit, I'm so sorry," I hiss, searching for something to dry her reddening skin with. I end up using my T-shirt, because Phoenix is busy studying her phone like it contains the secrets to the universe itself.

What does she see on that screen?

My heart does little bunny hops into my throat. Lux tugs her earlobe three times.

There's no question we should go. *Now.*

I stand and take Lux's hand, pulling her up with me. "Thank you so much for the tea and hospitality, Phoenix, but we might just get going now."

Phoenix glances up at us, looking utterly bewildered. Her voice comes out like the bang of a firework, making both of us freeze in place. "Well, hang on now, there's no need to leave! Did I scare you girls with my twenty questions?" She laughs, big and open, so I can see the rot forming at the back of her blackened molars. "I'm so, so sorry, girls." She flushes red and covers her face with her hands. Just like that, she's a little girl again. "I just get excited when we have visitors, is all. Sorry, sorry. Please. Please sit. Stay awhile. I have to go help some of the boys with some good cooking." She winks so we know it's not *the food* kind of cooking. It takes me back to my trailer-park days. Most people in the park were regular and clean, but there was one guy whose trailer always gave off a whiff of this terrible combination of rotting eggs, nail polish remover, and burning plastic whenever you walked past at dusk.

"I'll be back in an hour or so, my dears." Phoenix stands and smooths out her long peasant skirt. "Feel free to make yourselves at home. There's bread and jam in the cupboards if you want dessert. Oh, and the second door down the hall on the left is all yours. There's a sleeper sofa. Bathroom is across the hall."

I grit my teeth. "Thanks. So much."

Phoenix grins and giggles. As soon as she slams the front door shut, Lux and I both let out a breath.

"Jesus."

"Freaky."

"We shouldn't—"

"No. Definitely not. But we should at least see—"

"—if the room is okay. Yeah. I mean, she's freaky, but I really don't want to spend another night in the car." I rub my knotted-up neck and wince.

"Yeah, I mean . . . maybe she's just really curious," Lux says carefully. "Maybe we're overreacting?"

"The meth probably makes her like that, too."

"I mean, do we know for *sure* she's on meth?"

"Lux. Come on. Her teeth. *Cooking.*"

She sighs and spits her big wad of bubble gum into Phoenix's trash can. I rub the goose bumps on my arms and study the strange paintings on the wall.

"I had a nightmare like this once." I point at the oil painting of the snake eating the melon. His fangs are big and razor sharp. "Do you think she painted these?"

Lux shudders. "God only knows. This place is too weird. Too fucking . . ."

". . . absolutely bananas?"

We stare at each other for a moment, then burst out laughing. I feel like a big birthday balloon bursting with helium, drunk on something stronger than alcohol. Life is too fucking surreal right now.

"We're overreacting, aren't we?" I say. I open the cupboards, and sure enough, there's plenty of whole wheat bread and fresh jam, and none of it looks contaminated. There's peanut butter, too, and neat stacks of dishes and bowls. Nothing to suggest that a serial killer lives here. But, then again . . .

"Sure. I mean, she was nice enough to offer us a place to stay."

"Even if she did paint these, she has nothing on you."

Lux snorts and crosses the camper, sidling up close to me. I welcome her into my arms. "Oh, now you like my photography, huh? You never showed much interest before."

I press my forehead against hers, and she presses back. Our eyelashes brush and flutter. "And I'm sorry about that. I always did love your photos. I guess I never realized how—" I cut myself off, haunted by visions: Lux on a sunny campus lawn, reading a glossy photography book. Lux working in the darkroom. Lux huddled up in a computer lab at four a.m., chugging Diet Coke and ferociously typing her senior thesis. It comes out in a pained whisper: "Your future. I took it from you."

She shushes me. "Stop it. We've been over this, Trixie."

"*I* took it. I took everything—"

"Enough." She pulls away from me and crosses her arms over her chest, eyes filled with hurt. "Do you think that makes me feel better, when you do that? I've told you. It's over. It's not your fault and it's not mine. What's done is done. Every time you guilt yourself, you're not doing it for me. You're doing it to make *you* feel better."

My face burns. I wish I could crawl into the weird painting with the cozy winter home and hide away there forever, peeing dog or not.

"Look, it'll be fine, Trixie. We're both exhausted. Let's make sure the bedroom isn't filled with roaches or something and then we'll go get our stuff, okay? I'm tired. You're tired. Let's not make it weirder than it already is."

She holds out her hand, her nails chipped pastel pink. I bow my head in shame and take it, following her down the short hallway. She's right. I blame myself over and over, berate and beat myself up. An endless loop of self-torture.

I can't seem to stop it.

The guest bedroom is small but comfortable. Just as described, there's a sleeper sofa draped with a fuzzy afghan. A friendly wall clock shaped like a cat ticks and tocks. Two potted plants rest in the corner, next to a dresser covered in scratches.

I could melt, I'm so relieved. "It's fine. It's good."

"More than good." Lux's voice comes out like a long sigh, dripping with relief. We check the bathroom, too, and it's tiny but perfectly functional: a shower, toilet, and sink. Combined with the living room and kitchenette, it's downright cozy. I can't wait to get our bags, brush my teeth, shower, and collapse with Lux onto the sleeper sofa, drifting off into sweeter dreams and waking to the smell of a Denver omelet sizzling on a skillet.

Maybe we can even stay here a little longer, after all. We judged Phoenix too quickly, too harshly, I tell myself, pacing around the hallway. She has a right to know who's staying in her house. Plus, the other residents support us.

The door to what I assume is her bedroom is open a crack. Something in there catches my eye. That jumpy, jittery feeling is back. I press the door open slowly, as if whatever's inside might bite me. It creaks as it opens, revealing its insides.

"Trix?"

"Holy. Fucking. Shit."

Three assault rifles are mounted above the headboard of a bed.

Three AK-47s. Machine guns with long necks. Reliable and deadly. There's only one use for these.

Ketchup on mustard.

Little black dots dance in front of me as my brain connects the rifles to the black cardboard box perched on the coffee table. I race back into the living room, heart hammering, and yank it open. Inside are dozens and dozens of gold-tipped bullets. A few are missing.

Red splattered across my yellow shirt.

. . . in prison or in a body bag.

I choke out something between a sob and a scream.

Lux and I hightail it back to the stolen sunflower, racing each other down the long path like we're being chased by ghosts or frenzied murderers. The sweet night air fills my lungs and opens them wide, and the moon lights our way like a flashlight. The car is still there. Thank God. She's here. I open her up, shaking. Everything we own is still inside: the plastic bags of food and clothes, the duffel bags. But you can tell they've been moved and jostled around. I unzip my duffel and Lux examines hers. Things have been taken out and stuffed back in. Even the bloodstained yellow shirt. I want to tear it out of the bag and rip it to shreds, let them dance in the evening breeze, but I can't make my fingers do it. They stay frozen, holding open the duffel.

"The money, Trix." It's not very bright out, even in the glowing moonlight, but I can see all the color has drained from Lux's face. She stares at me helplessly, as if I can fix it. "The money. The money."

I tear the car apart, searching, knowing before I start looking that it's no use. All of it's gone. They took all of it. It wasn't much, but it was all we had, and that felt like everything.

Rage boils in the pit of my belly, intermingling with flashes of stone-cold fear. I stuff our things back in the car and open the door, firing up the engine of my trusty Razor Blade. "Let's get the fuck out of here. *Now.*"

I flip on the headlights and drive us back onto the highway, back into the open stretches of nothing and nowhere.

Slate City is not meant for girls like us.

Not even the Trouble Girls.

In another universe—a parallel dimension—Lux and I stop what we're doing right now. We wire up the engine of the stolen sunflower sedan and drive Razor Blade over a thousand miles back to Blue Bottle, West Virginia. Back to Sheriff's County, where we were born and lived the first phase of our insignificant, working-class lives.

We turn ourselves in to the local police station. We don't resist. We cooperate. Tears flow down our cheeks as we tell our stories slowly and carefully to the cops, then the lawyers, then the news.

I call Judy. I tell her I'm coming home.

I call Mama. I tell her I'll do my best to take care of her, and that I never wanted to leave her at all. That even if they send us miles apart, I'll find a way to visit her as much as I can in whatever home or hospital they stick her in. Stroke her hair and cut the crusts off her sandwiches.

In another universe—a parallel dimension—I feel guilty for stabbing Bryce Grimaldi. I am sorry that he died. I regret using Judy's knife to carve my name and pain into his flesh, letter by letter, line by line, even though at the time I had no idea I was creating such poetry.

The Youth Outreach Center in Burnsville is so much cleaner than I expected.

I don't know what I expected, really. The homeless shelters in movies and on TV are always filthy, cramped, full of mice and roaches and a sense of dread lurking around every corner. The looming threat of having your things stolen or being stabbed in the knife by an unhinged resident.

But this place is simple yet nice, tidy, made up of mostly kids our age, from what I can tell. Some have fantasy-colored hair like Lux's used to be, piercings and tattoos. A couple of them use wheelchairs to navigate the narrow hallways. The other kids shoot us wary looks, or give tight-lipped smiles, or just ignore us entirely. Most speak Spanish, are bilingual, or speak languages neither Lux nor I recognize. And, to my surprise and delight, little rainbow stickers pop up everywhere around here: on doors, in corners, on the cinderblock walls. I show Lux one and she nods eagerly, just as tight-lipped as all the kids around us.

A COEXIST graphic featuring all the religions in harmony has been placed next to a trans pride flag on a bulletin board. In parts of the shelter, the drab walls are covered in radiant art, no doubt done by the residents: incredible drawings, sketches, paintings bursting with shape and color, and long, flowing murals of landscapes and seashores.

We arrived soaking wet from a shocking desert downpour, teeth chattering, duffel bags dripping, explaining to the very short, very kind woman and her security team at the front desk that we had run for our safety and had no place left to go. She didn't ask too many questions or seem too frazzled by us and our vague admissions, just gave us both a friendly smile and asked if we'd like to sit in the staff room and have some hot tea and cookies while filling out intake forms.

She didn't tell us what to do. *She asked.*

"I'm Miss Nguyen," she said, her voice like iced tea down a painful sore throat. A rose gold cross hung from a chain around her neck.

She tells us there's a room we can share with another girl, named Autumn, for the night, "until we get everything sorted," giving both of us meaningful looks. It's small, bunk beds on one side for Lux and me. Autumn's side of the room has a twin-size bed covered in a cheerful quilt. Drawings, sketches, and little paintings of sunsets and horses cover her wall.

"Tomorrow after lunch, we can have you both speak to a counselor about your individual situations," Miss Nguyen says, gently as raindrops. "And hopefully soon, we can assign each of you a caseworker."

Lux forces a lopsided smile and I nod and I want so badly to trust this sweet, knowing woman, but she doesn't know the kind of girls we really are. If she did, would her voice remain as soothing, her eyes as crinkling with warmth? Those eyes of hers seem to say, *No matter what you did, no matter how bad you think you fucked up, we can help you.*

But I don't believe her. And either way, it's too late.

Lux and I are hardened girls now, husks of the smiling, open, easy girls we used to be. Our faces are lined with dirt and worry and fear. We stiffen at the slightest touch or movement and huddle close together like frightened animals as we follow her down the hallway, afraid to separate even to shower.

I shower anyway with lukewarm water and simple bar soap that feels luxurious on my sunburned, dry skin, then join the rest of the kids for dinner in an open dining room with long metal benches and tables. Lux and I sit side by side, nibbling our rice and carrots and chicken, noting the vegetarian soup option available. Once we'd have been chatting and laughing and making small observations to each other about everything and everyone in the room. Now our heads are bowed over our plates. There's nothing left to say. Nothing feels worth saying.

At dinner, I count how many others there are: maybe thirty or so. Some have their heads bowed while they eat without speaking, like us. Others are chatting and laughing. Still easy. Still open.

Or so it seems. I guess I don't know what anyone here has really been through, and it's unfair to assume. But still, there's something heavy and tangible that divides Lux and me from most of the others. Like we've both aged twenty years.

At dinner, we meet Autumn, our temporary roommate. She comes in late to the meal, dressed in bright green overalls and jelly sandals, her hair hanging loose and long down her back. It's impossible to miss her round, swollen belly.

"She's—" Lux murmurs in my ear, unable to finish her sentence.

"Yeah," I say, because there's really nothing else to say.

She's a baby herself.

But Autumn, who we discover is only fourteen, does not have the kind of demeanor I might expect from someone in her circumstances. She's chatty and cheerful, eager to tell us all about her day and the new mural she's been helping with in the outdoor rec area.

When we retreat to our room for bedtime, she sees something in the way we are with each other and says, "Oh, you two are together, aren't you? There's a lot of others like that here."

She grins when she says it, and it doesn't feel the least bit patronizing. She sits on her bed and watches us curiously as we change into nightclothes and get out our shoplifted toothbrushes and toothpaste and dental floss. When she sees Lux's Canon come out of its bag, she squeals. Lux's face relaxes into the first genuine smile I've seen in a while. A little bit of light sparkles back in her eyes.

"Oh my God, how does it work?!" Autumn begs to know.

Lux cradles the hulking camera, sidling over to Autumn. "Want me to show you? I can take some photos of you, if you'd like."

Autumn bounces up and down on her bed. "Yes, yes! Please!"

"Let's go out into the hall where the lighting is better." Lux winks at me before taking Autumn out of the room, and even though it's clear the fluorescent lighting is just as bad for photos in the halls as it is in ours, Autumn doesn't seem to notice. I sit on the floor, rearranging our dirty clothes, our messy duffels full of bags of chips and warm bottled water and little stashes of personal items—deodorant, mouthwash, tampons—all of it stuffed in alongside the sweaty T-shirts and worn-out shorts that badly need a run through the wash.

In the hallway, Lux instructs Autumn how to pose. She's a natural, this kid, angling her hips and swooping her arms to the ceiling. She finds her light even in the harsh brightness, tilting her head at an angle and shooting the camera a stealthy glare.

This kid.

Her pregnant belly swells underneath her overalls, wiggling as she moves. Bile crawls up my throat and threatens to make me vomit. A sweet little girl like that, pregnant. Homeless. It's not hard to put the story together.

"Yes! Gorgeous! Marvelous! Pose, darling, pose!" Lux takes shot after shot, her camera clicking and whirring. I watch as I walk down the long, winding hallway to the bathroom. I love watching Lux shoot. She's a natural. A gifted artist. My eyes well up with tears and I grin with pride.

A few kids come into the hallway to see what she's doing. Some stand shyly in the corner, observing or whispering among themselves. A couple of older teens pose and laugh loudly. They joke around and cut up until a staff member snaps her fingers and tells us it's time to get to sleep. The kids groan and a few complain, begging for a little while longer. Lux takes her time, photographing their faces, their silhouettes and shadows as they scurry back down the hall to their rooms. She looks so focused and professional holding that camera. For one agonizing second,

I let myself imagine the life she could've had, the art she could've made, if I hadn't ruined everything for both of us.

I know now that even if I'd stayed in Blue Bottle, I wouldn't have stayed for long. I'd have taken the little cash I had saved and hopped on the next train or bus across the country. I wouldn't care where I ended up, because no matter what I'd keep going.

Now our only hope is California, dangling before us like a golden carrot, so close yet so far away.

Autumn doesn't stop talking even after the lights go out. She blabs on and on about her day, her latest art project, what she might name her kid. She blabs herself to sleep, and it's comforting, the sound of another person's voice.

I press my face against the pillow, inhaling the scent of fresh laundry. It conjures old memories of home. Simple memories that contain fleeting moments of joy: the smell of Ivory soap in the bath as a toddler; dappled light through the blinds on a crisp fall day; the creak of the floorboards on the way to my room; the way everything hushes into stillness after I turn off the bathroom fan.

The house I rented with Mama may not have been the house that built me, but it contained me, held me. Held us together. And I left her and everything behind.

The pain is so sudden and sharp it's like I've been stabbed with Judy's knife.

And Lux. I can't lose her. I want to wake up every morning and press my face to her curls. I want to memorize every inch of her skin with my lips. I want to make her laugh until her dimples pop and she snort-laughs and can't stop.

I don't want to lose her.

I don't want Lux to hear me cry, so I stifle it as best I can, letting it pour out of me, a sweet and horrible release. Where the fuck did I think I'd go? What did I really think would happen?

I reach down from the top bunk for my girlfriend's hand.

She murmurs and rolls over, waking up from a half sleep, then grabs my hand back and gives it a squeeze.

The tears keep coming, soaking the pillow. Autumn is breathing softer now, though her breath is ragged, interrupted by little snores. I wonder if her baby dreams inside her womb, if her baby has any idea what's ahead in this horrible, painful, chaotic world.

———

At dawn, I'm disoriented at first when I see the cinderblock walls. My back and shoulders ache from the lumpy mattress, but it beats the car any day.

During breakfast, Miss Nguyen finds us again, reminds Lux and me of the meetings she scheduled with counselors after lunch today. "Separately," she adds kindly, watching my hand slide protectively over Lux's. "I know you girls are close, but we do want to hear from both of you. Each of your stories is just as important."

It makes my throat tighten and my scalp itch. We don't belong here. We chose this life on the run, this descent into chaos. We came from homes with food and clothing and parents and plenty of people in our lives. We aren't like the others.

We don't deserve to be sheltered.

Lux and I scarf down the breakfast of bagels and cream cheese and hot coffee like it's our last meal on earth. Afterward, we pack up and grab our duffels and sneak out of the shelter before Miss Nguyen can catch us again. We don't say goodbye to Autumn.

Sooner or later, they'd all learn the truth about who we are and where we're from and what we did. Even if they were on our side, agreed with every trip and stumble and terrible chess move we've made. Even if they still liked us anyway. Even if they believed me. Believed Lux.

Even then, they'd never let us stay.

———

It's blindingly hot and bright.

We're at a gas station in New Mexico right off the interstate, across from a pancake house and a casino with big neon lights that surely look better in the darkness.

It's windy as all hell, whipping back Lux's curls so much she had to tie her hair back into a knot. We circle our arms forward and backward, stretch them up to the sky. If only we could both sprout wings and fly to the ocean.

Though it's midday, and cars crawl along the road now and then, this gas station is a ghost town. The only other car is a dirty white sedan parked behind the dumpsters. Lux is inside using the bathroom and getting us cheap snacks with some of the meager $20 I swiped from one of the Youth Outreach Center staffers' wallet. People really can be careless sometimes, leaving their things lying around. We took a bunch of bagels from them, too, on our way out this morning, which I kind of still feel bad about, but my hungry stomach sure as hell thanks me for it now. Especially when I catch a whiff of those fresh pancakes—or maybe that's my famished imagination playing tricks on me.

I stand by Razor Blade, smoking my last cigarette from a pack I stole a day ago. Stealing has gotten easy as gobbling up Mama's homemade pie. I barely think about it when I see something I want: I just take it and tuck it away and act normal. No need to be cagey about it and get all nervous and paranoid and shit.

Sometimes the best crimes, I've found, are the ones done in plain sight.

The cigs are a real cheap brand and they taste nasty, but then again, they're cigarettes. I'm pumping pure filth and cancer into my lungs. May as well be reminded of that with every puff.

"Got a light?"

A woman appears behind me like a phantom and I nearly jump out of my skin. She wears red lipstick, crimson slacks, and a matching blazer even though it's hot as hell out here in the desert. Her burnt-orange shirt is buttoned conservatively all the way to the top, and her gray hair is pulled back into a tight bun. She smiles thinly at me with her mouth, not her eyes.

"Christ! You scared the shit out of me!" I gasp, squinting at her in the light. "You shouldn't sneak up on people like that."

The woman holds out a palm like an offering. "My apologies. You just looked like you had a lighter I might use."

Between her thumb and forefinger she holds a cigarette that's clearly not from the gas station or anywhere close to here. Way too fancy and thin-tipped.

That should've been my first sign to run.

The woman pins me to the dirt with her gaze and repeats, "You got a light? I could really use one at this hour."

The way she speaks . . . it's lilting, off. Like she thinks she's smarter than me. A creeping sensation goes up and down my spine. She doesn't break eye contact.

Fine. Whatever. I shrug and offer her a flick of my lighter, to show this strange phantom woman she can't spook me.

"May I get you a coffee?"

I blink at her. What does she think I am, homeless or something? I mean, I guess I look like a proper vagabond, with my grubby hair and face, my days-unwashed clothes. The dust and desert dirt caked beneath my fingernails that never seems to come out no matter how hard I scrub.

I shrug. "I'm fine."

She tilts her head and studies me, then takes a long drag off the slender cig. It scares me, the way she's looking at me like this. Little white-hot pinpricks pop up all over my skin. She could be one of those cultists, sussing me out, trying to figure how susceptible I am to brainwashing and all that. Maybe she'll ask if I want to come to a bereavement group with her or something and conjure my lost loved ones. Who fucking knows?

My head is spinning, and I'm so tangled up in my own daydreams I barely hear her when she says, "We can help you, Trixie."

That's when my heart stops beating. I think at first maybe I misunderstood, that the stress and the heat and the lack of sleep have started giving me real aural hallucinations. I try to keep my face and voice as neutral as possible as I ask, "What? Who's Trixie?"

The woman's brows narrow slightly, like maybe for just a second I threw her off, but then her face relaxes back into its placid form. She takes another drag and delicately taps some ashes out onto the concrete. She's in no hurry. She's been waiting for this, and she's going to take her time now. The cat has the mouse. My heart goes *thud, thud, thud* and blood pumps into my ears. I try desperately to send Lux telepathic signals to move faster and get out here so we can leave. I could run inside, but that would make me look more suspicious, wouldn't it?

Should I still be trying to play it cool? Why do I feel so frozen? Why won't my legs work?

I want to run, but I'm stuck. Rooted here. And this woman is still pinning me to the dirt with her gaze.

"There are people on your side, Trixie," she says. She doesn't make a move to grab me, or get out a gun or anything. She just stands there, puffing delicately, telling me this like we're having the most ordinary conversation to be had in the middle of New Mexico. "There are people who will listen to you and advocate for you. I'm one of those people. But we can't help you unless you allow us to help. Can I get you a coffee? Decaf or regular?"

I've been floating above my body again, I realize, and now I feel myself plunging headfirst into an icy river of sheer terror. The black dots wink and swirl around me. I take a ragged breath and try to steady myself as best I can, but I sway side to side, stumble a little. There's no hiding from this now, whatever the hell this is. I swallow hard. "You're a cop," I say.

She opens her blazer to reveal a badge resting inside a clear pocket. The badge looks shiny. Official.

It looks federal.

"Special Agent Diaz," she confirms, before offering a polite smile and smoothing out the blazer.

"Then why haven't you arrested me yet?" I ask. My voice is as shaky as my hands as I try to hold the nasty, cheap, no-good cig.

The fed lady scuffles her patent kitten heels in the dirt. She's way too nice and clean for this place. Probably came from a big fancy office in DC or something, with floor-to-ceiling windows and views of the Capitol building. Government healthcare for life and all that. Shiny Escalade or a BMW. A big house in the suburbs. Grandkids and indoor pools. And she gave all that up to come here, to this very spot, this dot in the dirt, to find me. And she did. Holy fuck.

Wake up. Wake up, Trixie. This is a dream. Jesus Christ. Please wake up.

The fed woman offers me a sad smile that makes her red

lipstick crinkle at the edges of her lips. "When I was around your age, I became involved in a situation that otherwise might have destroyed my life," she says. "But luckily, I had a lot of support around me. Other women who believed me and what I went through." She adjusts the ruffles on her burnt-orange blouse and I will my legs to work. It's so damn hard to breathe. This woman is a witch, sucking the magic out of the air with some horrible spell.

"I really do want to help you here, Trixie. You and Lux both. I know you have things left unsaid that are vital to the public's understanding of who you are and why you've done what you've done. You and Lux aren't criminals. You aren't monsters. But both of you are in way over your heads. People are on your side and more will be. We've seen your cries for help, your distress signals. That's what they were, weren't they? They helped us find you." *Our symbols. The graffiti.* "Let me help you."

This isn't happening. This isn't fucking happening.

A trucker honks his big-bellied horn and swerves past another car. It wakes me up just a little, slaps some life into me. Shit, I wish to God more than anything I was in that truck with him right now, speeding away. Being stuck with a road hog is better than the slaughterhouse.

"You've been following us," I manage to get out, swallowing a rock in my throat. "For how long?"

"Come inside," she says gently. "We'll sit together, talk about what happened. Coffee or tea, a sandwich. Whatever you want. We'll discuss what happens next. You must be hungry. Do you like ham and cheese? Or are you a vegetarian?"

When you wake up, everything will be all right.

"You're going to need me, Miss Denton." Miss Denton. Now we're getting real formal, with a sterner voice and look, but almost as if she's begging me, too. "If you don't take my help now, there's nothing I can do for you then. And *then* is going to be very soon."

I force myself to face her head on, to look into her steely gray eyes that I know won't turn me to stone. She won't cast a spell. She's not a witch woman, she's a fucking federal agent, FBI, and she's found me. We're caught.

We're over. It's done.

We're fucked.

"It happened to me, too, you know." Her voice is barely above a whisper. Here it comes. The sob story. She's going to relate to me, make me think we somehow know each other or met in a past life. "You aren't the only woman who has survived this, Trixie Denton. I hope that's a comfort to hear. I think your story in particular would resonate with a lot of people. This doesn't have to be the end for you."

"What do you mean, *my story?*" The words fly out like razor blades before I can stop them. If I were a cat, I'd be hissing, fangs bared. My hackles are raised now. I won't be patronized, not even by a fed lady with a shiny DC badge. I won't be talked down to like a silly little girl, and I certainly don't need this stranger coming at me like she knows my life when I damn well know she wants to lure me into confessing. I widen my stance and crack my knuckles, sizing her up, getting back into my body. In a fistfight, maybe I could take her. Maybe. "You don't know *my story*," I spit. "You don't know the first fucking thing about me."

"I know what happened to you when you were eight." She says it so matter-of-factly, like she's discussing today's weather patterns.

Sirens. Shouting voices. My nose in the cold dirt. Hog hands. Hog man. Bad man.

I wince like I've been struck right in the face. "You don't

know anything." My voice sounds ragged and raw, like it's coming from the mouth of a hunted animal, giving her last wounded
cry as she lies dying in tall grass. "You're lying."

Hog's blood.

I realize I've dropped my cigarette. The fed lady feels very
far away from me now, even though we're standing close. She
must've moved closer. I can almost smell the manure, His after-
shave, feel the scratchy stubble on His cheek.

I'm there. I'm there. Her mouth is moving, those red lips
forming shapes as soundless words come out. Words that form
the story, my story. Him. It. The day it all ended. The day the
world went to hell.

"I have to go."

Her eyes widen. She's as bewildered as I am, but that's when
my legs start to work again. I've crashed back down to Earth.

I sprint inside the gas station convenience store. The air-
conditioning smacks me in the face, but I'm already freezing,
teeth clattering, bone grinding on bone. I spot Lux's black-
licorice curls. She's bent over in the drinks aisle, hands hovering over a Diet Coke, but as soon as she sees the look on
my face, feels my tug on her wrist, it's like I don't have to say
a word.

Maybe I mouth it:

Cop.

Run.

Fucked.

Her face crumples, and everything inside of me I've been
holding too tight finally shatters completely.

We grab hands and race to the stolen sunflower, hurry to start
the stupid fucking engine that will electrocute me if I don't get
these damned wires right.

"Come *on*, Trixie!"

"I'm trying! I'm trying!"

The fed lady stands outside and watches us, hands clasped, face solemn. She waves and calls out our names but doesn't chase us. How could she, in those heels? In that burnt-orange blouse with all those ruffles?

A burning in my belly helps me finally connect the wires right. I watch myself do this like I'm in a theater viewing a scene in a movie.

I rev the engine and drive off the road, off the interstate highway. Into the open dust and dirt of the New Mexico desert, the stretch of forever that goes on and on for miles into nothing.

"She wouldn't have helped us anyway," Lux says softly, her eyes on the dusty horizon, on the burning road to nowhere. "We were right to run."

I feel like I've just swallowed a mouthful of sand.

I say, "Maybe it was our last chance."

I say, "I'm so, so sorry."

Lux says nothing.

She rests her head against my arm, the one I'm shifting gears with. It's so stiff and it hurts and I haven't stopped grinding my teeth for the past twenty minutes. Her hair is soft on my skin, though mostly I'm numb to things now.

Finally, she speaks again. "You need to stop blaming yourself for everything, Trixie. You need to stop taking on the whole world like everything bad that's ever happened is somehow all your fault."

What she doesn't say is, "Someone else will help us."

What she doesn't say is, "It wasn't our last chance. Everything will be okay."

What she doesn't say is, "I forgive you for always running."

———

I think I drove an hour or two, straight into the desert. Maybe longer. I know we stopped a few times, and Lux fed me chips and water and stroked my neck and felt my forehead with the back of her hand like Mama used to.

The sun's gone down. It's like I have the flu, but I'm not congested, just feverish and full of chills and cold sweats. My vision blurs now and then. Lux is in the driver's seat now. It's hard to remember how she got there or when. She tells me to keep drinking water.

In my hazy dreams, I'm in my bed back home with the soft purple sheets. They were always my favorite as a kid. Mama is singing to me, and the room smells like fresh-baked raspberry pie. I see the California mountains on the edge of the desert. There's a finish line there, the black-and-white checkered ones like you see at drag races. Mama and Judy are waiting, waving, big bright smiles on their faces. They don't need to say a word, and already I know this is a place where there are no snakes or hogs.

Things go black and still for a while, and then I open my eyes. At first, I think I must be hallucinating or fever-dreaming this, too, but no, there it is. I *swear* it. Just off in the distance but clear enough to see: a carnival in full swing; a giant pendulum glowing neon in the dark as it swings back and forth, a drop tower lit up yellow and orange. A Tilt-A-Whirl, a Ferris wheel of great heights, shimmering purple and pink, and best of all, a roller coaster. I inhale the cool nighttime desert air. My breath catches in my throat as the coaster car climbs the tracks and then speeds down.

Through the static and crackle of evangelical sermons and car wash ads, "Take Me Home, Country Roads" comes on the radio.

Lux's tears flow silently as she drives our stolen sunflower. We can't seem to find a road. This desert is a never-ending labyrinth, patterns repeating over and over, an old Windows screensaver. Even with all the streaks of red dirt staining her face and hands like desert tattoos, she is—in that moment—the second most beautiful thing I have ever seen in my life.

And that's when something inside of me breaks open, and suddenly my body is racked with sobs. I double over, cradling my head in my lap as the sounds and screams of the carnival fade, and Lux and I are back on this endless stretch of desolation, driving for miles and miles and miles into nothing, searching for an end that never existed.

———

That night, we finally go camping.

We have no choice. Our stolen sunflower is dead.

We should've had enough gasoline to last us a week, but filling her hungry belly wasn't enough. The battery is dead. There's nothing left to do now. We're stuck in the middle of the sprawling New Mexico desert. I don't know if we drove in circles for hours, or if there really is no exit now that we've gone off the grid. Maybe this is our penance for all we've done, our own special purgatory.

Luckily, my fever has broken. The water and the snacks helped, as did Lux's touch, but now we're out of food. We only

have the two half-full jugs of water from Slate City. I finished the
rest of the warm bottled water.

Lux and I have no sleeping bags, no tents. Just flashlights
meant for Fever Lake and the blankets from home that we lay on
the rust-colored earth, listening to the crickets, the cicadas, the
critters that lulled us to sleep in Blue Bottle. Now and then, the
soft call of a desert bird, though I have no idea what it's called.
And every once in a long while, the mournful cry of a coyote that
makes me shiver.

It's funny how coyotes out in the open desert have become
the least of my fears.

Lux and I inch closer together on the blankets, staring up
at the sugar stars. We've layered ourselves with several T-shirts,
made pillows from our duffel bags. My stomach growls and rumbles. There's a knot in it, a sharp hunger pang. I take another
swig of water from my jug to try to dull it a bit longer.

I hear rustling as Lux reaches into the pocket of her shorts
and pulls out a Snickers bar. She hands it to me. My mouth wa-
ters and I can almost taste the chocolate and peanuts, the sweet
caramel and nougat melting on my tongue.

"No, you have it," I say, shaking my head. I push it out of my
sightline. "Or we'll split it."

"I'm not hungry," Lux assures me. She shines the flashlight
at an angle so I can't see her face, but I know she's lying. I try
to resist again, but she opens my palm and places it inside,
locking my fingers over the candy bar. "You eat it. I ate the
last one."

I take a deep breath and finally nod, then unwrap and devour
the entire candy bar in about thirty seconds. It's the fastest I've
ever downed a Snickers, and I really love candy.

Lux links her fingers through mine and sighs up at the stars.

"Do you remember that time your mama had, like, a horrible day at work, and she ate our Halloween candy while we were taking a nap, and you cried and cried, and she felt so bad about it she took us both out for huge ice cream sundaes?"

I laugh. I do remember. Mama's forlorn face as I struggled to breathe through my hiccups and tears. Her abject guilt over what she did, which felt like a horrific crime to a six-year-old.

"I was a jar of jelly and you were a jar of peanut butter."

"No, *I* was peanut butter and you were jelly."

I shake my head. "No. That can't be right. I begged and begged Mama for the jelly costume at the mall in the city. She said, 'Maybe next time,' and next time we went back, she got it for me."

"And then you let me wear it, because I insisted that purple was my color."

"Maybe."

"Guess we'll never know."

"Maybe we will," I say, trying to keep my voice steady and calm.

I clear my throat, trying to will the tears away. Lux squeezes my fingers.

"Do you remember that time we found a skunk outside at lunchtime? I think it was fourth grade, Miss Peterson's class."

Lux giggles, the bells ringing in her laugh like a desert song. "And Maria Mendes got sprayed because she tried to pet it. And Miss Peterson, like, completely freaked out. I think she was terrified of animals."

"We couldn't even have a classroom gerbil! Or a goldfish."

"Imagine being scared of goldfish."

"The ocean's full of way weirder fish, though. Hermit shoe crabs, I think they're called. Creepy little things that burrow into the tides. Maybe when we go, you'll be freaked out, too."

Lux scoffs. "Please. I'll just kick them in the head."

That cracks us both up. We laugh and listen to the sounds of owls. There could be tarantulas out here, creepy lizards and scorpions scuttling across the desert floor. Once upon a time it would've scared me to death, but right now, I feel so in sync with the world, the ground beneath us and the massive black sky above us.

"Well, this sure beats Fever Lake," I say.

Lux just goes, "Mmm." Her breathing has slowed, and her head is nestled into the crook of my shoulder. She's drifting off peacefully, but I'm wide awake. I could run a marathon right now, sprint all the way to California.

I close my eyes and try to breathe, ocean's breath like Judy taught me, in and out. Lux shifts a little and asks all groggily, half dreaming, "We are going to see the ocean, aren't we, Trixie?"

I take the flashlight from her and flip it off, kissing her cheek and the top of her head, breathing in the faint scent of the peppermint shampoo she used at our last shower at the Youth Outreach Center. Savoring her. "Of course we are."

Even in the darkness, I can feel her smile. Minutes later she's asleep.

My heart thumps against my ribcage like an anxious steel drum. I wait as long as I can, making sure Lux is deep enough in slumber, then gently pry myself away from her and click on the flashlight. Back at the car, I fish around for a piece of paper, a pencil, something. My fingers itch to write, but I can't find anything. Lux might have a journal tucked away in her duffel, but I don't want to wake her.

Somewhere not so far off, an owl hoots.

I go for a little walk, studying the desert soil and shrubs that crunch beneath my sneakers. The moon is a milk-colored crescent in the sky. I swear I can feel its pull, its promised protection. This is the most peaceful place I've ever been, even more peaceful than the ocean. Even more so than Blue Bottle on hot summer nights. There are no mosquitoes or gnats, no stifling humidity. The air is crisp and clear.

I close my eyes and write a letter in my mind like a prayer:

Dear Mama,

I'm so, so sorry. For leaving you. For failing you. For not getting you the care you needed. Maybe if I'd tried harder, or gotten you to a real doctor sooner, things would be different. I know no matter what, things would've been better for you if I'd stayed.

You're probably wondering what happened to me, where I am now. A part of me hopes you forget I exist, so you can move on and be at peace. You always did worry so much about me. The selfish part of me never wants you to forget me at all, even if your mind retains nothing else, not even your own name. At least know my face, the sound of my voice. That you have a daughter.

I love you so much, Mama. I can't tell you that I'm safe, or that I'm going to be okay. I can't even really tell you where I am, because this feels like nowhere.

Tell Judy I'm sorry, too, and that I miss her a lot. I'll always miss her. I know she did her best for me, for you, for us.

Love, your daughter, forever and ever,
Trixie

I feel like a fish that's been gutted and left out to rot. I can't tell you how badly I want my mama.

At dawn, we leave Razor Blade behind.

I give her hood a few good pats, swig some water from our jugs, and take Lux's sweating palm in mine until the heat grows so intense I have to let her go.

We walk, sharing the little water we have left, wearing our sunglasses, Lux in her cat-eye ones she wore the first night on our way to Fever Lake. We don't talk much, because talking hurts and takes up that much more energy and precious water in our bodies. This sore throat is worse than the one I had when I had strep last year, and all I can think of is water. Streams. Rivers. Oceans and frozen winter lakes that would turn my body a beautiful blue.

Once upon a time I thought I wanted never-ending sunlight, a summer with long ligaments that stretch and stretch until they're bound to snap. But now all I crave is chills and cold air, ice and frost and a blanket of heavy darkness. I wish those looming mountains in the distance were covered in snowcaps, not desert scrub.

Time has no meaning here, not in Nowhereland. My watch says it's only been three hours since we started walking, but it feels like lifetimes. My T-shirt is completely soaked. My aching feet are cracked and bleeding inside my sneakers, and the skin on my face hurts something bad. Lux stops to smear some of her waning supply of sunscreen on my cheeks and around my ears.

"That's better," she says, her throat dry and voice scratchy as mine. She kisses the spot on my cheek where it burns the most. I try to squeeze some out for her, but she's used the little we have left on me. She takes a small swig of water, careful not to drink too much too fast. We're running low.

Lux trips and stumbles on a jagged rock and cuts up her knee real bad. I use her star-spangled bandanna to stop the bleeding, but we're so dehydrated she doesn't bleed much. Eventually we grow tired of carrying our bulky duffel bags and find a spot to dump out most of their contents onto the soil: stolen clothing, jewelry, bottles of shampoo and conditioner. I rip up my stained yellow T-shirt, tearing wraps for Lux and me to wear around our heads and protect us from the unrelenting sun. We wear the hog's blood like armor. With every step, the blood in my head kicks like a steel-toed boot to the skull.

I can tell it's heavy as hell, the hulking camera Lux carries in its bag, but she doesn't put it down and she doesn't complain. I hold the water jug in one hand and my duffel across my shoulder. It's so much lighter now, free from things we thought we needed in another life, when we were other girls with names I'm surprised I still remember.

Lux kneels down to rest and points. There's a cluster of little white houses several miles away, or so it seems. Distance is hard to gauge now, out here in the desert.

"Maybe they have water," she chokes out, and I nod and nod, imagining gushing faucets and pipes.

With each painful step, the houses seem to get farther and farther away, until finally . . . we're close enough to see the boarded-up windows, the crumbling foundations and rusty hinges on the doors.

They're husks of homes long abandoned.

Lux makes a garbled sound in her throat that's something between a cry and a scream. I put my arms around her and squeeze tight as she sinks to the earth, letting her camera bag tumble to the ground. She digs her fingernails into the red-brown dirt and gasps out a strangled cry.

I shush her and hold her, inhaling the sweet smell of her sweat, enjoying the softness of her burning skin.

"I'm sorry I couldn't . . ." I swallow back the scratchy mountain in my searing throat. "I'm sorry I didn't . . ." I hang on to her until she finally hugs me back so tight all the air is pushed out of my lungs.

––––––

Once, when we were little, I did my first awful thing for Lux Leesburg.

It must've been second or third grade. Lux had a brand-new shimmery pencil case that glowed in the dark, and inside were dozens of pointy, fancy colored pencils. The kinds with expensive names like "magenta" and "swamp green" and "robin's-egg blue." She carried that case with her everywhere, showing it off and babbling about it and its magical properties to anyone who would listen: patient teachers, jealous classmates, tired and grumpy lunch ladies.

We didn't have fancy art stores in Blue Bottle. To get a pencil case like that, you had to order online or drive to the nearest mall forty minutes out of town, in the city. Most of us kids at Blue Bottle Elementary had never held something that nice in our hands that was just for us, just for our own enjoyment.

During recess one day, Mikey Ruden approached Lux and asked in this sweet voice if he could see her pencil case. I could hear the venom mixed with the syrupy sugar, knew that he was baring his fangs while he smiled, but I couldn't stop Lux from gleefully handing it over. Just as soon as he had it, Mikey called for all the other kids to come and see. They circled around, excited, whispering, sensing the storm brewing while Lux just looked on blissfully unaware. Mikey Ruden took out each pretty, fancy pencil and snapped it in half right in front of her eyes, one by one. He grinned the whole time he did it, too, never broke his gaze from Lux's. He tossed each broken piece to the ground like it was nothing but trash.

"You're such a *loser!*" he hissed, spittle flying from his lips.

Lux stood there, dumbfounded, like what she was seeing was impossible, a work of dark magic. I expected her to cry, to scream, to fight for her pencils, but she was frozen, that smile still on her lips, as though if she acted like she couldn't see what was happening, couldn't hear the howls and jeers and shrieks from all the other kids in the circle . . . maybe none of it would be real.

Eventually a recess aide came over and broke it up, yelled at them both for littering. I regret not charging and pummeling Mikey Ruden in the face right then and there, but I would've gotten in trouble, and nothing would've salvaged Lux's broken pencils.

Mikey's family lived in an overcrowded mobile home parked behind the old Denny's before it was torn down. He had only one nice thing to his name, the one nice thing he loved more than anything: a bright red scarf his granny had knitted for him before she passed.

I bided my time as sunny fall faded out to darkened winter. Waited. Watched him carefully unwrap it from his neck each blustery morning, press his face into it like he could still smell his granny's perfume, then hang it lovingly in his cubby hole.

The day before winter break, when everyone was packing up their lunch boxes and pencil cases and bookbags, there came a shriek from the cubby nook.

Mikey Ruden stood dumbfounded as Lux had been, like he was seeing the impossible, shaking and pointing at the carefully cut-up remains of his precious red scarf that were littered around the corner of the room like bloody snow.

Who knew that would only be the first time? Who knew that was the least worst thing I'd ever do for the girl I loved?

And as for the worst thing . . . it haunts me even now: Did I really kill the hog for love? For Lux?

Or did I kill the hog for me?

"Do you see it, Trixie?" Lux croaks. Her eyes brim with tears, or maybe that's just a mirage, too. "Water."

If I raise my sunglasses and squint, I can almost see what she sees: little puddles of blue wiggling on the not-so-far horizon, the air rising with steam.

"The ocean," she breathes, then lets out a dry, hacking cough. "Let's just pretend, at least. For a minute."

I kneel in the hot dirt next to her and wrap my arms around her shoulders. It hurts to speak, but I say it anyway: "I told you I'd take you there, didn't I?"

The bells ring and clang in her tired, scratchy laugh.

I think it's late afternoon, judging by the way the sun is slanted across the distant mountains. My watch is stuck on noon or midnight, depending on how you look at things. Lux and I have been resting here for a while. We listen to the sounds of the open desert, the birds and the wind and all those strange desert bugs. Out there it's all so alive and asleep at once.

I stand and offer Lux my hand, and she grabs her camera out of its bag and spins me around, then snaps one last photo of the two of us: windswept, sunburned, dried out and hollowed and together.

"Can't wait to get these developed," she says, and we both laugh even though it hurts.

"They'll go viral for sure."

She rolls her eyes. "Better yet, they'll put them in the history books."

"Who knows? Maybe they will."

We hear a faint roar, a lion's roar. Tires crushing desert ground. Helicopter blades chopping up the sky. Plumes of sand kick up in the hazy horizon, where those mirage puddles were supposed to be.

They're coming.

Or maybe it's all part of the mirage. Either way, this all ends soon, and it only ends one of two ways.

"I love you, Lux."

She keeps her eyes on the horizon, on the imaginary pools of puddles in our shared hallucination. I love that we see the same things now, even if they're only delusions. When she says it back, it's soft and warm, like Mama's fresh-baked pie: "I'll never stop loving you, Trixie Denton."

Sirens scream behind us, distant at first. Growing closer.

Lux takes my hand, hers so solid and sure in mine. I try to memorize every inch of her face, every freckle and crease and pore.

I always thought this part would be the hardest, would be the heaviest to bear and would hurt the most. But right now, I feel light as air, scooped out clean like a pumpkin, just in time for a fading autumn in Blue Bottle and cold air and Halloween. I am fearless.

I take Lux Leesburg into my arms. God, I love her so fucking much. We kiss hard. It's a kiss that burns through centuries, back through time and forward into a hazy future. Her lips taste like everything I never thought I could have, and I savor it, because this could very well be the very last time I ever get to taste them.

She laughs and so do I. "Fuck," she says.

"Fuck," I answer.

Harsh male voices, amplified through a crackling mega-phone. The whine of police cruisers. Soon their helicopter blades will tear up the burning sky. Plumes of desert smoke will rise and dance and ripple around us like fountain water.

It's hard to hear, but Lux says it and I hear her, her lips pressed to my ear: "You ready, cowgirl?"

When they finally get us—when those sirens are no longer distant screams and the helicopter blades are roaring right over our heads—I hope that we'll both be ready. That they'll have mercy on us. That they'll listen.

Just two troubled girls, together on the edge of the world.

Acknowledgments

First and foremost, thank you to my editor, Sylvan Creekmore—from our very first phone call, I could feel your passion and energy for this story and these messy, complicated, troubled girls. Thank you so much for all of your guidance and encouragement, and for helping me shape this book into the best possible version of what it could be. I am so infinitely proud of what we created together, and I can't wait to work with you on more.

Immense gratitude to Saritza Hernández for supporting me and this project from the very beginning, and for finding *Trouble Girls* the perfect home.

Lauren Spieller, my agent extraordinaire: thank you for believing in me, working so hard, and welcoming me into the Triada US Literary Agency family. I am so happy to be here and am thrilled to be working with you and Uwe Stender, as well as the rest of the agency.

Thank you endlessly to my rock-star publicist, Sarah Bonamino; my equally spectacular marketer, Rivka Holler; as well as everyone else on the incredible team at Wednesday Books who went above and beyond for *Trouble Girls*: Sara Goodman, Eileen Rothschild, DJ DeSmyter, Brant Janeway, Chrisinda

Lynch, Adriana Coada, Melanie Sanders, NaNá Stoelzle, Rima Weinberg, Olga Grlic, Soleil Paz, and Devan Norman. And of course, thank you so much to Monet Kifner, the brilliant artist who illustrated the cover of my dreams. You're a legend.

Sophie Gonzales—where do I even begin? You've been my rock from the moment I first conceived of this book and ran the concept by you. Now, as fate would have it, we share the same editor and publisher, and I couldn't be prouder to call you my close friend and sister in publishing.

Thank you also to Sophie and the following YA authors who wrote me the most kick-ass, swoon-worthy blurbs imaginable: Demetra Brodsky, Ashley Schumacher, Hannah Capin, Lygia Day Peñaflor, Emma Berquist, Diana Urban, Dana Mele, and Emma Lord. You're all writing wizards.

My friends who've been the world's best cheerleaders for me and this book from the start: Darion Richardson, Lia Ryerson, Jamie Rabinovitch, Parrish Turner, Tyler J. Gasper, Zianab Sankoh, Ashley Lystne, Holly Rice, Chelsea Wolf, Kelsey Caine, and Sayoni Nyakoon. I love you all so much, I can't even tell you. Thank you to Max Mauro for taking such a stunning author portrait on short notice and then rambling with me about David Lynch films after. And of course, to the rest of my writer and non-writer (but equally creative) friends, who are honestly family to me, and to everyone else who has shown me love and enthusiasm for this book throughout this entire process and everywhere in between: THANK YOU! I LOVE YOU SO MUCH!

Thank you to my mom, dad, and sister, Jessie: You've always been my biggest fans and believed in me the most. I'm so excited to share this story with you.

And finally, last but never least, to you, the reader. I said this in the acknowledgments of *Burro Hills*, and I'll say it again: Thank you for holding this book in your hands or enjoying it in the format of your choice, and for giving me my reason to keep writing. This one's for you.